PEOPLE WE LOVE

PEOPLE WE LOVE

PREETI SHENOY

HARPER FICTION

An Imprint of HarperCollins *Publishers*

First published in India by Harper Fiction 2026
An imprint of HarperCollins *Publishers*
HarperCollins *Publishers* India, Cyber City,
Building 10-A, Gurugram, Haryana – 122002, India
www.harpercollins.co.in

2 4 6 8 10 9 7 5 3 1

P-ISBN: 978-93-7307-485-6
E-ISBN: 978-93-7307-320-0

Typeset in 11/15.1 Adobe Garamond Pro
by HarperCollins *Publishers* India Pvt. Ltd

Printed and bound at
Nutech Print Services Pvt. Ltd.

FSC
www.fsc.org
MIX
Paper | Supporting responsible forestry
FSC® C195953

This book is printed on FSC® certified paper
which ensures responsible forest management.

HarperCollins *Publishers*, Macken House, 39/40 Mayor Street
Upper, Dublin 1, D01 C9W8, Ireland

For Purvi,
My Ctrl+C and Ctrl+V, who somehow got all of me and still became entirely herself

CONTENTS

AUTHOR'S NOTE

EVERY BOOK BEGINS as a whisper.

It's never a grand idea, nor a carefully plotted outline. It's just a whisper. A sentence overheard in a café. A look that passes between two people on a street. A misplaced earring. My daughter and I, mid-conversation, turning to each other at the exact same moment and saying: *This will make a good book.*

A writer's mind is always awake, always quietly gathering and storing away the small, ordinary things that are, in truth, never quite ordinary at all.

But some stories don't announce themselves. They wait.

They lie quietly inside other books, between the lines you thought you had already read. They are patient. They have no urgency. They simply exist, dormant and unhurried, until the moment they decide that they are ready to be told. The book you are holding in your hands right now is made entirely of such stories.

I wrote *The One You Cannot Have* in 2013 and *It's All in the Planets* in 2016. They were stories about young people, restless, searching, wonderfully flawed, living in cities and grappling with questions that never quite leave us: Can you choose who you fall in love with? Do you stay, or do you go? And what do you do when the life you have and the life you want refuse to line up? The people in these stories, they are people you might recognize in your own life: an Aman, a Nidhi, an Aniket. Ordinary people living ordinary lives, until they weren't.

Both books found a deep, lasting place in my readers' hearts. And when the letters came, reader after reader said that they saw themselves in the pages of these books. They shared their own stories with me, and told me, again and again: I know this feeling. I have lived this.

What struck me as magical was that although I had written these stories years ago and had expected the readers to have moved on and forgotten all about them, it wasn't so. There were those who discovered these stories only recently, and those who went back to them, but for all of them, the words felt new.

And that's when my publisher came to me with an idea: You have created characters people fall in love with, they said. Could you write a book of short stories about them?

I agreed instantly, and went back to reading my own books.

What happened next was something I did not expect. I have written seventeen books till date. Years had passed in between and life had layered itself over memory. I had genuinely forgotten who these people, these characters were and why they mattered. And so, I read like a reader, with fresh eyes and no agenda. That distance, that beautiful, humbling distance, is what allowed me to see what I had missed the first time. The hidden rooms inside familiar houses. The stories behind the stories. It was a reunion, a homecoming.

Then I began to write.

And as I wrote, the stories grew and kept growing, revealing themselves to be far larger, and longer, than what I had initially planned. Clearly, they had no interest in being 'short'.

So, three long stories later, here we are.

These stories, titled 'Before the Planets Aligned', 'The One Who Changed Everything' and 'The One I Almost Missed', are not sequels. For they existed long before the first pages of either *The One You Cannot Have* or *It's All in the Planets* were written. Before the years, the moments, the quiet turning points that made the people in these stories who they are—the people we love.

Each of these three stories can be read entirely on its own; no prior knowledge is required. But if, when you reach the last page, you find yourself wanting more of these characters, well, those books already exist. They are waiting for you too.

There's one small thing that is worth mentioning here: The Subbu whose story unfolds in 'Before the Planets Aligned' is the Subbu from *It's All in the Planets,* not the Subbu from *A Place Called Home.* Same name, but different worlds entirely. You will know him the moment you meet him.

I hope these stories settle into you the way only certain books do. Slowly, gently, staying longer than expected, and warming your heart. I hope they remind you of someone you love, or someone you once were.

May they give you hope and bring a little lightness to your step. May they transport you so completely into another world that, for a while at least, you forget your own. And may you return to it feeling, somehow, just a little more alive.

Thank you for being here. For picking this up.

Preeti Shenoy
May 2026

BEFORE THE PLANETS ALIGNED

SUBBU

Error 404: Courage Not Found

I CANNOT LET Aniket make the same mistake I did. As painful as it might be for me, I have to talk to him. I decide to broach the subject in a language we both understand: computer programming.

After all, debugging code is easier than debugging feelings.

'You know how there are memory leaks in programming?' I ask Aniket, watching the first light of dawn slice through the cafeteria windows, casting golden rays over his exhausted face. It's been a gruelling night: no sleep, no relief, no trips home. All because the top management insisted that a project we're working on be ready by the end of the day. They've made promises to the client and, as always, it's us, the ones building it, who end up paying the price.

Aniket squints, shielding his eyes from the morning light. 'You mean when a program fails to release the memories it no longer needs?' He cradles his coffee mug like it's the only thing keeping him tethered to consciousness.

'Exactly,' I reply, leaning forward. 'You know what happens because of that?'

'Why are you quizzing me, bro?' Aniket groans, running a hand through his dishevelled hair. The messy strands stick up at bizarre angles, defying all attempts at control. 'This sounds like bootcamp hell all over again.'

'Just humour me, bro.'

'Fine. If a program doesn't release its unused memory, it starts eating up more and more resources. Eventually, it slows down ... and crashes.' He takes a long sip of the coffee, steam rising from the mug.

'Bingo. Full marks for you,' I say, leaning back in my chair. 'I asked because that's exactly how I see you right now. I watch you obsess over Trisha. It reminds me of everything I went through with Viji.'

Aniket shoots me a confused look, but I notice he doesn't ask who Viji is. The guy is more sleep deprived than I thought. His brain isn't firing on all cylinders.

'The hell, bro? I'm not obsessing over Trisha,' he protests, but his voice lacks conviction.

'I see you watching her, noticing every little change, monitoring her variables, tracking every minor update in her system. Yet you keep your distance like a firewall.' I hold his gaze, meeting his tired eyes. 'It's obvious that you like her, but you do nothing about it. I know you well enough, Ani. I've been observing your behaviour for weeks now.'

'Come on! It's not like that at all.' He shifts uncomfortably. 'And hey, who is this Viji anyway?'

Finally, his caffeine-starved neurons are connecting.

'Ah, Viji. Where do I even begin? It's a conversation we should have over beer. Your treat. Your place.'

'You know you're welcome anytime, Subbu.' Aniket yawns, stretching his arms above his head. 'But we need to close off this damn P0 priority task first. The one that bloody Semicolon assigned us.'

I chuckle at his nickname for our manager Amit, who's clueless about software development. Legend has it that he once asked in a standup meeting whether semicolons were absolutely essential. I had shared that gem with Aniket on his first day, and he had smirked, saying he had heard that Amit had told some engineers to 'stop putting bugs in the code'.

We had both laughed and known straightaway that we would be good friends.

That evening, I take an auto to Aniket's apartment in HSR Layout, a crate of beer balanced on my lap. Even though it's supposed to be his treat, old habits die hard. It doesn't feel right, showing up empty-handed. Besides, Aniket is such a good guy, I don't mind spending on him.

It's always easier taking an auto in Bangalore traffic than driving. Not that I own a car or a bike, even though I could easily afford one. Every rupee I save goes towards something bigger: buying a home for my mother.

It's been Amma's lifelong dream—one Appa never fulfilled. He had to borrow money just to put me through engineering college, despite my scholarship. Because hostel fees, books, food, clothes and the endless other expenses, they all added up.

Then, in my second year, Appa suddenly died. Cardiac arrest. Amma's cries from that night still ring in my ears, jolting me awake on some nights.

From that moment, I had promised myself that I would buy her a home of her own, no matter what it took. All our lives, we had moved from one rented house to another, packing up whenever a landlord decided it was time. We never belonged anywhere; never had a place we could truly call ours. But all of that ends with me. Amma deserves stability. A two-bedroom apartment in Coimbatore where she can finally feel at home. Lost in these thoughts, I arrive at Aniket's building. Looking around, I realize that this is exactly the kind of place I want for her.

I ring the doorbell. No response. I call Aniket's phone. No answer. Then I hear hurried footsteps.

Aniket yanks the door open, water still dripping from his hair, a towel barely clinging to his waist. 'Sorry, bro! Was in the shower.'

'I can see that. You could've finished your shower instead of rushing out half-naked,' I say, stepping inside.

'Says the man who was too impatient to wait and had to call immediately,' he grins, crossing his arms.

I roll my eyes, setting the beer crate on his table. 'Shut up and get dressed. We've got a long night ahead.'

His apartment is sparsely furnished with just a sofa and two bean bags. The mismatched maroon curtains came with the place, and, despite my nagging, Aniket couldn't be bothered to change them.

'How does the colour matter? They do their job. You change the curtains at *your* place,' he had retorted once.

'My place isn't as nice as this flat! I live in a PG accommodation. But yeah, when I get my own place, I'm definitely doing it up properly,' I had replied.

Aniket emerges from his bedroom in a pair of shorts and a T-shirt, his hair still dripping.

'At least dry your head, bro.'

'You sound like my mother,' he says, but he towels his hair anyway before plopping down on the other bean bag and booting up his PlayStation. The familiar *Street Fighter* loading screen flashes as he tosses me a controller.

'Come on, Subbu. Time to get your ass kicked,' he smirks.

I don't take the controller. 'Not in the mood today,' I mutter after a moment.

Aniket pauses, looking at me in disbelief. 'In all the years I've known you, Subramaniyan Venkataraman, when have you ever said no to *Street Fighter*? Especially against me?'

I shrug. 'I'm exhausted, Ani. I have a lot on my mind these days.'

He raises an eyebrow but still picks his fighter. It's Ryu, as always. 'Everything okay?' he asks.

'Yeah, I guess,' I reply vaguely.

'Let's play one round, then we can stop. What do you say?'

I know he's stalling. He knows I have something important to say. Maybe he's even guessed what. He's one of the smartest people I know, and this is his way of letting me ease into it, subtly acknowledging that while life is serious, it's good to have a little fun first.

'All right,' I concede, picking up the controller. I choose Ken just to annoy him. 'Let's settle this once and for all. Ryu versus Ken. Who's the real king of *Street Fighter*?' I tease.

'Ryu, obviously,' he scoffs confidently.

'We'll see about that.'

For the next half hour, we're totally engrossed in *Street Fighter*. I start strong, landing a clean shoryuken that sends Aniket's Ryu flying backward.

'Okay, okay, not bad,' he mutters, adjusting his grip on the controller with renewed focus.

'Not bad? That was a textbook uppercut,' I say, dodging his counterattack smoothly. 'I bet even Ryu felt that in his pixelated soul.'

Aniket suddenly lands a perfect hadouken, sending my Ken sprawling across the screen. 'And I bet Ken just regretted all his life choices.'

I let out an exaggerated groan. 'Ugh. Cheap move, man, cheap move.'

'Cheap? That's pure strategy, my friend.'

I lean forward, fingers dancing across the buttons on the controller, trying to land a complex combo. 'Strategy? Nah, that's like spamming CTRL and calling it coding.'

Aniket laughs but doesn't let up his assault. He corners me with a flurry of perfectly timed kicks, my health bar dropping dangerously low.

'This is it!' he yells dramatically. 'One final move to finish you off!'

Before I can react, he executes a devastating super combo finish. My Ken collapses in defeat, and the words 'K.O.' flash triumphantly across the screen.

Aniket throws his arms up in victory. 'And *that* is exactly why Ryu is the GOAT!'

I drop my controller. 'Fine, fine. You win this round. But next time, I'm taking you down.'

'You can never defeat the master, young Padawan,' Aniket gloats. Then his expression shifts, and he eyes me suspiciously. 'You didn't lose on purpose just so I would listen to whatever you have to say, did you?'

'Maybe!' I grin back mysteriously.

But we both know I would never do that. My competitive spirit runs too deep.

We crack open cold beers, the familiar hiss of carbonation filling the room.

'Let me order some pizza,' Aniket says, tapping away on his phone with practised efficiency. Thirty minutes later, we're both stuffed with cheesy pizza and pleasantly buzzing from the beer.

'Now,' Aniket says, settling back into his bean bag, 'what's really been on your mind?'

I take a deep breath, hesitating. This is something Aniket needs to hear, but sharing it means reopening old wounds.

'Don't think of this as a lecture or as me nagging—' I begin carefully.

'Bro, it definitely *is* a lecture when you start like that,' Aniket cuts me off with a knowing smile.

I shake my head ruefully. 'Do you want to hear about Viji or not? Here's a man trying to bare his soul and you're already interrupting.'

'Okay, okay, sorry! Shoot. I promise, no more interruptions.'

I take another breath, steeling myself. The words come slowly at first, then faster as the dam breaks.

'I spent four years of engineering college madly in love with Viji. I was naive enough to believe that life, like coding, followed logical rules. Input effort, output success. Debug, refine, optimize. I had it all planned out in my head.'

Aniket listens intently, his usual jovial demeanour replaced by serious attention.

'I kept thinking I would ask her out eventually. But two years went by like that. Two whole years, and I couldn't muster the damn courage. I worked on group projects with her, hovering in the background, helping her with problems she didn't understand. I would make witty comments in our group chat just to see her respond with a smile emoji. We went for coffee many times, but always in a group.'

The memories flow freely now, each one sharp and painful.

'My friend Divya noticed how I looked at Viji. She pulled me aside one day and asked if I liked her. I blushed like an idiot and couldn't even answer her properly.'

I pause, taking a swig of the beer to steady myself.

'Divya advised me to confess my feelings, but I told her I had to wait for the right time. Needless to say, that perfect moment never came, and then, my perfectly structured code ran into a broken server when Appa passed away. I had never deployed my feelings, bro. Never pushed them to production.'

Aniket's expression softens with understanding and sympathy.

'Then one day, during a casual group lunch in our final year, she dropped the bombshell. "My parents have found someone for me. He's an NRI working in San Jose. We're getting engaged next month." That day, Subbu.exe crashed completely.'

Silence fills the room. I can't look at Aniket directly.

'I haven't had the same feelings for anyone since then. Maybe it's silly, but I'm unable to dump those memories and move on. I'm caught in an infinite loop of regret. That's why I'm urging you, Ani. Go ahead and talk to Trisha. Ask her out on a proper date. Because if you don't try, the answer will always be no.'

Aniket remains silent for a long time, processing everything I've shared. Finally, he exhales slowly. 'I had no idea, bro. No idea at all … How could I have never known about Viji?'

'It's not something I ever talk about. But today, I felt I had to share it with you. For your sake, so that you can ask Trisha out.'

Aniket shakes his head doubtfully. 'Have you seen her? Have you seen me? She's way out of my league, man.'

'You're being too harsh on yourself. I see a tall, handsome, intelligent guy with a great sense of humour.'

'If only I could just CTRL + C your thoughts and CTRL + V them directly into her mind,' Aniket says, and we both laugh despite the heavy conversation.

'Just because she does modelling gigs, it shouldn't intimidate you. Plenty of studies reveal that conventionally beautiful women actually get asked out less, or don't get asked out at all!'

Aniket raises a sceptical eyebrow. 'Come on! You're just making that up now, aren't you?'

'No, bro, I'm serious! Apparently, most guys assume that beautiful women are sick of dudes hitting on them constantly, so they don't approach them because they don't want to be another random guy bothering them. Plus, guys have this paralysing fear of rejection. They think the more attractive a woman is, the more likely she is to say no.'

'Hmm …' Aniket says thoughtfully, lost in contemplation.

I can see the function running in his brain, processing all the parameters I've fed him. Now all I have to do is wait for him to compile his decision and push commit.

NIDHI

The Sensible Choice

I DON'T LIKE being here. I don't like the food, the ambience, the music, the view or, rather, the lack of it. The restaurant is trying too hard to be authentic, what with its gold Buddha statues (zero points for originality) and red paper lanterns swaying in the artificial breeze from the air conditioning. The walls are painted in a burnt orange with gold Thai motifs that somehow manage to look both expensive and tacky at the same time. The lighting is too dim, probably to hide the mediocrity of the food, I think uncharitably.

I pick at my pad thai listlessly, watching Manoj as he enthusiastically explains something about his latest project at his company; he is rather proud of his role as a senior technical business analyst. His hands move animatedly as he discusses project cost and technical deliverables in the same breath, using terms that used to make up my daily vocabulary until a few months ago. Now they feel like distant echoes from another life. A life filled with fluorescent lights, the constant hum of the air conditioning in glass-walled conference rooms, accompanied by the complimentary Monday morning panic attacks in the bathroom, where I had to calm myself, then walk out, pretend everything was fine and attend yet another pointless meeting. It was a life I detested and had, fortunately, left behind.

'The client wants us to migrate their entire payment processing system to the cloud, but the cost implications are huge ...' Manoj drones on, barely pausing for breath, completely oblivious to how I'm pushing the noodles around my plate.

I used to sit in on meetings like the one he is describing, my laptop open, pretending to take notes while my mind wandered to the pottery class I was taking on weekends. Back then, it was my escape. Now my escape has become my life, although trying to explain that to Manoj is like trying to explain colours to someone who only sees life in spreadsheets.

'... I spent the whole day building ROI models to justify the technical architecture. And guess what? It got approved!' He beams as he puts his fork down and adjusts his perfectly knotted tie—it's a midnight blue one with subtle silver stripes, and it matches his crisp white shirt and charcoal grey suit perfectly—looking at me expectantly, assuming I would share his excitement over this victory of numbers over chaos.

I manage a weak 'Wow, that's indeed impressive.'

The irony isn't lost on me. I left that world behind, yet here I am, still playing the role of the attentive—or captive—audience to my fiancé's corporate saga.

His phone buzzes and he cannot resist checking it. It's probably another email from his boss. He quickly scans it under the table (some habits never change) and I find myself remembering my own last days at my company. The resignation letter I had drafted and redrafted twenty times, the concerned faces of my colleagues when I told them I was leaving to teach pottery, the way my boss had asked if I was 'really sure' about this decision, as if I was choosing to jump off a cliff rather than follow my passion. None of them got it.

Manoj had been supportive then, or at least it had seemed that way. 'Take some time off, explore your options,' he had said. I had felt massive relief that he had understood. But I did not know then that he had presumed it was a temporary deviation, a short creative sabbatical. All along, he had been expecting me to return to the 'real world' of quarterly targets and performance reviews, once I had got it out of my system.

He has already sent me three LinkedIn job postings this week, each with a gentle note saying, 'Just in case you want to keep your options open.'

Manoj doesn't get why I still continue teaching pottery. He doesn't understand how much it means to me that my days now start with checking my class schedules, breathing in the earthy smell of clay and hearing the gentle whir of the potter's wheel, rather than anxiously checking messages on my phone.

My tiny studio, with its large windows and natural light, is my sanctuary. My students come from all walks of life. I have a retired professor who wants to make her own garden pots, a teenager dealing with anxiety and a young mother who needs a creative outlet. All of them, in their own ways, remind me of why I chose this path. The peaceful silence, the feel of the clay taking shape under my hands, the freedom to create what I want is priceless. In my pottery studio I don't have to be afraid to experiment, to make mistakes, to start over. There's no pretence here, no need to maintain a facade of perpetual efficiency and enthusiasm and, above all, no pressure to deliver.

How do I tell this man, who measures success in Excel sheets and PowerPoint presentations, that the irregular income from my pottery classes brings me more satisfaction than my six-figure salary ever did? That I don't wake up with knots in my stomach anymore? That I don't count days to the weekend, and that I've finally stopped pretending to be someone I'm not?

The waiter arrives with another round of prawn crackers that I didn't ask for. Manoj ordered them, just like he ordered the spring rolls and the tom yum soup. 'You'll love it,' he had said, not bothering to check if I wanted any of it. My stomach churns slightly at the overwhelming smell of lemongrass and fish sauce.

The words are right there on the tip of my tongue: 'Manoj, I don't really like Thai food.' Simple words. Honest words. Words that might make him pause mid-sentence and look at me with surprise because in the two years we've been together, I've never once complained about his restaurant choices.

I should speak up. Say something. But instead, I smile weakly and reach for my glass of water, washing down the taste of my own cowardice.

Later that night, long after Manoj has dropped me home, I open my laptop and submit my article, a technical piece of writing for a client. Thanks to my extensive corporate background, finding work has never been a challenge. My freelance writing complements the income I earn from teaching pottery classes. But my real writing—the kind that fuels my soul—is what I pour into my blog.

I started the blog to document my pottery projects and initially called it *A Pot of Clay*. But three months in, I realized I had more to say than just posting photos of my creations. So, I renamed it *A Pot of Clay That Holds Gold*, and soon, it became a space for my musings, reflections and anything swirling in my mind. My readership grew steadily, and now I have a loyal group of readers who eagerly await each new post. Secretly, I'm pleased about this, even though I don't make a single rupee from blogging. But that doesn't matter. Writing on my blog recharges me, and today, after that tiresome outing, a new blog post is calling to me.

But before I get to it, I change into comfortable pyjamas, arrange the pillows just right and settle into bed with my laptop. The soft glow of the screen illuminates my face as I begin to type.

A Pot of Clay That Holds Gold

Hi there. Hope you've done at least one nice thing for yourself this weekend. What? You haven't? Schedule it right now. You deserve it.

Too often, we hesitate to give ourselves what we truly deserve. Instead, we spend our time on things that don't really matter. We say yes to things we don't particularly enjoy because it's easier to go along with it, to keep the peace, to make the other person happy.

But what is the price we pay for our choices? When does that price become too high? How do we decide if it's worth it?

Saying yes can become a habit, creeping up on us until we're too deep in, just like the proverbial frog in the pot, unaware the water is heating up until it's too late. The frog could jump out at any time, but it doesn't. It stays. Till it dies a slow, painful death.

I didn't mean for this post to turn morbid, but these are things worth thinking about. We owe it to ourselves.

Until next time.

PS: So, tell me in the comments again: What's one nice thing you did for yourself this week? I'd love to know.

I feel better once I've written the blog post. It's a secret tool to help me process my feelings, but my readers don't know that. I mostly keep the happenings in my personal life out of it. I read the post thrice, check for typos and hit publish. Then, as always, I spot two typos the second after I've posted it. I'm convinced these typos have a secret hiding spot and emerge only when they please. I hurriedly correct them and republish the post.

The next morning, the first thing I do is check my blog for comments. Three have come in, and one of them is from my stepmother, Tara, who comments under the pseudonym 'Starry Nights', a play on her name.

Tara and I are more like friends than stepmother and stepdaughter. As I stare at her comment, I think back to the time after my mother died. My parents hadn't had a great marriage. Not as great as the one my father has with Tara. When I left for college at eighteen, he was all alone, and that's when Tara, a mid-level manager at his company, came into his life.

It didn't bother her that he was a widower with a grown daughter. She fell in love with him anyway. I liked her instantly because I could see how happy she made him. When they got married, I was twenty-two and she was thirty-six. She seemed too young to be a 'stepmother', so I called her by her first name, which she loved.

I remember the night I showed her my blog. We were on the terrace, sitting under a starry, moonlit sky. She was so fascinated that she grabbed my iPad and read all my previous entries in one go. Over the next few days, she went back and commented on almost every old post. Now, her comments are one of the highlights of my blogging experience. They are sharp, insightful and always making me think.

Today, she's written:

> Most of us don't weigh our options carefully. Deep down, we're scared of rejection. That's why we say yes, even when we want to say no. If you're secure enough in your relationship with the other person, saying no becomes slightly easier. But it has to be done with tact.

I read her comment and pause. She's right, as usual. Tara has a way of cutting through the noise and getting to the heart of things. But am I truly insecure about my relationship with Manoj? The thought sits uncomfortably in my mind, like a misplaced piece of a jigsaw puzzle, and sets me thinking about my relationship with Manoj. I mean, objectively speaking, I know he loves me. He remembers important dates, buys me the plants that I love, texts me 'good morning' and 'thinking of you'. He is indeed a master of all the thoughtful gestures that would make a girl feel cherished. He checks all the right boxes too: well-educated, smart, has a successful career, comes from a good family. In fact, before approving of him, my father even ran a background check on him when we started dating.

And yet, there's this persistent whisper in my head, a question I can't quite silence. Like when you feel you've forgotten something important but can't remember what.

I close my laptop and sink back into my pillows, staring at the glow-in-the-dark stars on the ceiling. I've always had these stars in my room, no matter where I moved to. Tonight, however, they fail to quiet my mind. I cannot help thinking about my ex.

Vir and I had six years together. The first four were like a perfectly choreographed dance. We had simply clicked, professionally and personally. Then came the long-distance phase: me in Sri Lanka, him in New York. That was when our relationship got reduced to scheduled video calls and time zone calculations. We tried so hard to keep it alive. I think about the miles and miles of late-night WhatsApp messages and the lengthy emails about our days which I used to carefully compose. I remember the virtual movie dates, the voice notes—we did it all. But ultimately, balancing a long-distance relationship and our busy careers turned out to be too difficult. Something had to go. And it was our relationship.

That very year, I had met Manoj at a fintech conference. I was in a phase where I was done with uncertainty. Manoj represented everything I thought I wanted at that point in time. He was decisive and articulate, someone who could match my corporate ambitions word for word. Back then, we made perfect sense together. But that was *before* I traded my corporate suits for my pottery classes and a blogger's life, before I started questioning what success really meant to me. Now, the differences between us feel like paper cuts, small but impossible to ignore.

Why am I dissatisfied? What am I looking for? I don't know. Am I too maudlin to desire the spark that makes your heart skip even after years together? I catch myself and sigh. This is exactly the kind of romantic nonsense I used to roll my eyes at. Love isn't supposed to be like the novels I read or the shows I watch. It's supposed to be about building something lasting, about choosing each other every day, about compatibility and shared values, I tell myself.

I stare at the plastic stars on my ceiling. I remember how Vir had once said they looked like scattered dreams. Ironically, years later, Manoj had pointed out that they weren't accurately positioned according to any *real* constellation.

Both observations were true. I just don't know which one matters more now.

ANIKET

A Shift

LONG AFTER SUBBU leaves, I sit with my laptop open, intending to watch a show. Then I decide against it. I'm not in the mood anymore. So, I shut my laptop and put it away.

What Subbu said about how his biggest dream is to buy his amma a house in Coimbatore keeps echoing in my head. 'Just two more years of savings and I can get it, bro.' He had made it sound so simple, as if buying a house was like ordering takeout. But then that's Subbu. He breaks down life's toughest challenges into clear, logical, manageable tasks and then takes action to overcome them.

I think about how he must have felt when his father passed away. One of my biggest fears is losing either of my parents. The very thought terrifies me. I don't know how Subbu managed to carry on. He was in his second year of college when he lost his father. That's what, nineteen? Or maybe twenty? I cannot even begin to imagine the trauma he has been through.

Now that he has opened up and shared his story with me, a lot of things about Subbu begin to make sense. I can see why he has always acted like some wise coding guru. Coding was probably the one thing that made sense to him when everything else fell apart. It would've given him structure, logic, a way to process a world that had suddenly become very uncertain. So, he probably built his whole philosophy around it, throwing around metaphors like 'Life is just a series of try-catch blocks' or 'Sometimes you need to reboot your thoughts to clear the cache.'

Perhaps wise guru Subbu has a point. Maybe I *should* ask Trisha out. I open Instagram and look at her profile. The moment I do it, I know it's a mistake. Yet I cannot stop.

Trisha's profile is a glimpse into a world that I could never be a part of. Her latest post is a professional shoot where she's wearing a leather jacket, black pants and boots, and posing on a Ducati. It has nine thousand eight hundred likes. The comments section is full of fire emojis and one-word responses like 'Queen'. I scroll further. She is at a tech conference, looking impossibly elegant in a pantsuit. Another is from a fashion show where she walked the ramp.

As I walk to the bathroom to brush my teeth, I look at my own reflection in the full-length mirror in my bedroom. A regular black T-shirt that's my standard, shorts I've had since college, hair that never quite behaves. My last Instagram post was about six months ago—a random sunset shot from my balcony. Eighteen likes, mostly family.

Trisha's Instagram posts show me how plain and ordinary my life is compared to hers. From her posts, it seems like all her friends are as stylish as she is. Most of them look like they walked straight out of a magazine, while the most fashionable thing I own is a shirt my sister gifted me last Diwali. Trisha's Instagram also had a few posts with pictures of her feeding street dogs and petting them. I, on the other hand, am terrified of them.

How do people like her end up in an organization like mine? She could be doing anything: modelling, acting in movies. And yet here she is. In *our* company through campus recruitment.

Trisha works in business development, which means she's the bridge between our clients and the tech team. She talks to telecom operators, understands their problems and then somehow translates their vague, often impossible demands into things we actually have to build. She's good at it too—confident, articulate and sharp.

Sleep takes a long time to come, and when it finally does, one thought settles quietly in my mind: Trisha ... I do want to ask her out. I've known it for a while, I think. Maybe tomorrow I'll do something about it.

The tech team is on the seventh floor, while the business development team is on the fourth. Trisha often comes to our floor, for explanations, feasibility checks or, sometimes, damage control. She reports to Mr Tiwari who closes deals, presents strategies and makes the company look good.

The next morning when I reach office, Subbu greets me with a questioning 'So?', raising his eyebrows.

'What?' I ask, even though we both know what he's talking about.

'You know what I'm talking about. Do it! Today is the deadline. You have until five,' he commands. I shake my head.

For the rest of the day, I'm lost in my work, the hours slipping by unnoticed. My half-eaten burger grows cold on my desk, forgotten, because I have to finish a high-priority task.

Around 3 p.m., a familiar energy ripples through the office. I don't need to look up to know that Trisha has arrived on our floor. As if a wave of electricity has washed over them, every man in the office subtly transforms: shoulders straighten, fingers smooth down hair, uneaten food gets swept into dustbins and screens suddenly become fascinating.

Then I hear her heels. Click-clack. Click-clack. Crisp, sharp and confident against the office floor in an assertive rhythm. Trisha.

I keep my eyes on my screen. I have to get this task done but her arrival has ruined my focus. My treacherous heart pounds away as she stops right next to my desk.

'Hey, Aniket,' she says, her voice smooth.

I think I'll never get used to the sound of my name rolling off her tongue so easily.

I glance up, keeping my expression neutral, professional. I pretend that my stomach isn't currently free-falling into an abyss.

'Oh! Hi, Trisha,' I nod, like I've seen her only then. Like we're just two colleagues. Like I didn't spend at least an hour last night scrolling through her Instagram and wondering what alternate reality she exists in.

She leans against my desk slightly, the scent of her expensive, intimidating perfume wafting towards me. 'Busy?' she asks.

'Only rewriting the same function five times because I don't like the font,' I say. 'So, no, not really.'

She laughs, and I try to tell myself that I don't care how nice it sounds.

'I have a favour to ask,' she says, tilting her head. 'That client presentation you helped me with last month? The one where you explained the technical terms instead of letting me ramble about "synergistic cloud solutions" for twenty minutes?'

I smile, remembering her mock-corporate voice during our practice run. 'You mean where I told you not to use "leverage" seventeen times in one sentence?'

'Exactly that,' she grins. 'Well, I have another one tomorrow. Much bigger client. They're going to ask actual questions this time, and I need your help again. I just want to make sure I don't sound like I learnt technology from a buzzword generator.'

'So, you're saying you don't want to tell them about our blockchain-enabled, AI-powered, quantum-ready platform?' I quip.

She laughs, shaking her head, and I join in. It's partly in relief that I've managed to keep this conversation *normal*, the bonus being that I managed to make her laugh.

'This is why I come to you. Everyone else just nods and says "yes" to whatever I'm saying. You're the only one who called me out for using too many buzzwords,' she says.

'All right, all right, let's make sure you survive tomorrow without seeming like you memorized stuff from the tech manual,' I say, pushing my laptop aside.

The next half hour whizzes by quickly. I'm so lost in explaining things to her that I forget, briefly, how drawn I am to her. I wish I had the superpower to slow down time. Trisha tilts her head and listens intently, asking questions that make me realize she is so much smarter than people give her credit for.

For a brief second, I let myself imagine what it would be like if I weren't a guy whose idea of fashion is picking the least-wrinkled T-shirt from the pile of clean laundry. If I had the kind of effortless confidence she does. If I could just say, 'Hey, Trisha! Want to grab a coffee?'

But instead, I clear my throat and lean back. 'That should cover it. Feel free to hit me up if you need more details.'

She grins. 'Thanks, Aniket. If I crash and burn on this call, I'm blaming you.'

'Perfect. I love being held accountable for things beyond my control. It's basically my job description.'

Another laugh. Then, just like that, she's gone.

I watch her disappear down the corridor, my fingers hovering uselessly over the keyboard. I exhale, shake my head and get back to work.

Professional. Always.

Even if it kills me.

Subbu materializes at my desk with a fizzy drink in hand, setting it down with exaggerated ceremony. 'Here,' he says, pretending to dab my forehead with an invisible handkerchief. 'To cool you down after that heroic performance.'

I reach for the drink and grin at him. Of course, Subbu has noticed the whole interaction.

'You know, you could channel some of that smooth explaining energy into actually asking her out instead of staring at your screen and pretending to work every time she walks by,' he suggests.

'Come on, Subbu. That's just work stuff.'

'Did I narrate Subbu.exe's whole life story last evening for nothing? Did you not get why you simply must ask her out?'

'I did, Subbu. I did. I appreciate you sharing your story with me. And trust me, I do want to ask her out. Maybe one of these days I will,' I say and turn to my screen. I don't want Subbu nagging me any further. I want to revel in the glory of having made Trisha laugh, for some more time.

The next day, we have a meeting with the business development team. The conference room is packed. It's the kind of meeting that no one wants to be in but cannot avoid as Mr Tiwari has called for it.

On one side is my team: developers who consider 'good morning' as excessive communication. On the other is the business development team, led by Mr Tiwari, with Trisha beside him, ready to take notes. She looks so elegant that I have to force myself to keep from glancing at her.

'We have an issue,' Mr Tiwari begins, adjusting his glasses. 'Meridian Global, our biggest client, wants real-time fraud detection within three months.'

Three months. My stomach performs the kind of flip that requires a rollercoaster.

'Not possible,' my manager Amit says firmly, much to my surprise. 'Look,' he continues, placing both his hands on the table, with the kind of serious expression he dons when someone tries to push code without testing, 'my team is already juggling three major projects, two critical bug fixes and whatever mysterious issues keep popping up in production at 2 a.m. Adding real-time fraud detection is like asking a donkey that's already carrying the washerman's load to turn into an elephant.'

I hide a smile. This is classic Amit. Using ridiculous metaphors to make his point while somehow maintaining a completely straight face. But he's not wrong and, more importantly, he's defending us for once, instead of his usual 'we'll make it work somehow' approach that ends with us sleeping under our desks.

Trisha glances at Mr Tiwari before speaking. 'We understand that, but can we phase it out? Deliver the basics first and expand later?' Her voice is steady, professional, but there's a slight hesitation. Like she knows she's stepping into dangerous territory. Her eyes meet mine across the table; I detect a small smile in her expression and a glimpse of the same person who laughed at my jokes yesterday.

Mr Tiwari nods approvingly. 'That's exactly what we need. It would be a massive win for the company if your team can deliver that.'

Amit exhales. 'Aniket, thoughts?'

I drum my fingers on the table. 'If we strip it down and prioritize key risk indicators, then maybe in five months, given our current workload. But that's a big maybe. It'll be tight.'

Trisha writes something down quickly, then looks up. 'Okay. What's the absolute minimum we can deliver in three months?'

Mr Tiwari raises an eyebrow but doesn't interrupt. He's watching her, assessing.

We break down the problem and explain what it will take. Mr Tiwari throws around possibilities. Amit talks about the actual work involved. Tension rises in the room, ideas clash, but through it all, Trisha holds her own with Amit, focused, nodding at the right moments, asking sharp, relevant questions. I'm impressed at how well she handles it.

By the end of it, we've agreed on a compromise: a basic prototype in four months, provided Mr Tiwari speaks to the leadership about getting two new resources allocated to our team. After that, we will meet to discuss full implementation.

Mr Tiwari sits back in his chair, satisfied. 'Thank you, Amit, Aniket. I'll handle the client. Trisha, summarize these points and send them to me by end of day.'

She nods. 'On it.'

As we leave, she lingers by the door for a second, turning to me. 'Thanks for that.'

I shrug. 'It's what I do best. You heard Amit. You've turned donkeys into elephants.'

She laughs. A genuine laugh, throwing her head back. 'But you always deliver, Aniket. We can all rely on you. You're a coding ninja.'

My heart does a somersault. I hope I'm not grinning like I've won a prize.

Then she's gone. Off to write reports, sit in on more meetings and probably post something effortlessly cool on Instagram while I go back to debugging a stubborn piece of code.

Two completely different worlds, somehow orbiting the same space.

SUBBU

A Plan

OF COURSE, ANIKET won't ask her out. The guy's stuck in his own head, running in endless loops of self-doubt instead of just making a simple move. He'll spend hours convincing himself he's not good enough for her, that she's somehow out of his league, completely unreachable. This is classic Aniket. He'll get excited for a moment, then slowly dismantle the possibility until nothing remains. It's maddening to witness, especially when you care about the guy as much as I do. Aniket's one of the best people I know. Brilliant, funny, genuinely kind, but he's got this self-sabotage routine down to an art form. If it were an Olympic sport, my man here would be a gold medallist.

When I had opened up about Viji—and it took me superhuman effort to do that—the guy had listened. Nodded at all the right moments. Even said he understood. Then he went right back to doing absolutely nothing about Trisha.

Someone needs to shake him out of this pattern and, naturally, that someone is going to be me. So, I've been doing a little reconnaissance. Not stalking, mind you, just paying attention. Gathering information like any good engineer would. And here's what I've noticed: Trisha leaves work alone every single day. No boyfriend picking her up, no quick phone calls to check in with someone special, no rushed exits to meet anyone. She just walks out, plugs in her earbuds and disappears into her own world.

That tells me everything I need to know. She's available. Still, I'm not one to trust a single data point. I need a corroborating source. And I know just the person to turn to: Jeena.

Jeena and I go way back. We were at the same engineering college, but in different departments. She was in industrial design, which, in college terms, meant she always had paint on her hands and a mild disdain for our 'boring code life'. But we bonded over shared detentions and a mutual obsession with filter coffee. Now, as fate would have it, she works in business development, the same as Trisha.

Perfect source. Credible. Observant. Not prone to exaggeration.

I catch her during my coffee break one morning. We're there for our daily caffeine rituals. She's pouring herself a masala chai; I'm going straight for the espresso.

We go through the usual small talk of office politics, Bangalore traffic hell and the horror of 8 a.m. meetings. But I'm itching to steer the conversation towards Trisha without making it obvious.

As if on cue, Trisha walks into the cafeteria. And like clockwork, a dozen male heads swivel in her direction. She, however, doesn't notice. She walks over to the coffee machine like she's immune to their attention.

I nudge Jeena slightly. 'Look at the number of guys turning to stare at her.'

'She's a model after all. What would you expect? She's glamorous, poised. See her cheekbones? You could cut glass with them,' Jeena smirks at her own joke.

I go in, subtle. 'Her boyfriend must be one anxious man.'

Jeena takes the bait. She sips her chai and lowers her voice just a notch. 'Truth is … they're taking a break. It's been a while now. I mean, I don't like to gossip, but yeah, she's single.'

Interesting.

'And what's she like to work with?' I ask, like it's an afterthought.

Jeena doesn't hesitate. 'She's really sweet, you know. Most people make assumptions about her because of how she looks. But she's drawn to people who can see past all that surface stuff. People who genuinely want to get to know her.'

Bingo!

That's the missing puzzle piece. Every guy who tries his luck with Trisha probably walks in with a generic pickup line and a compliment about her smile. They don't *see* her. Not really. They're dazzled by the exterior and never take the time to look deeper.

Aniket, for all his agonizing and hesitations, is exactly the kind of guy who would see her for who she really is. And suddenly, it becomes crystal clear to me that if Aniket won't step up on his own, I'm going to have to engineer the perfect setup. Just a gentle nudging of the variables to allow for a natural outcome. A space where he can be his usual funny and thoughtful self, and where she might see him for who he is.

He doesn't need lines or charm or some grand gesture. He needs to stop running those damn simulations inside his head and start showing up.

And if anyone can create a system where all the conditions align, where all the human and technical components flow into one coherent, elegant solution, it's me.

This isn't just a love story. It's a project.

And I always deliver.

NIDHI

An Invitation

Anjana is waiting by the door when I arrive at Mitti, my pottery studio. For a moment, panic grips me. Did I make a mistake? I check my watch, only to realize I'm thirty minutes early.

'Thank God you're here,' she says, wringing her hands. 'If I had your number, I would've called you.' At sixty-seven, Anjana carries herself with grace, but today there's a fragility to her. The morning sun catches the silver strands in her salt-and-pepper bob as she shifts anxiously from foot to foot.

'Rough day?' I ask, noting the shadows under her eyes.

'More like a rough night.' Her voice falters, tears welling up in her eyes. 'I dreamt of him. Again. And that feeling when I wake up and know I can never see him again …' she pauses, swallowing hard, 'that's the absolute worst.'

I nod sympathetically as I dig through my bag for the studio keys, the familiar jingling filling the heavy silence between us.

It's been only a month since Anjana lost her husband. Thirty-nine years of marriage and then he was gone. She'd joined my classes, starting with a trial session, in a desperate bid to outrun her grief. Her daughter, who was in the US, had gently suggested that she should try and do something new. But what had begun as a distraction transformed into something more. She had fallen in love with pottery, just as I had.

'Who knew clay could be therapy?' she had said in wonder, admiring her first completed piece, fingers still muddy with clay. 'Your studio is my sanctuary, Nidhi. God bless you for opening this place. I walk in here and all my sorrows disappear. At least temporarily. It's just me and the clay.'

'I know exactly what you mean,' I had replied, watching her hands smooth the piece she had created. 'The fact that you can shape it, crush it, dry it, wet it and start all over again, as many times as you please … It's strange how it gives us hope for our own future. Endless possibilities just from mud.'

Anjana had nodded then, understanding passing between us like a current. It was like we shared a secret that no one else knew. That sometimes, the simplest of things, like earth and water, hold the power to heal the deepest wounds.

Each of my students carries their own story, their own reason for seeking solace in clay. There's Devika, a corporate lawyer who comes in twice a week, her shoulders gradually loosening as she works the wheel, the tensions of legal battles melting away beneath her fingers. Then there's Rohan, a teen battling anxiety, who found that the methodical process of centring clay helped centre his thoughts too. Mrs Mehta, a retired bank official who didn't know what to do with her time, discovered a new purpose in crafting delicate kitchen sets. She had made a set for her granddaughter, and it had turned out so beautifully that many parents with young children requested her to make similar sets for them and insisted that she take payment for it. She is set to launch her own business soon, and I've been helping her with branding and social media.

Only the Sharma siblings, Aditya and Ananya, come with a different agenda. They're preparing for art school applications, methodically adding another medium to their repertoire. Their cameras are always ready, and they document each and every object they create so that it can go into their portfolios. Sometimes, I catch them watching the others with curiosity, perhaps wondering why someone would spend hours perfecting the curve of a bowl just to crush it and start over.

But they're the exception. For most who walk through Mitti's doors, pottery isn't about the final piece. Instead, it's about the journey. It's about the way the clay responds to gentle pressure, how it rebels against harsh handling, how it teaches patience and acceptance. Most come to heal, while some come to find peace and a few to rediscover themselves.

Like Anjana, they all find their own form of therapy within these walls, their stories gradually taking shape, much like the clay beneath their hands. I feel proud to be a part of their lives.

The best thing about having my own studio is the deliberate choice to open for only a few hours in the morning and a few hours in the evening. It gives me the rest of the day to pursue what gives me joy—my writing. It gives me the space and time to ponder, to breathe and to simply exist.

I feel a surge of gratitude for this lifestyle as I close the studio for the day and head back home. The evening air is crisp as I park my car and walk to my apartment. That's when my phone breaks the silence, its screen lighting up with an international number. My heart skips a beat when I see the name flashing on Truecaller: Vir.

I'm momentarily stumped. Why is he calling me out of the blue? It's been so many years since we broke up. I fumble with my keys, barely managing to get inside my apartment.

'Hello?' I say, trying to keep my voice steady, neutral. My bag lands unceremoniously on the sofa, a departure from my usual habit of hanging it in my wardrobe. I hate being untidy.

'Hey! How are you?' His voice is bright, cheerful and so achingly familiar that for a moment, I'm twenty-six again, answering the phone when he would call every evening.

'Uh ... good.' The words feel inadequate. I'm stuck between politeness and shock.

'No need to sound so guarded, Nidhi,' he chuckles, and I can almost see him running his fingers through his hair. 'I know I'm calling out of the blue. But I have something to tell you, and I thought it better to tell you over the phone than drop you a message ... I'm getting married.'

My breath, which I did not realize I'd been holding, escapes in a rush. Something tightens in my chest. It's a strange sensation; not quite pain, not quite relief.

'Oh, nice. Hearty congratulations, Vir!' I manage to say. The words are genuine. Memories flood unbidden. Our first date at the MBA college canteen, lazy Sunday mornings, fierce arguments that always ended in laughter and, finally, the quiet end of us. Six years of my life. We'd been so happy together. I did not imagine then that there would come a time when we wouldn't be in each other's lives.

But as painful as it was, both of us did move on after the break-up. I buried myself in my career because it helped me cope. But this phone call seems to have dug deep into those memories. And they close in on me, leaving me no space to breathe.

'Don't you want to know what she does?' he asks, oblivious to my inner turmoil.

'Eh, who?'

'My wife to be! Shreya.'

'Yes, of course,' I nod, trying to focus. 'Sorry, I've just got back home from my studio and entered my apartment,' I blurt out.

'Studio?' His interest piques. 'Did you have a corporate shoot?'

'Oh no, no. I quit my corporate career a while ago. This is my own pottery studio.'

'Wow! You managed to open a pottery studio? What about your career?'

'I quit, Vir. And I can't tell you how blissful it feels to have escaped the corporate rat race.'

Vir wants to know all about it. And just like that, we fall into conversation as if the years between us have melted away. It's always been this way with Vir, words flowing easily, thoughts connecting without effort.

For the next hour, I find myself asking him questions about his life, his work. I tell him the story of my transformation: leaving the corporate world behind, the move from Sri Lanka to Bangalore, finding peace while shaping clay with my hands. And then, almost casually, I mention Manoj and our engagement.

There's a small, petty part of me that feels satisfied, a childish tit-for-tat that makes me cringe inwardly. *See, I've completely moved on too.*

But Vir's genuine happiness for me dissolves that pettiness, replacing it with something warmer, more mature.

As our conversation continues, it dawns on me that we could be really good friends now. Time has smoothed the jagged edges of our break-up. The chemistry that once made us lovers has matured into a rare understanding that doesn't need the scaffolding of romance to stand by itself. It's like finding an old book that you once loved and discovering that it still speaks to you, just differently.

Vir tells me that I simply *have* to attend the wedding. He asks me to bring Manoj too. The wedding is to take place in Udaipur, nearly a year from now. 'I've given you plenty of advance notice, Nidhi. I'll be very upset if you miss it,' he warns.

I promise him that I'll speak to Manoj about it, and if Manoj cannot make it, I'll definitely try to.

'There's nothing like "try to". Just come,' he says.

The sun has set completely by the time we say goodbye. My bag still lies where I dropped it, a small rebellion against order that makes me smile. Tomorrow, I'll go back to my studio, shape clay into beautiful things and work on some articles for my clients. But tonight, I let myself sit with these memories. I don't see them as wounds anymore. I have healed. Perhaps they are stepping stones that have led me here, to this point in my life. And as hard as it is to accept, we grow from every heartbreak, every person we have loved.

ANIKET

Ambushed

'BRO, I NEED your help,' Subbu says, sounding unusually serious. His usual coding jokes are missing.

'What help do you need, my man? I'm at your service,' I reply as we walk to the office canteen.

We've just wrapped up a major project and, for the first time in months, I feel like I can breathe without feeling like my head will explode. Sure, I'm still busy—this is still a tech company after all—but it is a manageable kind of busy. The kind where I can, at the very least, enjoy my lunch break instead of wolfing down a burger while debugging code.

'I'll tell you the details when we sit down,' Subbu says as we take out our Sodexo coupons. Subbu gets a south Indian thali while I opt for a plate of chole bhature.

For all the work they make us do, the company does provide good meals. The aroma of fresh chole bhature makes my mouth water as we settle into our usual spot by the window. The garden below is in full bloom, a splash of colour against the monotony of the grey-and-white colour scheme of our tech park. I can see that they're also holding an art exhibition in the open space and I make a mental note to check it out later.

Subbu looks at me a bit sheepishly instead of digging into his thali.

'What's up? You look stressed,' I comment.

'It's a girl problem, bro,' he blurts out, absentmindedly breaking off a piece of pappad and crunching it. 'I'm ... umm ... going on a date.'

I can't help but grin. Now that I know Subbu's story, this is something exciting. 'Hey, that's wonderful! Does this mean Subbu.exe is functional again?'

He laughs, but it's tinged with nervousness. 'The system is trying to reboot, but it's running into some issues. That's where I need your help, man.'

'Sure, anything! What do you need? Help with your outfit?' I offer, taking a bite of the bhatura. It's as delicious as it looks.

'If only it were that simple,' Subbu sighs. 'So, Jeena from business development asked me out. I … umm ... I know her from our college days.'

'That's great, Subbu!'

'Wait, hold your horses. It's not really a date. But maybe something leading to one? She's bringing a friend along and asked if I could bring someone too. You know, to make it less awkward. Like a double date situation.'

'Ah, I see!' I raise an eyebrow. 'And you want me to go along?'

'Who else will I ask, bro?'

'When is it?'

'This Saturday, around 7.30 p.m.,' he says and hesitates. 'But the thing is, the place she has suggested is really far away.

It's close to the airport. Which means it would take us over an hour and a half to get there. Jeena's cousin owns the place. Apparently it's very good and she's been meaning to check it out.'

'No problem,' I shrug, taking a sip of water. 'We can take my car.'

'The thing is, she lives close to the airport, so it'll just be you and me heading there. I was thinking we could take a cab. Don't want to deal with having to drive back if we end up drinking.'

It made sense. 'Sure, bro. It's not a problem.'

The relief on his face is immediate and comical. 'Thanks, man! I knew I could count on you!' he says, and his smile is back to its usual brightness as he finally starts eating his meal.

On Saturday morning, my parents call me for our regular video chat. I jolt back instinctively as my sister's face appears front and centre on the phone screen, eyes wide with exaggerated horror, face smeared with a thick, dark grey mask that is part of her ever-diligent skincare routine. She's at that age where every tiny blemish feels like a catastrophe and a single pimple is nothing short of an emergency.

'What the f—Anisha!' I almost scream.

She bursts into laughter, her little childish antic having exactly the effect she desired. 'You should've seen your face!' she cackles.

My parents shake their heads, amused but used to her tomfoolery.

'Anisha, move. Let us see your brother properly,' my mother chides gently. But Anisha only grins, adjusting the camera to ensure all I get is an extended view of her self-care masterpiece.

'Your face looks better like this. I hope this thing you have on is permanent. You can compete for Miss India,' I say.

She sticks her tongue out at me and crosses her eyes in mock offence but finally steps back, allowing me the full view of my home.

My mother, sitting at the dining table, is methodically shelling peas. The familiar plink, plink of the peas dropping into the steel bowl is oddly comforting. My father, in his usual armchair, smiles at me, his glasses slipping down his nose. This is our Saturday ritual, allowing me a glimpse of a small slice of home even when I'm miles away.

'Are you eating properly?' my mother asks, right on cue. 'Or are you just surviving on bread and instant noodles?'

I grin. 'Ma, I had a full meal yesterday. Dal, rice, sabzi, even roti.'

'Hmm,' she says, unimpressed. 'And today?'

'Still figuring it out,' I admit.

She sighs. 'You need someone to take care of you, Aniket. If you were married—'

I groan. 'Ma, please, not this again.'

She exchanges a knowing glance with my father, who wisely stays out of it.

'I'm just saying,' she continues, rolling a pea between her fingers, 'it would be nice to have someone remind you to eat on time, someone to come home to.'

'Ma, I'm not thinking about marriage right now,' I say, rubbing my forehead.

Anisha smirks. 'Yeah, he's too busy dodging commitment and living his "independent" life.'

'Exactly,' I say, playing along. 'Freedom suits me.'

My mother shakes her head but doesn't push further. She knows me too well. She knows that if she presses too hard, I'll retreat. Instead, she moves on to her next set of questions.

'Is work stressful? Are you sleeping well? And what are you up to this weekend?'

'It's not bad at all, Ma. We've just wrapped up a major project and this evening I'm going out with a friend.'

'Guy or girl?'

'With Subbu,' I tell her.

I lean back, letting their voices wash over me. Ma updates me with our Chennai neighbourhood gossip: who got married, whose kid got into IIT, which aunty is feuding with whom. She asks about the weather in Bangalore, and I tell her about the unexpected rain last week. These calls, these simple, routine conversations, keep me anchored. No matter where I am, for these few minutes every Saturday, I am home.

Later, I stand before my wardrobe, deliberately picking the most basic white T-shirt I own, the kind I would wear to Big Bazaar or for a quick grocery run. This double date that Subbu has set up isn't worth the effort of dressing up. I'm going solely because it would be great if it helps him get together with Jeena. I run my hand over my stubbled chin and decide against shaving. Let her—whoever Jeena's friend is—see me as I am.

I'm dragging a comb through my hair when Subbu calls.

'Bro, I'll meet you at the restaurant,' he says, sounding slightly out of breath. 'Amma sent some special avakkai pickle through a relative who's landing at the airport, and I have to meet him as soon as his flight lands. The restaurant is close by.'

'Oh! All right,' I say, checking my watch.

'Don't be late, bro. Please don't leave me hanging. It'll be so awkward making small talk with them until you show up.'

'Relax, I'll be on time,' I assure him, though he calls twice more when I'm in the cab, each time with increasing anxiety in his voice, to check where I am.

The restaurant surprises me, but in a good way. It's built like a wooden chalet, nestled among carefully landscaped greenery. Warm, yellow lights twinkle from both the indoor section and the outdoor pavilion, creating an unexpectedly romantic atmosphere. Not exactly the casual dinner spot I'd imagined.

I call Subbu to update him. 'Just reached.'

'Thank God! Almost there, bro. Just ask for the reservation under my name.'

The hostess leads me through the restaurant, weaving between tables filled with couples and families. Our table is in a quiet corner, partially screened by potted bamboo. I settle into my chair, absently scrolling through my phone, mentally rehearsing small talk for when Subbu arrives with Jeena and her friend. The waiter asks me if I'm ready to order and I tell him I'm waiting for a friend.

Five minutes pass. Then ten. I'm just about to call Subbu but then I freeze. Nothing could've prepared me for what I see. For a few seconds I wonder if I'm imagining things. My heart nearly stops. Those confident strides, the click-clack of those heels. That characteristic sweeping glance as she enters, as though she expects someone to wait on her like she's royalty. I would know that entrance anywhere. And sure enough, like moths to a flame, the restaurant staff are already hovering around her, eager to please.

Trisha.

Here.

Walking towards my table.

She spots me and waves with effortless elegance. 'Oh! Hi, Aniket. Looks like we're early?' she says as the waiter materializes to pull out the chair. She slides into it with grace, and then thanks him while I sit with my mouth slightly open, trying to process this reality.

My brain is short-circuiting. Trisha acts like this is the most normal thing in the world.

For several seconds, all I can do is stare, my capacity for speech having apparently vanished along with my common sense.

'Hi, Trisha,' I finally manage, my voice embarrassingly croaky. I clear my throat and say, 'So, you're Jeena's friend! Of all the people, I never expected it to be you.'

'Jeena? Umm … yes, I do know her. I mean we're in the same team after all. But we barely work on the same projects. She's more of a colleague than a friend,' Trisha says, her brows furrowed, confusion writ large in her eyes. 'But what do you mean by you never expected it to be me?'

'Because Subbu didn't mention who the other person Jeena was bringing to the double date was.'

'Double date?' The frown deepens.

'Aren't you here for … umm … the double date?' I ask, feeling increasingly like an idiot.

'No! I'm here for the office party. Amit's team dinner? Subbu said your team insisted on treating us.' She glances suspiciously at the intimate setting, the flickering candles, the couples at the nearby tables. 'Though this place did seem like an odd choice for a team dinner.'

I'm silent for a few seconds. Then I find my voice. 'There is no team dinner, Trisha. At least none that I know of. Subbu told me he needed moral support for a date with Jeena because he's too shy to—'

At that moment, my phone buzzes, and then so does hers. We reach for our phones simultaneously, like actors in a badly coordinated play.

Subbu's message makes my stomach drop:

> Sorry, bro! Have fun with Trisha. You would never in a million years ask her out. So, I had to do it.

I want to crawl under the table and die. Or maybe find Subbu, kill him first and then die. I look up to find Trisha watching me, her expression shifting from confusion to pure amusement. There's something almost wicked in her smile, like she's enjoying watching me squirm.

'Trisha, I am so sorry. I had no idea about this at all. Subbu—I'm going to fucking kill him,' I mutter.

'But why?'

'Because … well, because …' The words stick in my throat. I'm not able to complete the sentence.

She just laughs, the sound warm and surprisingly genuine. 'You know what? I needed this outing. And they say the universe gives you exactly what you need, when you need it the most. I know it may sound lame, but I was, in fact, looking forward to this team dinner. I don't mind even if the "team" is just you.'

'Really?' I blink. 'You aren't angry?'

'Angry? Please. At least this elaborate ambush includes a nice restaurant and good food. Shall we order? I'm famished.'

'Yes, yes, of course!'

'So, what did Subbu tell you?' she asks as she studies the menu.

I tell her about his 'shy act' and she laughs again. The sound does something to my chest that I choose not to analyse too closely.

'How about the kebab platter with their special house chutney?' she suggests, looking up.

'Sure,' I say automatically. She could've suggested we order rocks from the moon and I would probably agree. I'm still trying to process how this evening has gone from an awkward setup to whatever this is.

'And paratha with paneer butter masala for the main course?'

'Perfect.'

'I'm ordering a margarita. What will you have?'

For a moment, I'm tempted to say that I'll have the same even though I dislike cocktails. But better sense prevails. I tell her that I'll have a beer.

As she waves the waiter over, I try to take a few deep breaths without being obvious. Because despite the embarrassment, despite wanting to strangle Subbu, despite everything, I'm secretly glad I'm here. I now know why Subbu deliberately chose a far-off place. He knew that since we would have travelled a long way, we would decide to stay.

'This Subbu deserves an Oscar,' I say as we wait for the drinks to arrive.

'Indeed, he does. He was so convincing. He even made me fill out an official-looking form, complete with the names of all the people from both teams, and a column for whether we would be attending or not.'

'What? No way!'

'Yes way! Although, I did wonder why the form had a column for filling in our phone number. When I asked him, he said that the restaurant would be sending out individual confirmations about time. I was busy and didn't think much of it. Now I know that it was only so he could text me an apology.'

'Oh my God. Subbu could be a criminal mastermind,' I say. 'He had the whole thing planned down to the last detail.'

The waiter arrives with our drinks. My beer is in a frosted glass, golden and inviting, tiny bubbles dancing their way up to the perfect inch of foam at the top, while the margarita that Trisha has ordered sits in a salt-rimmed glass, catching the light, glistening.

'Cheers, Aniket!' Trisha says as she raises her glass and clinks it against mine. The sound seems to break through some of the lingering tension.

'Tell me about yourself, Aniket. What do you do in your free time?' Trisha asks as she takes a sip of her margarita, watching me over the rim of her glass.

I take a long pull of my beer, letting the cool bitterness settle in before shrugging. 'Free time? What is that? I feel like I'm always working on something or the other.'

Trisha gives me an exaggerated disapproving look. 'Come on! Don't tell me you're one of *those* people? The ones who proudly wear the I-thrive-on-deadlines badge of honour?'

'No, no. I run.'

'Run? Like those marathon runners?'

'More like running away from responsibilities,' I quip, and immediately want to kick myself. But, to my surprise, Trisha laughs so hard she almost chokes on her drink.

'I feel that in my soul,' she says, still grinning. 'But what's the real answer?'

I wish I could dazzle her with tales of exotic hobbies. Maybe mention the gym membership I keep meaning to use, or the trek I almost went on last year. Anything that would make me sound half as interesting as her super-cool friends on Instagram. But I've got nothing. And maybe it's the beer, or maybe it's just the desperate desire to impress her, but what comes out is: 'I'm helping out at a dog shelter.'

The words hang in the air for a moment before her face lights up. She actually reaches across the table and pats my hand, sending an electric current straight up my arm. 'Oh, that's wonderful, Aniket! What do you help them with?'

I feel like I'm floating. I'm going straight to hell for this. 'Their website,' I say quickly, already plotting. 'I'm more on the tech support side. Don't have to physically go to the shelter.'

I had looked up the shelter she had tagged on Instagram, and they'd asked for volunteers for their website. Well, they've just got themselves a volunteer. I need to email them. Tonight. The moment I get home. Because this lie needs to become truth before karma catches up with me.

The rest of the evening proceeds so smoothly that I'm surprised. I feel a bit more relaxed as Trisha seems to be enjoying herself. Maybe it's the beer and the margarita, but we don't run out of things to talk about at all.

We swap horror stories about bad first dates. She tells me about a guy who brought a printed PowerPoint deck to pitch himself as her ideal partner. ('I respect the commitment, but no.') I tell her about a date from my college days who spent two full hours ranking her exes out loud. ('She gave me a detailed analysis of each one, Trisha. She had a little journal she carried with a page for each one.')

We discuss a movie we've both watched and discover that our tastes in movies and TV shows are surprisingly similar. We also agree that those badly rehearsed Bollywood dances at weddings should be banned, and then somehow we end up ranking our favourite childhood snacks.

As the evening rolls on, Trisha orders another margarita. And then another. And because her enthusiasm is endearing, I don't stop her. I just sit back and enjoy how she gets progressively more animated. I'm unable to keep up with her, so I just order another beer.

By the time she's on her fourth margarita, she's deeply invested in explaining why pigeons are agents of chaos.

'They're always watching, Aniket,' she says, leaning in like she's revealing a state secret. 'They sit on windowsills and balcony ledges and AC units and just watch you. Judging. I swear they have a group chat and *we* are definitely the topic.'

I bite back a laugh. 'So, what you're saying is … pigeons are the real villains?'

She nods solemnly. 'Yes. And you should never trust them. Especially guys who masquerade as pigeons.'

'Noted,' I say, smiling even though I have no idea what she's talking about. I can't remember the last time I felt this light, this happy in someone's company.

When the bill arrives, I insist on paying it.

'Aniket, you're a very good person. I … I really like you. But I want to pay for my own drinks. I'm fine. I mean I'm a financially independent woman, you know?' she says.

'I know,' I reply, handing my card to the waiter before she can protest. 'But let me be chivalrous. Just this once.'

She narrows her eyes, trying to decide if she'll argue. Then she just sighs dramatically. 'Fine. But next time, it's on me. I insist.'

Next time.

The words settle somewhere in my chest, warm and hopeful. I feel like dancing. Instead, I sit there, smiling at her, looking into her eyes.

Outside, the night air is sharp and cool against my skin. Trisha is slightly unsteady as she steps onto the pavement, and I instinctively reach for her elbow.

'Whoa there.'

'I'm fine,' she insists, even though she's leaning against me. 'I have to get home.'

'Where do you live?'

'Indiranagar.'

I glance at her, debating my options. There's no way I'm sending her home alone in this state. I call for a taxi, and it arrives quickly.

'Come on,' I say, steering her gently inside before climbing in beside her. 'I'll make sure you get home safe.'

She shakes her head. 'Can't go to my own house like this.'

'Why not?'

She sighs, her voice quieter now. 'My parents are strict. No drinking, no boys … especially since I'm modelling and all that.'

She exhales heavily, then adds, almost as an afterthought, 'Not that they know I broke up …'

'Oh!' I say.

The words hang between us for a moment.

'Where in Indiranagar?' asks the cab driver a little impatiently.

'Defence Colony, Indiranagar,' Trisha says, and then proceeds to give him the full address, which he puts into Google Maps. 'It's my friend's place. I stay with her whenever I go out; I have a key. That way my parents don't find out I've been drinking,' Trisha explains.

Then she leans her head against my shoulder and closes her eyes. And just like that, she's asleep.

I sit there, barely moving as the soft lavender scent of her hair fills the space between us. For the first time all evening, I let myself simply breathe. I can't believe I'm here. *With Trisha.* And that she trusts me enough to lean on me.

It takes us nearly an hour to reach her friend's place, the usual chaos of Bangalore's traffic finally easing after midnight. The city—usually buzzing with impatience—now hums with a softer, sleepier rhythm. Streetlights cast long, golden streaks on the pavement as the cab winds its way through near-empty roads. For once, I wish we had traffic snarls. I don't want this drive to end.

Trisha remains curled against my shoulder, her breathing slow and steady. I hardly move, unwilling to wake her, unwilling to break whatever this moment is.

When we finally arrive, I gently nudge her awake. She stirs, blinking at me in confusion before realizing where we are. 'You're a really nice guy, Aniket. We should do this again. Thank you,' she mumbles. Then she kisses me on the cheek and smiles sleepily as she climbs out of the cab.

I want to say something clever, something that will make her laugh again, but I'm so elated, so shocked that all I can say is, 'Get some sleep, Trisha.'

'Call me Trish. All my friends do,' she says, giving me a lazy wave before disappearing inside the building.

As the taxi pulls away, I lean back against the seat, exhaling slowly, grinning widely. Trisha kissed me!

The grin remains plastered on my face as the cab speeds towards home. It wasn't just the conversation or the laughter or even the fact that she trusted me enough to fall asleep beside me. It was the ease of it all. The way we just fit—easy, unforced, like it had always been this way.

By the time I reach home, my face hurts from smiling. I unlock my phone and type out a message to Subbu:

Thank you.

I give no details, no explanations. He'll anyway demand a full debrief tomorrow, complete with interrogation-level follow-ups. Tonight, I just want to sit with this feeling. To let it settle, sink in.

It's been years since I've had a date this good. Years since I've felt this alive. And the craziest part is that Subbu was right. I would've never mustered the courage to ask her out and this would never have happened without his devious little scheme.

SUBBU

A Year Later

LIFE HAS A peculiar way of unfolding, slipping past even the most careful calculations. I had made my peace with the arithmetic of sacrifice: two more years of pinching every rupee and denying myself small pleasures. All for the dream of buying Amma a proper home. The numbers were clear, unforgiving, and I had resigned myself to their tyranny.

Then the universe shifted.

A brand-new apartment surfaced in the market under circumstances that seemed almost orchestrated by fate. The owners—a young couple who had purchased the apartment as an investment—found themselves blessed with an extraordinary dilemma. The wife had secured a coveted posting in London, the kind of opportunity that comes only once in a career. Her husband, who had been casting his net wide across the UK job markets, suddenly found himself with an offer from a company in Birmingham. Not London, true, but close enough to nurture hopes of an eventual transfer.

Their windfall became my opportunity. They needed to liquidate quickly, and I sensed the desperation beneath their excitement. This was where my years of austere living—every declined dinner invitation, every mended shirt, every rupee counted twice—finally revealed their purpose. I negotiated with the focused intensity of someone who understood that fortune rarely lingers at the door after knocking. My savings formed a substantial foundation. A home loan would bridge the remaining gap.

Within weeks, my mother and I had transformed from tenants to proud homeowners. Amma finally had her own walls, her own set of keys, her own slice of permanence in this shifting world.

The joy of helping Amma move into our own home was indescribable. Our previous rent payments would now go towards our EMIs. Though I have to spend a little more than what I was spending as monthly rent earlier, the pride of owning our own home makes it worthwhile. Every weekend, I take the bus to Coimbatore to spend time with Amma in our two-bedroom apartment.

Amma has made the eighth-floor apartment truly our own. She faithfully draws a kolam outside it every morning, carrying a beautiful tradition meant for the earth, up into the sky. The apartment is blessed with abundant natural light and cross-ventilation, making even the hottest days bearable.

Amma is so proud. She insisted that I invite Aniket over one weekend. He agreed to come, though I suspect it was partly because Trisha was out of town on a modelling shoot. Her modelling career seems to have really taken off after she and Aniket started dating. Their relationship has blossomed beautifully over the past year, and I'm glad my friend didn't end up like me, forever regretting not expressing his feelings.

On the bus to Coimbatore, Aniket can't stop talking about Trisha. 'I still can't believe my luck, bro,' he says, shaking his head in wonder.

'The plan worked better than I hoped,' I reply. 'You'd have never approached her otherwise, even after I shared my story.'

'It could've also gone terribly wrong,' he reminds me.

'But it didn't! And you said it yourself that this has been your happiest year.'

'It is,' he admits, then hesitates. 'Though she's quite high maintenance.'

'Complaining so soon? It's just been a year,' I tease. 'How quickly things change.'

'No, no, not complaining exactly. It's just that relationships need a lot more work than I expected. Plus, those modelling agency people she hangs out with? Their lifestyle, the drugs, the drinking—I don't approve at all. And she can't handle her alcohol well. But I don't want to sound like a judgemental uncle. Trish keeps telling me to loosen up.'

'You can't control who she spends time with,' I advise gently.

Amma is waiting with freshly made filter coffee and her special vegetable pulav when we reach home. Watching her fuss over Aniket, treating him like a second son, warms my heart. She gives him a tour of every corner of our new home, proudly showing off the kitchen with its granite countertops, the balcony where she's started a small herb garden and the living room where sunlight streams in through the large windows.

Later that evening, as we sit on the balcony watching the sunset paint the sky in brilliant oranges and pinks, Aniket turns to me and says, 'Your mother is glowing with happiness, Subbu. You've done well, fulfilling her dream.'

I smile, looking at Amma humming in the kitchen as she makes dinner. 'Sometimes the best dreams are the ones we make real for others,' I reply, feeling contentment settle deep in my bones.

I feel blessed. To me, this apartment isn't just four walls and a roof. It is the ultimate manifestation of years of hope, hard work and a mother's prayers finally answered.

NIDHI

The Turning Point

I STARE AT pictures of myself on my phone. Professionally clicked photos from Vir's wedding that he has forwarded. He has thanked me for attending and told me how much it meant to him that I was there. My burgundy saree does look stunning. Tara had helped me choose it, and I'm glad I went with her choice. I swipe and look at more pictures. They have all turned out splendidly. Just like the wedding. But I'm alone in all of them.

Manoj had sent me a casual message:

> Something came up at work. Sorry, babe. Won't be able to make it.

This was *after* I had booked our flight tickets to Udaipur and packed my clothes. He had said that he would come straight from work and join me at the airport. He had assured me that he had packed all his outfits too. Perhaps he had never meant to go all along.

My mind wanders to the day when Vir had called to invite me to his wedding. I had brought up the conversation with Manoj that very evening when we were having dinner at his place, with music playing softly in the background. His reaction had caught me completely off guard.

'Who in the world calls up their ex and insists that they come to their wedding? What is he trying to prove?' Manoj had scoffed, his fork pushing the pasta around on his plate.

I had just finished eating and it took an effort to keep my voice level. 'He isn't trying to prove anything, Manoj. He's genuinely happy, and he wants me to be a part of his big day.'

'You know what, Nidhi,' Manoj had looked up from his plate, his expression unusually serious, 'I would never invite my ex to our wedding. It's over and it's in the past. Why would I do anything of the sort?'

'That's because you had a nasty break-up, Manoj. My break-up with Vir wasn't like that.' The words had come out sharper than I had intended, and he had flinched slightly.

'It's not about whether it's a nasty break-up or not,' he had said. His voice had taken on that patronizing tone that I hated. 'It's about whether you want that person to be a part of the new life you're starting with someone else. Looks like he hasn't gotten over you at all.'

A small smile had played on my lips then. Trying to lighten the mood, I had said, 'Come on, is that jealousy I detect?'

'I can tell, Nidhi …' He had leaned back, his face serious. 'I don't know what you think, but if a guy invites his ex, it's definitely because he still has a thing for her.'

'Manoj, there's nothing between us now except perhaps affection,' I had said before excusing myself from the table and placing my plate in the sink. 'Like I said, it was nice talking to him, catching up. At one point, we did mean a lot to each other.'

'I don't think it's a good idea, Nidhi. Why rake up things that are in the past?'

I had walked up to him and pressed his shoulders then. 'Please, Manoj. I promised him I would come. And it would really mean the world to me if you came along too.'

I had felt him relaxing under my gentle touch. His voice had softened. 'Not every promise has to be kept, Nidhi. But fine, I'll come along if you want me to.'

Then that cocky grin I'd found charming spread across his face as he turned towards me. 'You can show me off.'

I had been so elated that I immediately RSVP'd for the both of us. When I called Vir to confirm, his joy was palpable through the phone. 'That's wonderful, Nidhi! I'll put both your names down right away. Shreya has been wanting to meet you too!'

But at the last minute, Manoj had backed out with a text message that seemed so hollow. I was forced to go alone.

The wedding itself was beautiful. Shreya turned out to be everything Vir had described and more: brilliant, warm, with a smile that lit up the room. Watching them, I could see how perfectly they fit together, how their eyes followed each other across crowded spaces, how their hands naturally found each other's. It made me happy for Vir, truly happy, but it also stirred something uncomfortable in my chest. I felt abandoned by Manoj. How could he do this to me?

Throughout the evening, old friends and also Vir's parents asked about Manoj: 'Where's your fiancé?', 'Vir had said you'd both be coming?' Each question felt like a small needle prick, forcing me to smile and make excuses I didn't believe myself.

The couples' dance was the worst. As pairs filled the dance floor, I stood at the edge, clutching my cocktail like a shield. Vir noticed. Of course he did. He tried to include me in a group dance. But it wasn't the same. I felt like I was surrounded by happiness while standing in a bubble of sadness and solitude.

Now I'm back home, and the anger I've been suppressing keeps rising up. Every time Manoj tries to talk to me, I find myself snapping at him. He acts bewildered, as if he doesn't understand why I'm upset.

'It was just a wedding,' he said last evening over dinner. 'Why are you making such a big deal of it?'

But it *wasn't* just a wedding. It was about trust, about keeping promises, about being there for each other. It was about Manoj prioritizing his career over my happiness. Most of all, it was about realizing that maybe it was time for me to have a long conversation with Manoj about keeping his word, respecting each other and perhaps even what we mean to each other.

As I sit here with my blog open, I can't help but wonder whether this is what growing apart feels like. When did Manoj's charming confidence start looking a little bit like insecurity? When did his protectiveness begin to feel like possessiveness?

The wedding invitation still sits on my dresser, a beautiful cream-coloured card with gold lettering. Next to it lies the little keepsake that Vir and Shreya had handed out to the guests.

The small card reads: 'Your presence made our day even more special.'

I trace the words with my finger, thinking about promises. I had promised Vir that I would attend. Manoj had promised me that he would go along with me. But how do we decide what promises to keep?

A Pot of Clay That Holds Gold

Hello there! Hope you're all doing well. I must apologize for the slight delay in this post. I've been travelling and have just got back.

I used to believe that a promise was a sacred thing. That once given, it had weight, an invisible thread tying two people together. A promise was trust, spoken aloud. A contract, not of paper, but of the heart.

But life has a way of testing even the strongest of promises. It puts us in circumstances where we need to make choices. Do we keep our promises no matter how hard it is? Or is it okay to not keep a promise?

Not all broken promises come with loud betrayals. Some unravel so gently that you don't realize it's happened until you wake up one day and notice the gap. Some break, not because of deceit but because circumstances change.

Then there are those promises that endure. The ones made not just in words, but in actions. They live in the small, everyday choices we deliberately make: a call returned, a kindness offered, a hand held even in silence. And, sometimes, it is simply being there for a friend because you promised them that you would.

Maybe the real test of a promise isn't whether it's kept forever, but whether it was honest when it was made.

And maybe the promises we make to ourselves matter the most.

What do you think? Do you always keep your promises? I'd love to know.

ANIKET

An Ending or a New Beginning?

SOMEONE SHOULD WRITE a book called 'The Unwritten Rules of Being a Boyfriend'. I'd grab it in a heartbeat and study every chapter. Trish is so different from any woman I've ever known. My last relationship had been when I was in college—practically ancient history—and it had lasted a mere four months. But surely some rules of dating remain constant? With Trish, I never know what to expect. She keeps me on my toes.

I find myself reorganizing my entire weekend schedule based on what she has planned. If she's out of town and is set to arrive on a 2 a.m. flight, I'm there at the airport, armed with flowers or her favourite perfume. The dark circles under my eyes from these late-night airport runs have become a permanent fixture, but seeing her face light up makes it worthwhile.

And yet, I can't help the knot that forms in my stomach whenever she mentions Vishwa, this guy she's been spending considerable time with. She insists it's strictly professional. When I had asked about his role, she had explained with practised patience: 'He's the creative director, Ani. He develops the visual concept and works with photographers, stylists and designers to execute the campaign's vision.'

'Does that mean he'll be with you on every shoot?' I had tried to keep my voice neutral, but the jealousy seeped through anyway.

'Look, I'm getting fabulous opportunities because of him. Come on, Ani. He's a colleague. Don't get so jealous,' she had said and kissed me. She's been doing that a lot, kissing me whenever I raise any concerns. And like magic, my worries dissolve.

Today, though, Trish has decided to pick a fight with me only because I sent her multiple messages asking what time she would be done. Surely that's not wrong? I did it only because I was concerned.

'Ani, that's not cool. You're not my parent; you don't have to keep tabs on me. What in the world are all those missed calls and messages supposed to mean?'

'I … I didn't mean anything by it. I just wanted to know when you'd finish,' I stutter.

'That's exactly what I'm talking about!' Trish throws her hands up in exasperation. 'You're always hovering, always checking. Do you realize how suffocating that can be?'

I sink into the couch, her words hitting harder than I expected. The room feels smaller suddenly, the distance between us expanding with each word.

'I don't mean to suffocate you,' I say quietly. 'I just … I care about you.'

'Caring doesn't mean controlling, Ani.' Her voice softens slightly, but the anger remains in her tone. 'When you keep messaging me, asking when I'll be done, it puts crazy pressure on me. I had to put my phone on silent, and everyone made fun of me because of the constant calls and messages.'

'I didn't think—'

'That's right. You didn't think,' Trish cuts me off. She paces the room, her footsteps echoing against the hardwood floor. 'I need space to breathe, to grow in my career. I need you to trust me.'

The word 'trust' hangs heavy between us. I think about all those late nights at the office, the shoots with Vishwa, the constant text messages I send and the calls I make to her. Maybe she's right.

'I'm sorry,' I say, and this time I mean it differently than all the other apologies. 'I know I've been … intense. It's just that you're so different from anyone I've ever known, and sometimes I worry I'm not enough.'

Trish stops pacing. Her expression shifts from anger to something conflicted, more complex. 'Ani, being enough isn't about monitoring me. It's about supporting my independence and being there when I desperately need you. And you always are. I'm happy about that.'

I nod slowly, understanding dawning. 'I promise I'll be more mindful. Give you the space you need.'

'That's all I want,' she says, sitting beside me. 'Just be my boyfriend, not my guardian.'

The knot in my stomach begins to loosen. Maybe this is one of those unwritten rules that I need to learn: love doesn't mean constant surveillance. Sometimes it means stepping back, setting the other person free and trusting that they'll return.

That weekend, during our usual Saturday video call, my mother begs me to come home. Her voice carries that familiar mix of love and reproach over the phone. 'It's going to be almost a year since we last saw you, Ani. Come home this weekend,' she pleads. The guilt settles heavily in my heart. I've been meaning to go home for weeks now.

I give her my usual response about checking my work schedule, the words feeling hollow even as I utter them. The truth is there's only one person whose plans really matter to me right now.

The perfect opportunity arises a few weeks later, when Trish tells me that she's going to Leh for a shoot. 'I'll be gone for a few days. It's a big campaign,' she says.

'Leh? That's so cool, Trish! I've always wanted to visit,' I say, watching her rummage through her bag.

'Umm …' She pauses as she finds the lipstick she has been looking for. 'But I'm going to be extremely busy. I don't think it's a good idea for you to come along.'

'Oh! No, I wasn't suggesting that at all,' I say, taken aback by the sudden sharpness in her voice. The memory of our fight is still fresh in my mind. 'I was thinking of visiting my parents while you're gone.'

Her shoulders relax visibly. 'Oh, you must!' She opens her compact mirror and uncaps the lipstick. Dark pink, I notice, different from her usual flaming red. 'They must be waiting so eagerly to see you.'

I watch her apply the lipstick with quick precise strokes, using the moment to gather my courage. My heart pounds so hard I wonder if she can hear it. 'Yes, and Trish …' The words stick in my throat, but I force them out anyway. 'I'm thinking about telling them. About … us. It's been a year and a half, you know.'

She stops applying the lipstick and freezes. I see her eyes widen and, for a moment, neither of us breathes. She goes quiet for a moment and my stomach clenches. I wonder if I've pushed too far, too fast. The last time I brought this up—that was a few months ago—she said the timing wasn't right.

Then her smile returns, easy and bright. 'Sure, you should tell them,' she says, as if we're discussing something as simple as the weather.

'Are you sure?' I ask, barely daring to believe it.

'Of course,' she smiles as she puts the lipstick away in her make-up pouch and places it inside her bag. Then she reaches up to straighten my collar in that familiar gesture that still makes my knees go weak. 'Just don't show them those terrible Instagram photos from my last shoot. I look awful in them.'

I hug her so tightly that she says, 'Ani! Let go! You're crushing me.' I can't stop smiling for the rest of the evening. I take her out to dinner at an expensive Italian place that she loves. My Trish. She deserves the best.

Subbu thinks I'm going overboard with the whole Trish thing.

'Ani, while I'm thrilled that you've found happiness with Trisha, I don't know if you realize that you're completely at her beck and call,' he says during lunch. 'Remember when we used to spend weekends playing *Street Fighter*? When was the last time we did that?'

I laugh and deflect. 'That's because you're rushing off every weekend to Coimbatore!'

'Touché. But that's different, bro!' His voice softens. 'You know how much those moments in our apartment mean to Amma and me.'

'I know, bro. I know.' I fidget with my fork. 'It's the same for me. I just love spending time with Trish.'

'I understand that, but you're turning into an errand boy, doing every single thing for her.'

'This is what you do when you're in love. You make sacrifices.'

Subbu stiffens, concern etched into his face. 'It should be a two-way thing, bro. You've been with her for what, a year and a half now? And when was the last time she did anything nice for you?'

'It's not like that at all,' I protest. 'She's genuinely a nice girl. I'm sure she'd do stuff for me if I needed it. She's just juggling a lot right now, between her modelling career and work. Besides,' I add, 'it makes me happy to see her happy.'

Subbu isn't convinced, but he sighs and lets it go. 'Do whatever makes you happy, bro. I just hope nothing changes our friendship. Not me rushing off to Coimbatore, and not you rushing off to Trisha.' He smiles good-naturedly, but there's a hint of sadness in his eyes.

I make a mental note to visit his place one of these weekends. It's a promise I've made to myself countless times over the past few months. Back when I was single, we used to hang out constantly. Now time seems to follow different rules. Weekdays blur into a haze of deadlines and meetings, and weekends—those precious forty-eight hours—dissolve into moments with Trish. I can't seem to get enough time with her.

I'm going to miss her so much when she goes to Leh. I'm leaving for Chennai the same day. But I don't tell Subbu that.

The morning I'm supposed to catch the train to Chennai, I oversleep. The moment my eyes spring open, panic surges through me. There's no time to change. Thankfully, my bag is already packed. I hurriedly brush my teeth, sling the bag over my shoulder and dash outside to hail an auto.

As I settle into the seat, trying to catch my breath, I glance down at my phone and freeze. Something sinks inside me. I can't believe what I'm seeing. I read the email once. Then again. The words blur as a wave of unease washes over me.

By the time I reach the railway station, my hands are clammy and my heart hammers in my chest. I feel light-headed, on the verge of a panic attack.

Usually, I'd grab a coffee before boarding the train, but not today. This message has rattled me to the core. When the train arrives, I board it in a daze, barely aware of my surroundings. I find my seat and sink into it. Then I dial Subbu and we begin to speak.

It's only when the train starts moving that I realize how loud I was being. By then, I've been talking for at least fifteen whole minutes, and am mid-way through my life-and-death conversation with Subbu. My fellow passengers are giving me death glares. Damn! I feel like such an idiot now as I lower my voice.

'No. I'm not okay. How can you tell me to calm down? She has said that she needs time to think about this. Do you know what this means? How can you? You've never even been in a relationship!'

Anyone in Subbu's place would have hung up on me by now and told me to take a walk. But Subbu? He loves me too much. Subbu—my wingman, my relationship philosopher, my guide and now my therapist—has been listening patiently to me going on and on about my issues with Trish. My last remark was below the belt. I immediately try to make amends.

'I'm sorry, bro. That was uncalled for. I apologize,' I say. I should not have made that remark, but I'm too upset and distraught at Trish's missive, which I now look at again, expecting the words to change.

Ani,

I'm really, really, really not dumping you. (Well, not yet! Just kidding!) Please don't get scared and please don't think of this email as that. But I need time to think about this relationship. I honestly do.

You don't give me space to breathe. You send one mail, then follow it up with a message, then three links, and before I've even had time to check them, you're on the phone, calling me. If I don't pick up, there are fifteen WhatsApp messages waiting for me.

I have a life outside of our relationship ... I need time on my shoots. I can't respond to you instantly. And I've told you that Vishwa is a friend. Yet you insist on keeping tabs on him and me. Why in the world did you send him that message, asking him when he'll drop me off? What was that supposed to mean?

I know you love me, Ani. And I've told you that I love you too. But please understand that you can't bind me like this. Make me accountable to you for everything. I don't keep tabs on you, do I?

I leave today for Leh. The whole team is travelling with me and, yes, Vishwa will be there too. Please don't worry if I don't message you. The internet, I'm told, is patchy. I will be coming back to you in two weeks. That will give us both enough time.

Please treat this dispassionately and please don't drink too much. Work out and lose that gut. Or at least try. Twenty-seven is no age to have a beer belly, as slight as it is. If you don't take care, you'll soon be a plump, overweight, roly-poly Ani. Heh heh.

Muaaah.

Trish

What the hell does she mean by this? Why does she need 'time to think'? How could she do this? That too when I'm on my way to Chennai to meet my parents and tell them about us? That's what we'd agreed on. And now she pulls this stunt on me.

I definitely don't recall flooding her with links. I had sent her one on anamorphic sculptures and two *XKCD* comics. How can that not be funny? And how long does it take to read two comic strips anyway? And what did she mean that I call her and inundate her with messages? I think any guy would definitely care about when his girlfriend is going to get home, especially when she was out drinking with a whole bunch of unknown idiots like Vishwa and his gang.

And what Trish has conveniently forgotten is that she was so drunk that day that she wasn't even able to stand. I drove all the way to Yelahanka to pick her up and then dropped her off at Indiranagar. I drove fifty-five bloody kilometres to ensure she was safe, but she does not remember that. This was too much.

Subbu listens patiently, despite being woken up at the crack of dawn with my Trish-troubles. And now, as a reward for listening to me, I have snapped at him. But he brushes it aside.

'No problem. Look, bro, what you've given me is a bug report where you think you know everything about system Trisha, but you don't!'

As upset as I am, it's hard not to laugh at what he has said. Only Subbu can come up with such techie jargon when I'm in the middle of telling him that my relationship is in danger.

'No, I haven't. I've given you an accurate report. But we have to admit that what we have here is a Reality 101 failure. She misunderstands every single thing I do. I wish I hadn't gone on that stupid office trip and had instead taken her paragliding or wherever she wanted to go. Damn.'

'My dear Aniket, what we have here is the Mad Girlfriend bug. We need to sort out these strange happenings to fix the reality. And this is not failure. This is an experiment. Now we know what works and what doesn't. Give me an hour or so.

I'll call you right back. I have a call with a client,' he says and hangs up.

I sink into my seat, push the button to recline it and stretch my legs. The Shatabdi Express is one of the nicest trains in the Indian Railways. No sooner have I settled in than the attendants bring a bottle of mineral water and some newspapers.

To distract myself, I pick *The Times of India* and am about to open it, when a voice next to me asks the attendant, 'Don't you have *The Hindu*?'

It is only then that I notice her.

NIDHI

A Journey

THE GUY IS nice-looking. Slightly plump maybe, but only ever so slightly. He's tall, and seems to have a five-day stubble. If he loses a couple of kilos and makes a little more effort with his clothes, he would definitely be attractive.

Hell, what am I saying? Compared to Manoj, this guy *is* attractive. Manoj dresses well but isn't what I'd call good-looking. This guy looks decent, though I must admit that he could've chosen better clothes than a T-shirt on its last legs, knee-length checked shorts and rubber flip-flops. He looks like he has just tumbled out of bed. And, from his conversation, it seems like his girlfriend has just dumped him. Over an email, no less. I wonder if he is overreacting though.

It's hard to tell as he seems genuinely upset. It's rare to find guys this sincere, guys who care this much. This one clearly does. I wonder what his girlfriend looks like. What was their relationship like? She wanted to go paragliding, but he went on an office trip instead. Would anyone break up over that?

The attendant brings out newspapers and water, and he hands me *The Times of India.* I always read *The Hindu*, and so I ask him if he has that instead.

'Yes, madam,' he says and hands me a copy of *The Hindu*. The guy I had been observing is now looking at me. He smiles sheepishly at me. I smile back.

'Sorry if I was loud. I didn't mean to be,' he says.

'No worries, you clearly seem to be having girlfriend trouble,' I reply, much to my surprise. I don't usually pry, but there is something so refreshing about this guy, it makes me want to pat his back and tell him that things will be fine. I don't think Manoj would quite appreciate that, though. I don't want to think of Manoj right now, but things have reached a stage where any interaction of mine with a person of the opposite sex is mentally measured against how Manoj will react.

Stop it. Manoj doesn't own you, even though he acts that way. Heck, you aren't even married to him yet.

'Yeah, my girlfriend says she needs space,' he says.

I laugh.

'What's so funny?' he asks.

'I said the same thing to my fiancé! I'm Nidhi, by the way.'

'Hi, Nidhi. Nice to meet you. Aniket,' he says and extends his hand.

His handshake is firm. You can tell a lot about a guy by the way he shakes a woman's hand. His isn't a bone-crushing grip like most men have, nor is it a weak, wishy-washy, delicate handshake. This one radiates a kind of trustworthiness and confidence. Somehow, I also get a sense that he's kind and sensitive. I like this guy! And I've barely spoken to him, nor do I know anything about him.

Yet I have surprised myself by revealing something that even my closest friends don't know: that I told my fiancé that I needed space. That's the thing about journeys. You open up a lot more to strangers. It's a weird kind of trust, and perhaps it's got something to do with anonymity—everyone's a stranger and chances are you'll never see them again. There's also a sense of adventure that you feel on every journey you embark on. I guess he feels the same way.

'What do you do, Nidhi? And, seeing that we're both travelling to the same place, what is your connection with Chennai, if I may ask?' he says.

He's looking at me now, and his gaze is direct, honest. I know then that I was right about his trustworthiness. I can always tell from the eyes.

'My dad lives in Chennai, and I'm going to spend some time with him. It's my hometown,' I answer. I'm usually wary of people I've just met, and normally never reveal details about myself. But this guy seems different. Either that or it's the train-journey effect acting up again.

'Oh, I see. And what about your mother? Where does she live?'

'I lost my mom,' I say.

There's a pause.

'I'm so sorry,' he says.

'It was a long time ago. It happened when I was fifteen. Besides, I have a stepmom now,' I say, and I see the expression on his face. It's a familiar look, one that I've seen on most people when I tell them that I've lost my mother.

'You didn't answer my first question though,' he says. 'About what you do for a living.'

'Oh, that. I teach a pottery course at a studio in Bangalore.'

'That's very interesting and unusual. How nice.'

'So, I presume your job is something usual and uninteresting?' I quip, and he laughs.

'I wouldn't say it's uninteresting, but yes, the usual. I'm a techie.'

'I guess it's true—every second person you meet in Bangalore really is a techie. And what is your company into? Where do you work?' It is my turn to probe now. Surprisingly, the conversation between us is flowing smoothly. *Well done, Nidhi—for a shy, introvert person, you're doing well.*

'I work for an organization called Connect Technologies.'

'And what does Connect do? Software development?'

'Well, not exactly software development. We provide a global business support system for telecom operators. We're pioneers in this field, and, if I'm not mistaken, also the only company that does this kind of thing. Right from fraud management to asset assurance, capacity management, route optimization, partner settlement and cost management, we give end-to-end services to our customers,' he says.

God, that sounds so boring. How can anyone want to do such stuff? I nod and try to appear interested.

The attendants begin serving breakfast, so we put our seats upright and open the tray tables in front of us. Both of us opt for the vegetarian meal. The food tray has a thermos flask with hot water, a cup, a cutlery packet, sachets of milk-powder and sugar, and a teabag, apart from the packed parcel of food. When

I open mine, I discover it is khara-bath, a speciality of Karnataka that I love. As I dig into the food, I see that he seems to be enjoying it too. I notice how neatly he has laid out his cutlery, and how he eats with his mouth closed. For all the sloppiness of his dressing style, his dining manners are impeccable.

'So, what does your fiancé do?' he asks as we sit sipping our tea after finishing our meals.

'He's a techie like you. Works at a multinational,' I reply.

'Aah, I see. Very different from your field, right?'

'You bet.'

'So, do you work with adults or kids? And how long is a typical pottery course? Tell me more about it,' he says. He appears to be genuinely interested; it doesn't seem like he is making conversation for the sake of passing time. I hate it when people do that. I have my book ready to fend off such people.

'We have several programmes, for kids as well as for adults.'

'And when you say adults, do people do the course as a one-off thing or do they pursue it further?'

'See, it all varies from person to person. We do corporate workshops; we host children's parties; and then we have full-length courses that typically run over eight weeks. And that's a basic course. Once you complete the basic course, you can go for an advanced course, if it interests you. We also have glazing, a potter's wheel foundation course and something called "bring clay to life", which is free-hand sculpting. And yes, to answer your question, many start off with a trial session, but then find that they enjoy it so much that they come back.'

'Wow! I didn't know there were that many options. I haven't even seen a potter's wheel—except in movies—or ever touched clay. When you say "potter's wheel", I can only think of Demi Moore in *Ghost*,' he says.

'Oh yes, it is very sensual. You must try it sometime! Working with clay is very therapeutic. Clay originates from the earth, the source of all things. Ancient civilizations used clay for everything, right from their buildings to their vessels and jewellery. There's something very primal about giving it form. It's very soothing.'

I'm surprised that I have talked so much to him. Then again, this is something I'm passionate about, and I feel like I have to explain just how wonderful it is.

'I think you've convinced me. I'll definitely give it a try sometime,' he says.

'We have a lovely sun-drenched rooftop studio with a lot of potted plants and terracotta objects scattered around. Drop by anytime. We're closed on Mondays, but are open on all other days, including weekends,' I say.

He asks me for the name and address of the studio. 'It's called Mitti, and it's in HSR Layout.'

'Oh! That's next door to where I live,' he says, and adds that he lives in Bellandur.

'Then the studio is only a five- to six-minute drive for you. Twenty, if the traffic is bad,' I say, and he laughs.

When you live in a city like Bangalore, you measure distance by the time taken to reach your destination, which in turn depends on traffic conditions. Knowing the actual physical distance is a useless bit of information, best confined to Google Maps.

His phone rings. I recognize his ringtone. It is Avicii's 'Waiting for Love'.

'Excuse me, I have to take this call, and this time I promise I won't be loud,' he says.

'Please go ahead,' I tell him, and he smiles, almost embarrassed to take that call.

'Bro, I can't talk right now,' I hear him say. There's a pause, then, 'I'll tell you later. I'm with someone.' After another pause, 'I'll call you back.' He practically hisses the last part and turns back to me apologetically.

When we finally arrive at Chennai five and a half hours later, it occurs to me that this conversation has been so interesting that for the first time in my life, I haven't opened my book on a train journey.

To know what happens to Aniket, Nidhi and Trisha, meet them again in *It's All in the Planets.*

THE ONE WHO CHANGED EVERYTHING

AMAN

Spotlight

FOR YEARS I'VE rolled my eyes at the romantic clichés that saturate our movies, TV shows and books. The protagonists lock eyes across crowded rooms; an orchestra playing in the background signals something special happening and, if it's a Bollywood movie, gusts of wind tousle the heroine's hair as she gazes dreamily into the distance. The rest of the plot is a drawn-out chase. I'm convinced it is all absolute nonsense.

'The screenwriters should be a bit more imaginative,' I declare with smug certainty as I enter my room and catch Chandan, my roommate and a self-proclaimed romantic, watching yet another cheesy romcom on his laptop. He doesn't have his headphones on.

'Bro! Let go of your cynical attitude a little. Allow yourself to be swept away by something unabashedly sentimental for once,' he replies, not bothering to look up from his laptop.

'You're just echoing Sonam's thoughts. She has filled your head with romantic delusions,' I retort, sitting down at my desk.

He pauses the latest tear-jerker he is watching. Then he turns serious. 'We're doing long-distance. It's hard enough without your cynicism. If movies and their so-called clichés give us a language to keep our connection alive across these miles, then so be it.'

The slight hurt in his voice is unmistakable. I realize I haven't exactly been sympathetic to his situation. His folks live in Bhutan and so does his girlfriend Sonam. He misses his home, and I know he misses his girlfriend intensely.

'Okay, okay. I'll try!' I laugh, trying to defuse the tension.

But deep down, I still think movies like the one he is watching are absolute nonsense. Real romance is never instant; it's built slowly over years. Like the one my Ma and Baba had. Even though he passed away when I was seven, the countless stories that Ma has told me about Baba make me feel like he has always been a part of my life. It's the little things Ma would share, like how Baba would always wake up early to make her tea before she even opened her eyes, or how he would leave small handwritten notes in her books with observations he thought she would appreciate. Their love wasn't about grand gestures or perfect romance; it was built on thousands of small moments, disagreements worked through with patience and a deep understanding that grew stronger with each passing year.

Sometimes when Ma speaks about him, the look in her eyes and the way she smiles make me think that their connection transcends his physical absence. Through her stories, I've learned that real love isn't just passion or convenience. It's about showing up every day and choosing each other again and again.

I hope, someday I'll find someone who will build that same slow, steady flame with me. Not the dizzying rush of infatuation that burns out quickly, but something sustainable that can weather life's storms. Something worth waiting for.

And then it happens to me. When I least expect it.

One moment I'm a rational person with evidence-based opinions about love, and the next moment, poof! I become a living example of how screenwriters aren't completely delusional.

It's during our farewell party, which our juniors are throwing for us, that this transformation takes place. The hall is alive with pulsing music, and laughter flows as freely as the fruit punch, the kind that's usually innocent but now carries a mischievous kick, thanks to someone sneaking in something extra. The mood is light, carefree and ebullient. Since our placements are already done, and most of us, including me, have bagged exceptional offers, we're all basking in the rare freedom that comes with endings and beginnings aligning perfectly. The constant pressure that defined our college years has dissolved into glimmering hopes for the future.

'The next item on the agenda is a special quiz for our seniors. And this one comes with great gift hampers from our sponsor Titania Industries,' a female voice announces, cutting through the ambient chatter. The crowd erupts in cheers as she gestures towards the oversized hampers displayed on stage.

I look up, and it is in this moment that everything changes.

There she stands on the stage in a pale-yellow salwar kameez, her presence calm, yet commanding. When she tucks a wayward strand of hair behind her ear with effortless grace, something shifts inside me. I feel an unexpected hammering of my heart that catches me off guard. The background noise seems to fade as though someone is turning the volume down. Chandan and my other friends continue talking beside me, but their words are unintelligible murmurs.

Despite years of mocking these exact clichéd moments in Bollywood films, I find myself now living in one. In that instant, all the theories I've had about what love should and shouldn't be, disappear. I stand and stare at her, mesmerized.

Suddenly, I find Chandan's hand beneath my jaw, pushing it upward. He leans in and murmurs with a grin, mimicking a famous Hindi film dialogue, 'Muh toh bandh karo, uncle.' Then he bursts out laughing.

I know my expression must be ridiculous. But I can't help it, because, for the first time, every single thing I've ever scoffed at, feels real.

'Who is she?' I whisper.

'Shruti Srinivasan, second year, Eng lit,' Chandan says.

'How do you know her?' I ask.

'If you had joined the film club instead of the math club, you too would've known her,' Chandan replies with a smirk. 'And guess what? *She* loves romance films too,' he adds with a chuckle.

I look at him, unsure if he's kidding.

He bursts out laughing. 'I was joking, bro! Look at your face! Remember I helped the Cultural Committee organize that trip to Bhutan? She was part of the planning committee.'

By now, Shruti has begun to explain the quiz rules.

'It's an interesting format, so put on your thinking caps and listen carefully,' she announces. 'This isn't your standard Trivial

Pursuit.' Her eyes move steadily over the crowd, as though taking in every single detail. 'Here's the twist. The first answer? It's going to be child's play. But each subsequent answer will begin with the final letter of the previous answer. Something like a chain of knowledge.'

'Teams?' someone calls out from the back, their voice tinged with hope.

Shruti shakes her head. 'You're all on your own today. Raise your hand, catch my eye, and once I pick, you can give me the answer,' she says. 'Ready for this?' she challenges.

Lukewarm murmurs of 'Yes' ripple through the crowd.

'Louder, please! I want *more* enthusiasm. Come on, guys! This is a celebration. And look at the size of the hamper to be won,' she says, gesturing to the package. 'Are you ready?' she raises her voice and asks again. She knows exactly how to sway the crowd.

'Yes! Yes! Yes!' the crowd chants.

A satisfied smile plays at the corner of her lips. 'That's better. First question. An easy-peasy one coming your way: Which Renaissance master painted the Sistine Chapel ceiling?'

Several hands shoot up. I know the answer to this one.

'This is your chance to impress her. Go, bro, go,' Chandan urges.

But Shruti doesn't pick me. She selects a girl near the front of the crowd. 'You, the girl in red, third row,' she says.

'Leonardo da Vinci,' the girl answers confidently.

'What the—she gave the wrong answer, bro!' I whisper.

'WRONG!' yells Chandan before I can stop him. Everyone turns to look at us, wondering which one of us has spoken.

'Yes, unfortunately, that's incorrect,' Shruti says. 'But would you be able to tell us the right answer?' She looks in our direction.

My throat constricts as her eyes lock with mine, waiting. The distance between us seems impossibly vast, yet strangely intimate.

Chandan's elbow finds my ribs as he nudges me, and I feel the sharp jab of bone against bone.

'It's Michelangelo,' I say, my voice emerging stronger than I had expected, carrying across the room like it belongs to someone else. Someone entirely braver.

A smile breaks across Shruti's face. It's not the polite quizmaster smile she has worn until now, but something genuine. I notice immediately that it is warmer, more real.

'Perfectly correct!' She gestures towards me with an open palm. 'Let's give a round of applause for ...' she pauses, her expression softening with curiosity. 'What's your name?'

'Aman,' I manage, the two syllables of my own name suddenly foreign on my tongue.

'Let's hear it for Aman!' Shruti says.

The crowd's applause washes over me in waves, but I barely register it. My heart is pounding hard. She *said* my name. I cannot believe she has noticed me.

'All right, here comes the next question,' Shruti continues. 'Which American talk show host is famously known for her long-running daytime TV show and book club? Remember, the answer to this one begins with the last letter of the previous answer.'

Fewer hands shoot up this time. Somehow, the stakes feel higher.

'Fifth row, blue shirt,' she says, picking a guy at the front.

'Oprah Winfrey,' he answers confidently.

'And that is correct!' Shruti confirms, her voice carrying a note of approval. She sweeps her gaze across the room. 'Looks like we need to raise the stakes a bit. These questions are clearly too easy for such a knowledgeable crowd.' Her smile turns challenging. 'We'll have to work a bit harder for that prize hamper, won't we?'

A quiet, vindictive pleasure blooms in my chest. Childish, I know, but I cannot help it. She hasn't asked for *his* name! Hasn't invited the crowd to applaud him. The distinction shouldn't matter, yet it does. I savour this small victory, knowing fully well how petty it is.

Shruti, blissfully unaware of the drama playing out in my mind, is already moving forward, her focus entirely on maintaining the quiz's momentum.

The next question she asks has only two hands going up. Me and Blue Shirt. He turns back and looks at me, sizing me up with a cool confidence that makes my stomach knot with insecurity. His effortlessly styled hair and relaxed smile scream social butterfly, the kind who thrives in a room full of strangers. Me? I'm more of a wallflower, content to blend in.

But I can't let him win. Not this time. I *have* to win this.

'Here's the next one: Which Israeli prime minister won the Nobel Peace Prize in 1994 for his efforts in negotiating the Oslo Accords?'

Beside me, Chandan frantically types into his phone. 'Yitzhak Rabin,' he hisses urgently. 'Put your damn hand up, now!'

My arm rises up as if pulled by an invisible string. Blue Shirt has put up his hand too. Shruti's eyes find mine immediately, as though she'd been waiting for it.

'Aman,' she says with a hint of teasing in her voice. 'Let's see if it was beginner's luck. What's the answer?'

A flush of heat crawls up my neck as every head in the auditorium swivels in my direction. My palms have turned cold and clammy with nervousness. My mouth feels dry. For a moment, I fear that I've forgotten the answer that Chandan has given me. Then I remember it. When I speak, my voice seems strangely steadier compared to how I feel inside.

'Yitzhak Rabin,' I answer.

Something shifts in Shruti's expression. Her eyebrows lift, and she leans a fraction closer to the mic. 'And that is absolutely correct!' she declares. I let the moment wash over me, barely believing I have beaten Blue Shirt.

'Okay, here's the next question,' Shruti says. 'And this is a tough one.' She pauses dramatically. The audience is completely silent.

'Which 1959 Alfred Hitchcock thriller follows an advertising executive who is mistaken for a government agent and becomes embroiled in a chase involving spies and a famous scene atop Mount Rushmore?' she asks.

Chandan whispers the answer. My hand shoots up before Blue Shirt can react. This time mine is the only hand that pierces the stillness that has descended all around us.

Shruti's gaze is fixed on me once more, a spark of something—surprise maybe—lighting her eyes. Sweat gathers on my forehead, a slow trickle sliding down the side of my face. My heart beats so fiercely I'm sure the entire auditorium can hear it.

'Yes, Aman?' she says, her voice softer. Am I imagining the intimacy in her voice? How is this even possible? Am I going crazy? My pulse races even faster.

Chandan nudges me again, gently this time.

'*North by Northwest*,' I answer, the syllables tumbling out with clarity.

The audience erupts into spontaneous applause. A thunderous wave that rings in my ears. For the first time in my life, I'm the centre of positive attention. As much as the sensation is terrifying, it's also intoxicating. But more importantly, is that admiration I spot in Shruti's eyes? I feel like I'm floating on air.

But what she says next brings me crashing to earth.

Shruti tilts her head slightly, her brows drawn together. 'You've been doing exceptionally well, Aman,' she says, a note of suspicion creeping into her words. Or perhaps it's my imagination playing tricks on me again. 'But for the final two questions, I need to make extra sure that you're not getting some help with the answers. So, may I please request you to come up on stage?'

The crowd lets out a collective 'Oooooh' that resonates through the room. My stomach plummets as though I've missed a step while climbing a staircase. The brief taste of glory is replaced by the harsh, acrid taste of panic.

Blood rushes into my ears as I swallow hard. I feel like every single pair of eyes in the auditorium is boring into me. Expectant. Judgemental.

I want to scream. Run away. But I find myself smiling and nodding. Pretending it's all okay. The twenty steps to the stage stretch before me like miles of treacherous terrain. I look at Chandan, and he gives me a look of half-apology and half-encouragement.

I force my leaden legs to move. With every inch I cover, my heart sinks further. I wish I had never raised my hand to answer that first question. But it's too late now. I climb the steps to the stage.

The stage lights glare down on me with merciless intensity, their heat prickling my skin. Without Chandan to whisper the answers, I know I'm destined to fail. Spectacularly. And yet, despite the panic gnawing at me, I can't help but notice how close Shruti is.

For a moment, the world narrows down to just her. The glint of her gold earrings, the slight unevenness of her smile that somehow makes her even more beautiful. Her perfume drifts towards me, warm, citrusy and utterly distracting. I force myself to focus, but my mind feels like a static-filled radio.

'All right, here's my question, and good luck!' Shruti says, her voice bright and clear.

I nod, blinking hard. *Focus. Focus.* I whisper a silent prayer, pleading with Hanuman to help me. Then doubt creeps in. Shouldn't I be praying to Saraswati instead? *Please, any god listening, help me now.*

Shruti glances down at the card in her hand. 'Which optical illusion, first created in 1832 by a Swiss crystallographer, depicts a cube that can be interpreted from two different perspectives, switching back and forth in the viewer's mind?'

The audience falls silent, a hush so deep I can hear my own heartbeat pounding in my ears.

I can't believe it. My gods haven't abandoned me after all. I want to jump for joy. I resist the urge to scream in relief. This was *exactly* what I had explored in my wireframe design and 3D modelling paper back in my second year.

'The Necker cube,' I say, my voice full of genuine confidence for the first time that evening.

'Wow! That's *incredible*!' Shruti says as the audience bursts into applause once more.

Then she covers the microphone and whispers, 'What's your full name?'

'Aman Mathur,' I say, standing straighter.

'Now the final question for Aman Mathur,' Shruti announces.

Even if I fail this one, I at least got the other one right. *It can't be that bad. Calm down.*

'Which UNESCO World Heritage site, located on an island near Mumbai, is famous for its rock-cut cave temples dedicated to Lord Shiva?' Shruti asks.

Another massive wave of relief floods through me. During our eighth-grade field trip, we'd visited this very place. I remember the boat ride across the harbour, the humid air heavy with salt and the cool caves cut into ancient stones.

Suddenly, I spot Chandan who has made his way to the front of the auditorium, joining the students standing by the side. He is discreetly trying to imitate an elephant trunk with his hand. His expression is so strained that I almost laugh despite being so tense. But I do not need his help. Not this time.

'Elephanta Caves,' I answer.

Shruti's smile widens, transforming her entire face. 'Ladies and gentlemen, we have our winner!' she says with theatrical flair. 'Give it up for Aman Mathur!'

She raises her hand for a high-five, and for a few seconds I just stare at her, still processing everything that has just happened. Then I raise my own hand to meet hers, the brief contact sending an electric current through my fingertips as the applause crashes around us, drowning us.

'And I request you all to stay for the Western dance competition coming up after a short ten-minute break,' she continues, her professional face back in place again. 'After the winners have been picked for the Western dance competition, the prize distribution for all events, including this quiz, will take place.'

As the crowd begins to scatter, she turns to me, switching off the microphone. The sudden intimacy of her undivided attention is more overwhelming than facing the entire audience had been.

'So, where are you from, Aman?' she asks, looking genuinely curious.

'Gwalior,' I reply, surprised that my mind can still answer coherently.

'Oh! Sorry. I meant to ask what department are you in? What are you studying?'

Her simple question has somehow breached the last of my defences. The stage beneath my feet seems to tilt slightly. I feel exposed. Unmasked. And, suddenly, also very foolish to have misunderstood what she had asked.

'I … I should go. I'm late for something,' I blurt out. Then, I say, 'Thank you for the quiz,' and rush down the stairs.

Confusion clouds Shruti's expression but I cannot bear to look back. I practically flee the stage, taking the steps two at a time, narrowly avoiding a collision with a student who is walking. I make a beeline for Chandan, grabbing his arm with more force than I intended.

'Let's leave!' I hiss; my voice is strained and foreign even to my own ears.

'What? But bro …' His eyes dart between my face and the stage. He is baffled.

'Now!' The single word carries all the panic, embarrassment and confusion swirling inside me. Fortunately, he understands.

We push through the crowd, leaving behind a trail of mumbled excuse-mes and sorries. I feel like I'm unable to breathe as we weave our way out. It's only when we burst through the heavy double doors and step into the evening air that oxygen seems to flow properly into my lungs.

The campus ground stretches before us, bathed in the gentle glow of twilight. The carefully tended flower beds seem surreal after the intensity of what has just transpired. I inhale deeply and exhale.

'Dude! What the hell?' Chandan asks as we make our way towards the parking lot. His exasperation and bewilderment are already melting into laughter.

'I have no idea what just happened,' I mutter.

'What just happened was that you blew up a chance to get Shruti Srinivasan's number.' Chandan's laughter is warm and familiar. Without judgement.

'I panicked, okay?' I defend myself. The adrenaline is still coursing through my veins. 'It was all too much. I'm not used to being in front of people like that. On top of that, she asked me something and I think I made a fool of myself.'

Chandan shakes his head, his expression a mixture of amusement and affection. 'The great Aman Mathur, unfazed by differential equations but terrified of a pretty girl?' he teases as he pulls out the keys to his bike.

I shrug.

'Come on, let's get you out of here before your admirer comes looking for you,' he says as he turns the key in the ignition and the engine sputters to life.

'She's not my admirer!' I say, getting on the pillion. The vinyl seat is warm from the day's sunshine.

'Sonam won't believe this,' he says.

'You're not telling anyone,' I warn.

'Oh, I'm telling everyone,' he replies cheerfully, revving the engine for emphasis. 'The day Aman Mathur fell in love and ran away. I'm writing a movie plot!' He chuckles as we speed away from the campus.

'I really messed up, didn't I?' I shout over the engine's rumble. But my words are carried away by the wind.

As the college disappears from view, I realize with startling clarity that this is the first time in my life that I'm not content to remain invisible. The realization terrifies me more than any spotlight ever can.

SHRUTI

An Escape

'I DON'T BELIEVE this! Are you really hiding here, Shruti?' my mother asks, finding me in the secluded back hall where coffee is being served for the staff. It's tucked away in a hidden corner of the sprawling venue at Palace Grounds that my cousin has chosen for her wedding. Meticulously manicured gardens, crystal-draped pavilions and a grand hall where guests dressed in silk and gold jewellery worth small fortunes mingle with each other in a display of casual opulence. This venue is massive. And elegant.

There are countless places one can disappear into on this vast, beautiful estate, its many acres of gardens offering refuge from the overwhelming festivities.

'No, Ma!' I lie, adjusting the pleats of my Kanjeevaram saree, the peacock blue one with a shocking pink border that Ma insisted I wear, along with the traditional gold jewellery she has forced upon me despite my protests about wanting to dress 'simple'. I catch my reflection in a distant mirror and wince. I look like a Christmas tree with all these shiny baubles.

Except these are real gold, worth millions. The thought makes me uncomfortable.

'The Muralidharans are asking for you,' Ma says, her voice dropping to a conspiratorial whisper. 'Their son Vipul is here.'

I stiffen. 'Ma, I do not want to meet him. I agreed to attend this wedding provided there was no matchmaking involved.'

'Kanna, where am I making a match?' She places a hand on her chest, feigning innocence. 'Just chat with him. Ten minutes. They are very keen. Don't make your Appa and me look bad,' she pleads.

'And what will the chat lead to? I'm not like Aishu who agreed to get married so soon. It's ridiculous.' I roll my eyes.

'Shruti ...' My mother's voice is a warning now, though her pleasant expression never wavers. 'He has done an MBA from London and has a nice apartment overlooking the Thames. His mother showed me photos.'

She squeezes my arm, her grip betraying the steel beneath her smile as she guides me in the general direction of the gazebo.

I sigh, knowing there's no point arguing with her and telling her that I don't care for his apartment or his fancy foreign education. I simply want to have my own career before I get married. I'm already rehearsing polite conversation as I march reluctantly towards the designated meeting place.

I stand at a gazebo decorated with cascading jasmine and vibrant marigolds, a little distance away from the main hall where my cousin's wedding is taking place, wishing I could escape. The wedding decorators have transformed every inch of the place into a scene from a fairytale. Rows of luxury cars fill the expansive parking area, their polished exteriors gleaming under the evening lights. The air is thick with the mingling scents of expensive perfume, incense and that unmistakable 'rich-people fragrance', a heady mix that's beginning to feel cloying.

I think all of this is a stupid waste of time and money. And my cousin? She's foolish to be over the moon. She's just nineteen! I can't believe how happy she looks in her wedding finery: a red and gold saree, her jewellery making tinkling sounds as she poses for the photographers. It's not even like she is in love with the guy. It's an arranged marriage. Both families have known each other for ages. Their grandfathers were classmates or something equally quaint. The guy she is marrying, Bharath, is filthy rich. His family owns industries all over India, from textile mills in Coimbatore and Tirupur, and automobile businesses in Mumbai, to tech parks in Bangalore. After the wedding, she and her husband will be living with her in-laws in their ancestral home that supposedly has more bathrooms than some apartment buildings have flats.

I recall our conversation when the marriage had just got finalized. She'd been sprawled across the bed in her room, scrolling vacation destinations on her iPad, while her mother, my aunt, bustled around feeling important, like her daughter had won a prize.

'Don't you even want your own house? What made you agree to this?' I had asked her, perching on the edge of her bed, watching her perfectly manicured nails tap at the screen.

'Akka, it's a great life,' she had replied without looking up, her voice light and unconcerned. 'Bharath and I have already planned our vacations for the year. We'll be going to Milan, Santorini and Bali.' She had said the names with practised precision, her accent shifting slightly to accommodate the foreign syllables.

'But Aishu, don't you want to have a career, a life?' I had pressed, leaning forward.

She had finally set down her iPad, giving me her full attention. A small, knowing smile had played on her lips. 'Akka, tell me something. You want to have a career, right?'

'Of course!' I replied.

'What would you be working towards?'

'What do you mean? I'll make my own money, have my own house. And I'll take care of my parents.'

'That's exactly what I'm getting!' She had smiled triumphantly. 'I'm getting my house, my money. The freedom to do what I want. Bharath's parents are extremely nice people.'

'Come on, Aishu. It's not the same,' I had argued, frustration creeping into my voice.

'If you change your perspective a little, you will see it from my POV.' She had leaned back against her pillows, serene and confident. 'We all have to get married anyway. When I met Bharath, I liked him … really liked him.' A faint blush had coloured her cheeks then. 'I didn't see any point in waiting. Some of us find what we want early, some take time. Neither is wrong.'

I had sighed then, defeated by her simple logic. 'All right.'

'Better not miss even one event at my wedding, okay?' She had sat up suddenly, grabbing my hands, her eyes intense. 'I want you there for every single thing. Promise me, Shruti akka.'

And so there had been multiple events to attend in the past four weeks. Mehendi, where her hands were painted with intricate designs while we sang old songs; the sangeet, where both families performed choreographed dances that had been rehearsed for weeks; a party for 'close people' that somehow included two hundred guests; and now the actual wedding with its seven-course meal and imported flowers.

We don't have any of these customs in our south Indian weddings. It's all borrowed from Bollywood. A bastardization of traditions where nalangu becomes mehendi, and simple family gatherings transform into extravagant sangeet performances. People simply want to emulate the big fat weddings they see on screen with no regard for authenticity or meaning.

And now this. I'm being forced to have a conversation with some guy I barely know. The aunties, including my mother, have told me multiple times to 'have a chat' and 'just see'. 'He's from a very good family,' they had whispered, as if that was all that mattered. There was no way out other than causing 'a scene', which I don't want to. So here I am.

'Shruti?'

I turn to see him approaching, adjusting the gold cufflinks on his navy blue sherwani, the kind that looks like it costs more than an entire semester's tuition.

'I'm Vipul,' he says with a practised smile. 'Your mother pointed you out to me.' His voice drips with the polished accent of someone who's spent years abroad. Smooth, confident and just a little too self-assured.

I'm already annoyed. The last thing I want to do is make small talk with this stranger who thinks his designer sherwani and foreign degree make him irresistibly impressive. I force a tight smile. He steps closer, his cologne, something sharp and expensive, invading my space.

And suddenly, I know what to do.

It's only after the wedding festivities are over that my parents broach the subject again. We're driving home, the streetlights flashing across my father's face, which is a study in concentration, in the driver's seat. My mother, meanwhile, twists around to face me in the back.

'So,' she begins, her voice carefully casual. 'How was meeting Vipul?'

I gaze out of the window, watching the gleaming office buildings slip past. Tall glass towers glowing with lights, part of a sprawling corporate campus. Someday, I tell myself, I'll be working there.

My mother is waiting for me to answer. I consider lying. Then I settle for a half-truth. 'It was good,' I tell her.

Hope blooms across her face. 'Really? I knew you would hit it off! His mother mentioned that he's just been promoted at—'

I feel bad. 'Ma,' I interrupt, guilt gnawing at me, 'he's a nice guy but he is not for me.'

Her face falls so quickly I almost take my words back.

'What do you mean he is not for you? What kind of guy is "for you" then?' she asks. I can sense her irritation.

I sigh. 'I don't know, Ma. Marriage isn't on my mind right now. I have tons of college work, plus all the Cultural Committee activities. I don't have time for any of this.'

'Don't let all this Cultural Committee business affect your studies,' she warns, her favourite refrain. 'Extra-curricular activities are fine, but ...'

'Meenakshi,' my father interjects, 'when has she ever disappointed us with her academics? You know she's always excelled.' His eyes meet mine in the rearview mirror and I shoot him a grateful look, mouthing a silent 'thank you'.

'Besides,' I add, seizing the opportunity to change the subject, 'being the cultural secretary will look impressive on my application for my master's.'

My mother perks up at this. 'Kanna, the UK has excellent colleges. You could do your master's there after you get married. Just think about that option.' She has found a way to steer the conversation back to my marriage.

'No, Ma. I am *not* considering that path.' The words burst out louder than I intended. I modulate my tone. 'I want some work experience first, then I'll apply for my PR course.'

My mother shakes her head, her expression settling into a familiar disappointment. 'I really wish you would follow Aishu's example. They are even allowing her to study after marriage.'

I grit my teeth.

'The more you delay,' she continues, 'the more you will get the leftovers. All the good men will be taken.'

I don't respond, even though I'm seething inside. Who are they to 'allow' or 'not allow' Aishu to study? My cousin's marriage feels more like a transaction than a partnership, with permissions granted like favours.

My mother senses that she has pushed too far and pivots smoothly. 'The biryani at the wedding was too dry, don't you think? And did you see Rekha's saree? That shade of purple with her complexion ...'

As she dissects the wedding detail by tiny detail, my father catches my eye in the rearview mirror again and gives me a small, conspiratorial nod. His silent support is a lifeline I cling to.

The next morning, my college campus buzzes with post-event energy. I'm hurrying across the quad, mentally reviewing my presentation for brand management strategies, when I spot Latha ma'am heading towards the humanities building.

Latha ma'am is the faculty advisor for the Cultural Committee, a responsibility she executes with military precision and unexpected creativity. Under her guidance, we've transformed the committee from a glorified party-planning group to a serious cultural force on campus. The Indo-Bhutan cultural exchange programme we organized last semester earned us a feature in the national education supplement.

'Shruti!' she calls, changing course to intercept me. Her crisp cotton saree and perfect posture make me stand straighter automatically.

'Good morning, ma'am.'

'Congratulations,' she says, her usually stern face relaxing slightly. 'Everything went very smoothly yesterday. No untoward incidents like last year when security had to get involved after discovering those rum bottles circulating.'

I feel a rush of pride. 'Thank you, ma'am. It's all thanks to your guidance.'

'No, no,' she dismisses my thank you with a wave of her hand. 'You students put in the work required. Your leadership was evident.'

I don't mention my stern pre-event talk with the seniors, specifically about keeping alcohol consumption discreet and making absolutely sure that there were no visible bottles on the premises. Some battles are best left unmentioned.

'Have all the prizes been distributed?' she asks, businesslike again. 'I thought I saw something remaining in the stockroom this morning.'

The quiz competition. The memory surfaces: Aman Mathur answering question after impossible question, then disappearing before the award ceremony.

'Everything has been collected except the Titania Industries prize, ma'am.'

Her eyebrows draw together. 'Well, find the winner and get it collected soon. We can't hold onto it indefinitely. I will be answerable to the auditors reviewing our inventory next week.'

'Yes, ma'am. I'll handle it today. I'll get it done.'

As she walks away, I remember that Aman had been with Chandan, who had helped me plan the Bhutan trip. Their hasty departure seemed so odd.

I pull out my phone and text Chandan:

> Hey, can I get Aman Mathur's number?

Three dots appear immediately, then:

> Why? Are you so impressed by his quiz knowledge? 😜

I smile despite myself. It wasn't just his knowledge that had impressed me, even though that alone had been remarkable. There was something about Aman that lingered in my mind. He had a calming presence that seemed to still the chaos around him. His tall, lean frame and the shy smile when he answered difficult questions—not smug, but certain, as though he knew he would get it right.

But Chandan doesn't need to know any of that.

> It's to give him his prize, silly. Cultural Committee business.

Chandan replies:

> How about I tell him to meet you during lunch break tomorrow?

I frown at the screen.

> How about today? Latha ma'am wants this wrapped up ASAP. Need to clear out the stockroom.

> I can check with him.

> How about you give me his number and I check directly?! Why are you acting like his agent? 😒

There's a pause before his reply:

> Fine, fine. Don't bite my head off.

He sends the number.

I save it, then compose a carefully casual text:

> Hi Aman, Shruti here from the Cultural Committee. Let me know what time works for you to collect your quiz prize? That was quite an impressive performance yesterday, by the way.

I hit send and spend the rest of the day half-distracted, checking my phone between classes. Nothing. By the time my last lecture ends and I'm heading towards the bus stop, I've nearly forgotten about it.

When I push open our front door, I sense that something is wrong. The house is too quiet, the air too still. I step inside, my bag slipping from my shoulder as I spot my mother standing in the living room, arms crossed, face etched with an expression I know all too well.

'There you are,' she says, her voice unnaturally calm. For a few seconds I'm puzzled. Then it hits me. Vipul. My mother knows. Her network of aunties has worked at lightning speed.

But I pretend to be ignorant. 'Hi, Ma,' I say, hoping I sound nonchalant.

My father sits in his favourite armchair, the newspaper he is reading held up like a shield. He is watching us warily.

'What in the world were you thinking, Shruti?' My mother's voice rises, her calm facade cracking.

I consider my options. I know denial is futile, given the thunderous expression she sports. But I try anyway. 'What, Ma?' I ask, blinking innocently as I set my bag on the dining chair. 'What are you talking about?'

'This is outrageous, Shruti, simply outrageous.' She takes a step towards me. 'Do not pretend you don't know what you did. You actually thought it was a good idea to conduct a *quiz* on the man who could potentially be your husband?'

'Ma, he didn't get any of the answers right,' I reply. Despite my mother's anger I cannot help the mischievous satisfaction that I experience. 'Not a single one.'

My father's newspaper lowers slightly. I detect a glimmer of amusement on his face, quickly suppressed. My mother, however, is incandescent with rage. I swear I can see steam coming out of her ears.

'Meenakshi,' my father mutters weakly. A gentle warning.

But my mother is too angry to pay heed. 'You're a foolish, foolish girl. This is what I deserve for pampering you all these years, for listening to your every single whim.' She paces now, her bangles jingling angrily. 'You know very well that what you did was disgraceful. Beyond disgraceful!'

I sigh, suddenly tired. 'Ma, I'm sorry. Can I please have some tea first? We can talk about this properly ...'

'What is there to talk about?' she snaps, throwing her hands up. 'Go inside, change your clothes and have your tea. You blew a fantastic opportunity for your own future. Like a bomb. Boom!' She makes an explosive gesture with her hands.

Despite everything, curiosity gets the better of me. 'What ... what did he say to his mother?' I ask.

My mother's eyes narrow. 'That he doesn't want to marry a quizmaster.'

Laughter bubbles up before I can stop it. I clap a hand over my mouth, but it's too late.

My mother looks at my father in shock and helplessness.

'Shruti! How can you laugh?' my father finally speaks up.

'I'm sorry,' I manage to say, turning my laugh into an unconvincing cough. 'I think I need to lie down for a bit.'

I grab my bag and retreat to my room before my mother can respond, closing the door behind me and collapsing onto my bed. The laughter I've been holding back escapes in waves as I recall Vipul's expressions throughout the ordeal.

His initial bewilderment when I suggested we play a game: 'A quiz? Right now?'

The transition to interest when he thought he might impress me with his knowledge: 'Sure, I watch *Who Wants to Be a Millionaire* sometimes.'

His growing frustration with each wrong answer: 'Well, that's not really important in daily life, is it?'

And finally, his defeated expression when he couldn't even name the artist who painted the ceiling of the Sistine Chapel: 'It's da Vinci, right? Everyone knows that.'

I had saved the easiest question for the last thinking it might give him a chance to redeem himself.

I press my face into my pillow to muffle my laughter. Poor Vipul. He probably thought he was meeting a potential bride, not sitting for an exam he hadn't studied for.

As my laughter subsides, I roll onto my back and stare at the ceiling. My mother's disappointment weighs on me, but not enough to make me regret my actions. If Vipul and I are supposedly compatible, shouldn't he share some of my interests? Or at least know that Michelangelo painted the Sistine Chapel?

My phone buzzes, pulling me from my thoughts. A text message. Curious, I open it.

> Will you go out for a coffee with me? I can collect the prize then.

Aman Mathur. The quiz champion. The guy who had made it look effortless.

I sit up, re-reading his message. Coffee. With Aman.

I don't hesitate as I type my response, oddly pleased.

AMAN

A Date

THE CLOCK TICKS. My palms are sweaty, knees weak, arms heavy. And then her reply arrives. Chandan whoops for joy, jumping up and down like a child. 'I told you! I told you!'

It was Chandan who had played a pivotal role in this whole thing.

'Bro, you've got to do this,' he had urged, slapping my shoulder with too much enthusiasm. 'I tried to set up a meeting for you, but she asked for your number directly. Deffo she's interested in you. Trust me.'

I had rolled my eyes. 'Come on, Chandan. Your brain is a romantic mush with all those movies you've fed it. She asked for my number because she had to give me the hamper. Nothing more to it.'

'She could've given me the hamper and asked me to pass it on to you,' Chandan had commented.

'Maybe you looked like a thief who would vanish with the hamper?'

'Arey waah! If I am a thief, then what are you? Prince Charming?' He had snorted, and I had laughed at his expression.

Just as I was about to reply to Shruti, telling her I could collect the hamper the next morning, Chandan had grabbed the phone from my hand and sent her a text asking her out for coffee.

'I'm fucked!' I had whispered, terror washing over me. 'Not only is she going to turn me down, but she's also going to think I'm a creep.'

'Relax bro, she's going to say yes,' Chandan had assured me, but I could hear the uncertainty in his voice.

Therefore, when her reply arrives, Chandan is happier than I am. He knows how mortified I would've been had she turned me down.

I stare at the phone and read her message several times:

Sure, let's do it.

I still can't believe she has said yes.

For the next hour and a half, Chandan and I zero in on the place. It's about three kilometres from our college. A café done up like a dhaba, with colourful truck art on the walls and traditional charpoys instead of chairs. Chandan insists I borrow his bike.

'Bro, it would seem like a proper date then,' I protest weakly.

'Well, dude, news flash! It *is* a date if you ask a girl out. Now do it in style,' he retorts, tossing me his keys.

I text her the name of the place and ask if I can pick her up after college. She replies almost immediately, saying she's always wanted to try the place and yes, it works for her.

The next afternoon, when it's time to pick her up, I'm so nervous I can barely breathe. I've memorized the Google Maps route like my life depends on it, terrified that I'll mess up and have her think I'm a fool. My palms are clammy on the handlebars as I park outside the college gate and pull off my helmet.

When she finally appears, my heart leaps a little. She's in faded blue jeans and a short floral top that reveals a hint of her midriff when she moves. Her hair is tied back in a ponytail that sways rhythmically with each step. She looks nothing like she did on stage, yet somehow, she is just as captivating. And effortlessly stunning.

'Hey, Aman!' she says, her smile warm and easy as she walks up to me. 'You made it.'

'Yeah,' I manage, hoping my voice doesn't betray my nervousness. 'Right on time.'

'You got a bike? Nice!' Her eyes light up as she sees Chandan's Royal Enfield.

'It's Chandan's,' I admit, rubbing the back of my neck. 'He insisted I borrow it. Figured it's better than chasing autos or cabs.'

'What fun,' she grins. 'But what about a helmet?'

I pull out an extra helmet from the storage compartment, Chandan's foresight saving the day once again.

'Got that too,' I say, handing it to her. 'Safety first.'

'Always. How lovely that you came prepared!' she says, slipping it on. Then, with a playful grin, she strikes a pose, arms stretched out in front like a robot.

'How do I look?' she asks.

I pretend to study her seriously, then grin. 'Like an astronaut. You can apply to NASA. You're sure to get in.'

She laughs. 'About the hamper, it's quite big. Can we come back here after coffee and get it?'

'Sure.'

She climbs onto the bike behind me, and I nearly jump when she wraps her arms around my waist.

'Is this okay?' she asks, her voice close to my ear.

'Perfect,' I croak. I'm so thankful that she cannot see my face, which, I'm sure, has turned a beetroot red.

The ride is exhilarating. The wind rushes past us. At a traffic signal, the breeze shifts, carrying a faint hint of her perfume. It's citrusy, the same one she wore on stage. I catch it before it disappears. I focus on the road. At other traffic lights, when she points out interesting buildings or street art, I have to strain and turn my head slightly to hear her. She is so comfortable around me that by the time we arrive at the café, my nervousness has dissipated. The evening rush at the Dhaba Café hasn't started yet. The place is decorated with string lights and old Bollywood posters of *Sholay* and *Mera Naam Joker*. The scent of cardamom and cloves hangs in the air, mingling with the soft hum of distant conversations.

'This place is adorable!' Shruti exclaims, looking around with delight.

We find a quiet corner with a traditional charpoy that has quite a few bright cushions kept on it. A low table made from what looks like an old wooden door sits in front of it.

Shruti adjusts her top at the shoulder as she settles in, the afternoon light catching the flecks of gold in her deep brown eyes. I have to tear my gaze away from her face.

'So,' she says with a playful smile that catches me off-guard, 'is this where you bring all your dates?'

I nearly choke on air, feeling heat rush to my face. All at once. 'I don't … I mean, I haven't … This isn't …' I stammer. 'This is Chandan's recommendation. He swears by their chai,' I flounder.

She laughs and the corners of her eyes crinkle. 'I'm only teasing you, Aman.'

A waiter appears just then.

'What would you like to have?' I ask Shruti, grateful for the distraction.

She considers the question for a moment. 'Masala chai, extra ginger, less sugar. And what's good here?'

'The samosas are supposed to be legendary,' I offer.

'That sounds great,' she says with a decisive nod.

'Two masala chais and two plates of samosas, please,' I tell the waiter, who nods approvingly.

As he walks away, Shruti leans forward, propping her chin on her hand. The silver bangle on her wrist catches the light. 'Your performance in the quiz the other day, it blew me away,' she says, her eyes bright with admiration. 'Have you always been into quizzing?'

I feel all the guilt in the world gathering like storm clouds in my chest. I also hear Chandan's voice in my head when he had instructed me just before I left: 'Don't you dare confess that we cheated. Take the win, take the glory, take the girl.'

But, looking into Shruti's earnest eyes—eyes that see something in me that I'm not sure exists—I know I can't do it. I can't build whatever this is on a foundation of lies. If she thinks less of me, so be it. This girl deserves the truth.

'Actually, Shruti,' I confess, my voice dropping, 'we did cheat for a couple of the questions. Not all of them, though.'

Her eyebrows shoot up, and I feel the familiar trepidation building up.

'What?' she asks. Then, to my utter surprise, she laughs. A full-bodied sound that turns heads at nearby tables. 'You know, I did suspect it! That's why I called you on stage.'

'Sorry,' I say. 'Why did you suspect us? Were we that obvious?'

'The way you and Chandan kept huddling together, the way he was looking at his phone. You weren't exactly *Ocean's Eleven*.' She's still chuckling.

'You know, I nearly died of fright when you asked me to come up on stage,' I admit. 'Those ten steps to the stage felt like crossing the Sahara desert. My legs were lead, and I was convinced that everyone could see right through me.'

'You did look like you were walking to your own execution, I noticed,' she says, nodding sympathetically. 'But then you rallied.'

I expect her to be at least a little annoyed but instead, she seems almost … impressed. 'You didn't cheat on stage though,' she says softly.

'No, no, of course not,' I reply earnestly, sitting up straighter. 'Those two final questions, I did know the answers to them.'

'The Necker cube. That was a tough one,' she says with a smile. 'I must say I didn't expect that. Well done!'

Our order arrives, the waiter setting down two steaming cups of chai, the surface shimmering with a film of spices, and a plate of golden-brown samosas surrounded by mint and tamarind chutneys. The aroma is intoxicating, the smell of cardamom and ginger in the chai mixing with the savoury scent of the samosas.

Shruti wraps her slender fingers around her cup and takes a careful sip. 'Perfect,' she murmurs, closing her eyes briefly in appreciation.

I can stare at her forever.

'You know, Aman,' she says after a moment, her expression turning thoughtful, 'I'm so intrigued by your utter honesty. You could've easily pretended that you knew all the answers. Why confess? Most people would have simply kept quiet.'

I sip my chai as I consider her question. She stares into my eyes, and it's suddenly hard to focus on anything else. I could get lost in those deep brown eyes framed by impossibly long lashes. But she's waiting for an answer.

'I don't know,' I say finally, setting my cup down. 'Maybe it's because my mother raised me to believe that a lie of omission is still a lie. Or maybe it's because I'm simply terrible at deception. My face gives everything away. But mostly …' I pause, surprised by the truth that's about to come out of my mouth, 'I felt you deserved to know. There was something about the way you looked at me, like you saw something worthwhile … and I couldn't bear the thought of that being based on something false.'

Her features relax, and the faintest smile tugs at her lips. 'I appreciate that, Aman,' she says, her voice warm. 'Honesty is rare. Especially when it costs you something.'

She breaks off a piece of her samosa and dips it delicately in the mint chutney. 'So, you're from Gwalior?'

'How did you …' I start, then remember my stammered introduction on the stage. 'Oh right, that day. I'm sorry I ran away so quickly afterwards. I was nervous, and being on stage was overwhelming enough without the added pressure of talking to someone like you.'

'Someone like me?' she asks, her eyebrow arched in question.

I feel my face heating up again. 'You know … smart, articulate, beautiful.' The last word slips out before I realize, and I hurriedly take a large bite of my samosa to stop myself from saying anything more embarrassing.

Her cheeks flush slightly, and she tucks her hair behind her ear, a gesture I'm beginning to recognize as a sign of slight nervousness. It's endearing to see that perhaps I'm not the only one feeling the butterflies.

'I know what you mean about stage fright,' she says, gracefully changing the subject. 'I ran away after my first public speaking attempt too. This was when I was in Class XI. I literally ran. Out the door, down the hall, and I didn't stop until I reached the bus stop a kilometre away.'

She launches into a story about how terrified she used to be of speaking in front of crowds, how her palms would sweat, her voice would shake and her mind would go completely blank. 'Then, one day, I decided I was tired of being afraid. I joined

Toastmasters, a public speaking forum. I was so nervous at my first meeting that I spilled water all over the person sitting next to me.'

'No way,' I laugh, imagining the scene.

'Yes way,' she counters with a grin. 'Poor guy was soaked. I apologized profusely. Then, week by week, speech by speech, I got better. Now I enjoy it. There's something powerful about holding an entire room's attention.'

I nod, captivated by how animated her face is as she speaks. She's radiant when she's passionate about something, and I find myself wanting to discover all the things that make her light up like this.

She asks me about Gwalior, and I tell her about growing up in the shadow of the fort, about the Hanuman temple that my house faced, the unbearable summers, the freezing winters and the street food that no place in Bangalore has quite managed to replicate. She listens with genuine interest, asking questions that make me see my hometown through new eyes.

She tells me she's lived all her life in Bangalore but has always dreamed of travelling. 'I have a huge map on a wall in my room, and I put a pin on all the places I want to visit,' she confesses. 'It's getting quite crowded.'

'What's the first place you want to go to?' I ask.

'Japan,' she answers without hesitation. 'Cherry blossoms, ancient temples and the culture. What about you?'

'New York and London,' I admit. 'Cliché, I know, but there's something about the energy of these cities that calls to me.'

We discover that we're both only children and laugh about the similar experiences we've had while growing up, with all the pressure and privileges that come with it.

'In my case, I lost my father when I was seven. Although Ma has never made me feel his absence,' I tell her.

'You must be very close to her,' she observes.

'Yes, she is quite a strong woman.'

'For me, my parents, mostly my mother, had my whole life planned out by the time I was five,' she says, rolling her eyes. 'Doctor, engineer, or eternal disappointment were my options.'

'And yet here you are, studying literature,' I note.

'My greatest act of rebellion,' she says with a wink.

The café has filled up around us, the afternoon crowd bringing a pleasant buzz of energy. We barely notice it though, lost in our own world, the conversation flowing as easily as if we've known each other for years. We discuss books (she loves Murakami, while I'm more of a Wilbur Smith fan), movies (I tell her about Chandan's love for romcoms) and music (she introduces me to indie bands I've never heard of, and I promise to listen to them as I make a note on my phone).

We talk about the excellent placement record this year in our college. Our entire batch has got great offers.

'And how does it feel to get through campus recruitment so early?' she asks, absently tracing patterns on the table with her fingertip.

'I can't tell you how good I feel about it,' I tell her, surprising myself with my enthusiasm. 'I really liked Vikram, who interviewed me. He's sharp but fair, and seems to genuinely care about developing new talent. I'm going to be a management trainee for a few months, after which I'll move into one of the divisions. I'm so excited to start working and get my own apartment.'

'You know, it's my dream too. To work at a good corporate organization and have my own place.'

'I get it. I've had enough of college life. I'm so ready for the next chapter.'

I realize how comfortable I feel with her and how the anxiety that usually sits on my chest like a weight has lifted. With Shruti, I can just be.

A little later, when we glance at our watches, we're both shocked to see that two and a half hours have just evaporated.

'I can't believe we've been here for so long,' she says, her eyes wide. 'It felt like minutes.'

'Time flies when—' I start, then cut myself off, suddenly self-conscious.

'When you're in great company?' she finishes with a smile that makes my heart somersault.

'Exactly,' I say softly.

Then reality comes crashing back as she remembers the purpose of our meeting.

'Oh no, the stockroom will be closed by now,' Shruti says. 'I need to give you the hamper today or Latha ma'am will finish me off.'

'What do we do now?' I ask, genuinely concerned. 'I'm so sorry I kept you talking for so long.'

'No, no, I enjoyed every minute,' she assures me quickly. 'Don't worry about it. I know Ramalingam, the security guard; I can get the key from him. Let's head back and get you your hamper.'

I insist on paying for our chai and samosas and take her back to the campus. The way she holds on to me as I drive sends electric currents through my body.

We find Ramalingam at his post near the administration building, reading a newspaper, with his feet propped up on a small stool. He looks up as we approach, his weathered face breaking into a smile when he recognizes Shruti.

'Ramalingam sir,' she greets him warmly. 'We need a small favour.'

'Anything for you, Shruti ma'am,' he replies, folding his newspaper. 'You helped my daughter with her English homework last semester. How can I ever say no to you?'

She smiles, and I'm struck by this new piece of information, this glimpse of her kindness that extends beyond our little bubble.

'We need to get into the stockroom,' she explains. 'I have to give Aman his prize hamper from the quiz.'

Ramalingam nods and detaches a single key from the large ring of keys in his pocket. 'No problem, ma'am. Here's the key. I cannot leave my post, else I would've opened the stockroom for you myself.'

'We'll be back soon. Thank you!' she replies with a grateful smile as she takes the key.

We hurry across the campus. The sun has already set and the long shadows across the quadrangle lend the college building an air of mystery. The stockroom is in the basement of the old science building, down a corridor that smells faintly of chalk dust and ageing textbooks. I feel fiercely protective of this girl who trusts me enough to go along with me.

It's dark near the stockroom door, and Shruti fumbles with the lock. I pull out my phone and switch on the flashlight, illuminating her face as she focuses on working the key into the stubborn lock.

'There,' she says triumphantly as the key finally turns. The door creaks open, revealing a room filled with shelves of supplies and neatly labelled boxes.

Shruti navigates the space with confidence, heading straight for a corner where a large gift hamper sits wrapped in cellophane, tied with a ribbon. 'Here you go,' she says, handing it to me with a flourish. 'Your rightfully earned prize.'

'I want to open it now,' I declare, suddenly feeling a childlike excitement bubble up.

'Here?' she asks, glancing around the dimly lit room.

'Yes, why not? I'm too curious to see what's inside.'

She shrugs. 'Go ahead then. The suspense is killing me too.'

I set the hamper down on a nearby table and carefully untie the ribbon. The cellophane crinkles loudly in the quiet room as I pull it apart. Inside, the hamper is packed with treasures: three 2TB external hard drives nestled in protective foam, three sleek headphones with noise-cancellation technology, three power banks in different colours, a strategy board game that I've been eyeing for months, a compact travel backpack, a plush sleep mask, a universal travel adapter, a box of imported gourmet chocolates, a leather-bound journal with an elegant pen, a puzzle book full of brain teasers, and gift cards for online shopping websites.

'Wow,' I breathe, genuinely impressed as we go through the contents. 'This is such a lovely hamper. They really went all out with this one!'

'Worth cheating for?' Shruti teases, her eyes sparkling.

I laugh. I want to tell her that this date was what was worth cheating for, not the hamper. But I don't.

Then, without overthinking, I pick out one of the headphone sets, a power bank and an external hard drive and hold them out to her.

'My gift to you. Please take these,' I say.

'Aman, I can't possibly take these,' she protests, her eyes widening.

'Why not?' I ask.

'Because … because you won it,' she says, gesturing to the hamper. 'It's yours.'

'Precisely. I can do what I want with it,' I counter. 'And I want to give these to my friend.'

I can see that she catches on the word 'friend' and her expression shifts, just barely, but I notice.

'So, I'm a friend now?' she asks, a note of something I can't quite identify in her voice.

'Unless you're saying you don't want to be one,' I tease. I'm astonished at how comfortable I feel around her now. Like I've known her all my life.

'No, no. I didn't mean it like that,' she says quickly, her hand reaching out to touch my arm briefly. 'I just … I don't want to take your prizes.'

'Listen,' I say earnestly, 'there's so much stuff in here. It's much more than I can use. If you don't take these, I'll end up giving them away to random people. I'll put up a flyer on the notice board with a "free to go to a good home" sign.'

She bites her lower lip, considering. 'Well, in that case, all right, I'll accept. Thank you,' she says, her eyes meeting mine in the dim light. For a moment, the air between us feels charged with possibility.

Then the spell is broken by the buzzing of her phone. She checks it and sighs.

'My mom wants to know why I'm late. We should get this key back to Ramalingam before he sends out a search party.'

We lock up the stockroom and return the key. Ramalingam gives us a knowing look that makes me wonder how transparent my feelings for Shruti are. At the college gates, just as she is about to leave, I offer to drop her home.

'Aman, you've done so much already.'

'It's really late, Shruti, and your mother is waiting. It'll be faster if I drop you.'

'You're right. Thanks again,' she says, already rummaging through her bag. She pulls out something small and folded, and holds it out to me.

'What's this?' I ask.

'I always have a couple of these with me. Open it.'

Curious, I take it from her and unfold it. It's a huge, sturdy bag with long handles.

'I never use plastic bags,' she says. 'You can keep the hamper inside it and hang it from the handlebar of your bike.'

I nod and do just that.

We weave our way through Bangalore's chaotic traffic. Her home is only fifteen minutes away. She makes me stop a little distance away from her street.

'I don't want my mother to know that a guy dropped me off,' she explains.

I stop and remove my helmet. She hands her helmet over to me, and we stand at the entrance to her lane. The evening air carries a quiet tension.

'So,' she says as she looks at me.

'So,' I echo, suddenly tongue-tied again.

'This was nice,' she says, clutching her gifts to her chest. 'Really nice.'

'It was,' I agree, wishing I could come up with something more eloquent.

'I should go,' she says, taking a step back.

'Right, of course,' I nod. 'Goodnight, Shruti.'

'Goodnight, Aman,' she replies with a smile that stays with me long after she's gone.

When I get back to the hostel, Chandan is sprawled on his bed, listening to music. He looks up as I enter and stops the music.

'How did it go?' he asks, sitting up eagerly. 'Did you charm her?'

I set the hamper down, lost in thought, replaying moments from the afternoon in my mind: the way she laughed, the touch of her fingers, the look in her eyes when she had said goodnight.

'Here, take whatever you want from this hamper.'

'The hamper can wait,' Chandan says, waving his hand. 'Details, man. I need details.'

'It was …' I begin, struggling to find words that could possibly capture the last few hours. 'It was nice.'

Chandan groans. 'Nice? That's all you've got? You spend an entire afternoon with your heartthrob, and all you can say is "nice"?'

I shrug, a smile tugging at my lips. 'Okay, okay. I owe you one, my friend. It was … magical,' I admit.

The next morning, I wake up late, a luxury I can afford now that placements are done. My heart leaps into my throat as I see a message from Shruti on my phone:

> Lunch today? I don't have classes after two. My treat this time. I know a place that does the best biryani in Bangalore.

My fingers hover over the keypad; a grin spreads across my face, so wide it hurts.

This time, I'm not nervous. This time, I know exactly what to say.

SHRUTI

A Hundred and Thirty-Two Dates Later

'YOU WERE RIGHT on our first date, Aman,' I say, resting my head on his shoulder. His scent, warm, comforting and unmistakably his, surrounds me. It's a fragrance I've grown to cherish. 'Time really does fly when you're with someone you love.'

The cool breeze skims over the waters of Ulsoor Lake, sending gentle ripples across its surface. The faint scent of wildflowers lingers in the air, and the soft murmur of distant voices blends with the sound of rustling leaves.

Aman shifts slightly, just enough to bring his head closer to mine. 'We must've been on what, 120 dates since then?'

I chuckle softly, threading my fingers through his. 'It's 132 to be precise. In a year and three months. I kept track, you know.'

He is surprised. 'Wait. You genuinely keep a count of the number of dates we've been on?'

'Of course I do,' I say with a laugh. 'Do you remember what you said on our second date?'

He is quiet for a minute as he thinks. Then he says, 'That two dates a week keep the blues away?'

I nod.

'I was joking that day,' he confesses, giving me a sheepish grin. 'But somehow, we've stuck to it.'

'I know. And you know what? I can't believe I've even got my dream job offer. I can't wait to join them, start my career.'

Aman's face lights up like he's the one who got the offer. 'Of course, I knew you would crack it!' he says, squeezing my hand. 'All those late nights of preparation. The panicked texts at 2 a.m. I knew you had it in you.'

His words make my throat tighten. 'I couldn't have done it without you,' I say quietly. 'You always believed in me. Even when I didn't.'

'We've come a long way from when we first met,' he says.

'I think we're both blessed,' I tell him. 'You've grown so much too. You bought a bike, you're thinking of investing in a home, *and* you've been promoted to a manager at your company. These are all real adult milestones. I simply can't wait to achieve all of these myself.'

'We've both worked very hard, Shruti,' he says, taking my hand in his and bringing it to his lips. 'And we deserve every bit of happiness that's coming our way.'

For a while, we sit in a comfortable silence, watching the water shimmer. The world feels quiet, yet full. Like everything is exactly as it should be. I feel lucky to have got an entire day with Aman, which is rare. He has a day off from work due to a local festival.

My phone buzzes, reminding me of my responsibilities. I've been entrusted with an important task today: escorting Mr Sanjeev Adani from his hotel to our college's entrepreneurial summit.

'It's Latha ma'am, checking if all is good,' I tell Aman as I glance at my phone.

He grins. 'She should know by now how efficient and reliable you are. When it comes to Shruti Srinivasan, there's no need to reconfirm anything.'

'If only the world had as much confidence in me as you do, Aman Mathur,' I reply.

'Who is this Adani guy again?' Aman asks.

'Only one of the most respected entrepreneurs in the country,' I explain, feeling a sense of awe. 'Sanjeev Adani. Padma Shri awardee, founder of Sneha Kutir and several other organizations focused on social welfare. His work with destitute women and children has transformed thousands of lives. He's on the Forbes list of most influential social entrepreneurs in Asia.'

'Impressive credentials,' Aman nods appreciatively.

As instructed by Latha ma'am, I had arrived at the hotel at 11a.m. and had contacted Mr Adani from the lobby, feeling slightly nervous.

'What time is the event?' His voice had been warm, lacking the intimidating edge I'd expected.

'Sir, your talk is scheduled for 6.30 p.m.'

'Then is it fine if we leave at 5.30 p.m.? Will that be enough time? I do not like being late.'

'That will allow for plenty of time. I'll be in the lobby if you need anything before then, sir.'

'Oh, dear girl, there's no need for any of that,' he had replied with unexpected kindness. 'I'll be ready around five-fifteen and will call you. After my talk, I'll leave for the airport from your college itself. And please, there's no need for you to accompany me to the airport.'

'Thank you, sir.'

After that call, I had immediately texted Aman. These days we grabbed every opportunity we could to spend time together. We simply couldn't get enough of each other. Aman had arrived within thirty minutes, and we had spent the last few hours at Ulsoor Lake.

My stomach growls and I remember that I've not eaten anything since morning. I had woken up late because Aman and I had been talking well into the early hours of the morning, and then I had rushed to the hotel to greet Mr Adani. Getting Sanjeev Adani to speak at our college's entrepreneurial summit is a big feather in the cap for us. He has travelled from Mumbai just for this, and Latha ma'am did not trust anyone but me with the task. 'We can't take a chance by leaving this to the second years. You have to go there as our college representative. The car we have arranged will be at Mr Adani's disposal for the whole day. If he wants to go anywhere in Bangalore, you will have to take him around,' she had instructed.

'Let's find something to eat, Aman, I'm starving,' I announce, standing up.

We walk to the road outside the lake and find a street food joint where the aroma of spices fills the air. We order two plates of aloo tikki chaat and sit on plastic stools, savouring each bite.

'If you like this chaat, you'll absolutely love what my mother makes. That stuff is out of this world,' Aman says. His eyes light up as he speaks about her. 'She has magic in her hands, not just when it comes to cooking, but gardening too. Our small balcony is always overflowing with plants. Neighbours come just to see what she is growing.'

'She sounds wonderful, Aman,' I tell him. 'I wonder what she'll think of me.'

'Oh, she'll absolutely love you, Shruti.' He reaches for my hand, his fingers warm against mine. 'I can't wait to take you to Gwalior so you can meet her.'

'Let's see,' I reply, gently pulling my hand away as a family walks past.

Aman is always talking about me meeting his mother, painting these beautiful pictures of a future that seems just out of reach. He doesn't understand that the gap between his world and mine isn't just about the geographical distance between our hometowns. I don't see how we can practically make this meeting happen when I have such a hard time hiding our relationship from my parents.

I've told him several times now that my parents are *extremely* traditional when it comes to finding a match for their only daughter. They've made it clear since I was old enough to understand such things that I should marry a nice boy within our community. Someone with the right background, the right family values, the right 'everything'. Just like Aishu had done.

But Aman, having been raised by a very liberal mother, doesn't get these invisible boundaries at all. To him, love should be enough to overcome any obstacle.

'When the time comes, I'll speak to your parents and convince them,' he always says with that unwavering confidence of his. As if my father's decades of firmly held beliefs will simply melt away in the face of his earnest charm.

I don't tell him that I've already imagined that conversation a hundred times, and none of the scenarios end well. I dislike thinking about it.

The afternoon stretches before us, golden and unhurried. I glance at the time.

'I still have a couple of hours left before I meet Mr Adani,' I say, subtly changing the topic of our conversation. 'What shall we do until then?'

'Cubbon Park?' Aman suggests.

'Let's go. It's been ages since I went.'

We make our way to Cubbon Park, walking beneath ancient trees, their branches creating dappled shadows on the ground. We find a quiet bench and watch children playing, dogs being walked and couples strolling hand in hand.

As the hours pass and 5 p.m. approaches, we reluctantly head back towards the hotel.

'You know what?' Aman says suddenly, motorcycle keys jingling in his hand. 'You ride in the car with Adani. I'll follow on my bike. I'll hang around until the talk is over and, after he leaves for the airport, we can go to my place. I'll cook us dinner.'

I smile. That sounds like a great idea. I'm already making excuses in my head about what I will tell my parents: *The talk at the college went on longer than expected. Latha ma'am asked me to stay back to help with some things.*

'What are you thinking about?' he asks, looking at me with eyes filled with love.

'What will you make?' I ask, even though I already know the answer to that one.

His grin is infectious. 'Pav bhaji. Mom's special recipe.'

'With extra butter?'

'Double butter, extra spicy, just how you like it.' He smiles, eyes crinkling at the corners.

'I can't wait,' I say, standing on tiptoes to kiss his cheek.

It's a little after 5 p.m. when Aman and I enter the luxurious hotel lobby. I fiddle nervously with my dupatta. But then I remind myself to let it go and sit up straight. The lobby features an elegant coffee shop that blends seamlessly into the reception and waiting area. The space is grand yet inviting, with towering floral arrangements and soft golden lighting. Aman waits a discreet distance away, and when our eyes meet, he flashes me an encouraging thumbs-up.

When Sanjeev Adani emerges from the elevator at precisely 5.15 p.m., I'm struck by how approachable he seems. His salt-and-pepper hair and simple linen shirt make him look more like a favourite uncle than one of India's most celebrated entrepreneurs and philanthropists.

'Ms Shruti?' he asks when he spots me, extending his hand.

'Yes, sir. It's an honour to meet you,' I say, shaking his hand firmly.

He glances at his watch. 'We have a bit of time. Would you like to join me for a cup of coffee?'

'I'll join you, but no coffee for me, thank you.'

'Then perhaps a glass of orange juice?' he suggests with a kindness that immediately puts me at ease.

'Yes, sir. Thank you.'

To my dismay, he selects a table right next to where Aman is seated. I have no choice but to follow, painfully aware of how Aman is studiously avoiding looking in our direction.

Despite my best efforts to focus solely on Adani, I cannot help but steal glances at Aman. His performance of nonchalance is almost comical, the way he suddenly finds the potted palm beside him utterly fascinating and how he scrolls through his phone with exaggerated concentration.

Adani, sharp as the rumours suggest, catches me mid-glance and follows my gaze. His eyes twinkle with mischief when they return to mine.

'And who is the young man trying very hard to look like he's not with you?' he asks, voice lowered conspiratorially.

Heat rushes to my face. 'Sir, I'm so sorry … he's a friend …'

'A friend?' Adani raises a sceptical eyebrow.

'My boyfriend, actually,' I admit. I've realized denial is futile. Something about Adani's demeanour makes lying to him feel impossible. I then motion for Aman to join us before I can second-guess myself.

Aman approaches our table with the careful dignity of someone walking into an important job interview. His shoulders are squared, his expression inscrutable.

'Sir, this is Aman Mathur,' I say. 'Aman, Mr Sanjeev Adani.'

Aman extends his hand with perfect professionalism. 'It's a great honour, sir. Your work with Sneha Kutir is commendable. The way you've transformed women's empowerment in rural communities is truly inspiring.'

My jaw nearly drops. Aman had barely known who Adani was when I first mentioned this assignment. The smooth confidence with which he delivered this compliment has, therefore, left me momentarily speechless.

Adani's face lights up. 'You know about Sneha Kutir? Most young people only know me from the Forbes list.'

'Social enterprise is something where my heart is, even though I work for an FMCG company now,' Aman says with a slight nod. 'But someday I hope to be more involved.'

'Come sit,' Adani invites Aman.

To my astonishment, the two of them launch into an animated conversation about sustainable business models and community investment. I find myself sitting there, utterly amazed at how quickly they've connected, how Aman has transformed from nervous boyfriend to engaged professional in seconds.

'You must join us while we drive to the college,' Adani finally says to Aman. 'I would love to continue this conversation.'

We exchange a quick glance, both of us not knowing how to mention that Aman has his motorcycle. Then, both of us simply nod.

And just like that, Aman finds himself in the front passenger seat of a luxury sedan, while I sit in the back with one of India's most distinguished entrepreneurs. As we pull away from the hotel, Aman catches my eye in the rearview mirror and gives me an understanding look that makes my heart flutter despite the absurdity of the situation.

'Sir, your talk is scheduled for 6.30 p.m.,' I tell Adani, consulting the programme brochure just to make sure. 'We should reach by six-fifteen to ensure everything is set up properly.'

'Plenty of time then,' Adani nods. He suddenly pats his stomach. 'I didn't realize it earlier when we were having coffee at the hotel, but I'm a bit hungry. Is there anywhere good we can stop for a quick bite?'

Before I can suggest something appropriately upscale, Aman turns around. 'Sir, if you don't mind something casual, there's a café on the way that makes an incredible spinach and cheese sandwich.'

'Perfect! I hate stuffy restaurants anyway,' Adani declares. 'Do we have time?' he asks me.

I check my watch. 'Yes, sir. We can make a very quick stop and still reach on time.'

At the café, which is tucked away on a tree-lined street, we find a quiet corner table. The aroma of fresh bread and coffee fills the air. Adani insists we all order something, and soon we're enjoying the café's famous sandwiches. The conversation flows easily, and I'm struck once again by how down-to-earth Adani is.

'So, how long have you two been together?' he asks suddenly, taking a bite of his sandwich.

Aman and I exchange glances, surprised by the personal question.

'A year and three months,' I reply, warmth flooding through me at the thought.

'Ah! A long time for young love,' Adani says with a nostalgic sigh. 'And what are your plans?'

Somehow, sitting there with this kind-eyed man who's accomplished so much yet remains so humble, both Aman and I find ourselves opening up.

'We hope to get married in another two years or so,' Aman says, reaching across the table to take my hand.

'After I've worked for a bit,' I add. 'And hopefully convinced my parents.'

Adani's eyebrows rise. 'They don't approve?'

I shake my head slightly. 'They don't know yet ... They've always talked about me marrying a nice guy from our community.'

'And your family?' Adani asks Aman.

'My mother will welcome Shruti with open arms,' Aman says with such confidence that I have to blink back unexpected tears. 'She's been asking to meet "the girl who lights up my world" for months now.'

'I wish I could say the same about my parents,' I sigh.

'I think the most important thing here is that both of you stand together. As long as that stays, no person, be it your parents or anyone else, can come between the two of you,' he says. There is so much empathy in his voice.

I'm not sure if I can detect a hint of sadness in his eyes when he says that, but he definitely has a faraway look.

'I agree completely, sir,' Aman says earnestly, his eyes lighting up. 'This is exactly what I keep telling Shruti.'

'Don't worry too much about your parents, Shruti,' Adani says. 'Time has a way of transforming even the hardest of hearts.'

His words settle over us like a blessing, and for a moment, I allow myself to believe that it will all work out exactly as we both hope.

After our impromptu meal, we arrive at the college with fifteen minutes to spare. Just as we are about to enter the campus, Aman says he would like to be dropped off.

Adani chuckles knowingly. 'Yes, yes, you don't want to get caught in your girlfriend's official car. Don't worry, we've all done this in our younger days.'

The way he says it, like we are all sharing a delightful secret, makes me giggle despite my professional demeanour. Aman grins and promises to meet me after the event before he quickly gets out of the car and leaves.

Adani's talk is a resounding success. The auditorium is packed, and he speaks with such passion about finding purpose beyond profit-and-loss statements that even the most cynical students are hanging onto his every word. When he mentions me by name, thanking me for my 'impeccable hospitality', I flush with pride. Latha ma'am looks at me and nods approvingly.

After the event, as Adani prepares to leave for the airport, he thanks me again and shakes my hand. 'Thank you for a wonderful day, Shruti. I'll be waiting for your wedding invitation,' he says with a wink before climbing into the car that will take him to the airport.

Aman is waiting for me outside the college. He had gone back to the hotel and brought back his bike. My heart hammers with joy and anticipation as I climb onto his bike and we make our way to his apartment. I love spending time here.

Aman's apartment is small but immaculately kept. Plants line his balcony, all of them gifts from his mother. He loves them and has inherited a green thumb from her. I've been here many times before but tonight feels different somehow. More intimate. More like this is my home just as much as it is his.

In the kitchen, Aman moves with practised ease, chopping vegetables and heating the pan. I sit on a counter stool, sipping the glass of wine he has poured me, content to watch him work. There's something incredibly sexy about a man who knows his way around a kitchen.

'So,' he says, stirring the bhaji mixture, 'how quickly Adani caught us! Are we that obvious?'

I laugh. 'It's only because you kept looking in my direction with those love-filled eyes that he spotted us.'

'No way,' Aman protests, pointing the ladle at me accusingly. 'You were not as inconspicuous as you thought. You were the one who kept looking at me with heart-shaped eyes.'

'I did not!'

'Did too! Every time I looked up, you were staring at me with this dreamy expression,' he says, mimicking what I assume is supposed to be my face, eyelashes fluttering, lips pursed in a pout.

I throw a dish towel at him, which he dodges effortlessly. 'You're one to talk. You practically gave him our life story within five minutes of meeting him.'

'He's easy to talk to,' Aman shrugs, then adds with a mischievous grin, 'besides, I needed to impress my future wife's VIP guest.'

My heart skips a beat at the casual way he says it, like it's a foregone conclusion. He looks up from the stove, his eyes meeting mine with such intensity that I can barely breathe.

I slide off the stool and walk over to him, wrapping my arms around his waist from behind and resting my cheek against his back. I feel his joy and warmth, and his deep love for me. My world feels complete.

We sit cross-legged on his balcony and have our pav bhaji. The moon casts a luminous glow over the city, transforming ordinary buildings into mysterious silhouettes. The food is delicious. Spicy, buttery and perfect. Bollywood classics play softly in the background, the familiar melodies weaving through our conversation as it drifts from Adani's talk to our future dreams. Does everything appear more beautiful when we're in love? I do not know.

'I want this to last forever, Aman,' I tell him.

'Me too,' he says. 'Whatever happens in this life, Shruti, we'll face it together,' he promises.

After we've cleared the dishes and cleaned the kitchen, I put my arms around him, hugging him tightly. He cups my face in his hands and kisses me gently. First on the forehead, then each eyelid, my nose and, finally, his mouth finds mine. His kisses are gentle, slow, deep and full of promise. My hands find their way under his shirt, taking in the warm skin of his back, feeling his muscles shift as he pulls me closer.

We move to his bedroom in a dance we've perfected over our time together, shedding clothes along the way. When we fall onto his bed, the sheets cool against my heated skin, he hovers above me with a look of such tenderness that tears prick at my eyes.

'What?' he asks, concerned, brushing a strand of hair from my face.

'Nothing,' I shake my head. 'I just love you. So much that it scares me sometimes.'

'It scares me sometimes, too,' he admits, lowering himself to kiss a path from my collarbone to my breast.

Afterwards, we lie tangled in each other's arms. We're both so content, so satisfied, that it feels like even in the silence, we are speaking a language only we understand.

Outside, the Bangalore night continues its symphony of distant traffic and singing insects, but in this small apartment, we have created our own perfect world, if only for a few hours.

AMAN

Hometown

'I CAN'T BELIEVE you're this nervous,' I say as I take Shruti's hand in mine, the slight tremble in her fingers betraying her anxiety.

The lady at the check-in counter has been accommodating, making sure we're seated together, and Shruti has even scored her coveted window seat. I've taken it as a cosmic sign that our forbidden weekend is blessed, that everything will unfold perfectly. But Shruti sits beside me rigid with tension, her face almost ashen as she stares fixedly out the small oval window. The retractable walkway is being pulled away from the aircraft now, and the cabin crew moves through the aisles with practised efficiency, demonstrating safety procedures that neither of us is watching.

Shruti sits with a haunted look etched across her face. I hate to see her eyes dull with worry and her lips pressed into a thin line. A part of me wishes that I had not insisted on this trip. But it's been long enough since we started dating. And it's time. Had I not pushed for this, she would never have taken the initiative on her own, even though we've been talking about it for over a year now.

She grips the armrest of her seat, as if the floor of the plane might suddenly drop out from beneath us, even though we haven't begun to taxi yet. But I know it isn't the flying that has her on edge. If only I could ease her tension, even a little.

'Come on, Shruti. How many times have you flown for work in the past eighteen months?' I ask, trying to sound cheerful. I brush my thumb across the back of her hand in small, soothing circles.

'Over fifty times, maybe,' she murmurs, finally turning to face me. 'But those were just routine trips to Delhi and Mumbai. For work, Aman. This is …' she hesitates, swallowing hard, 'this is different.'

'Well,' I say, leaning closer, 'instead of the flight landing in Delhi or Mumbai, it will land in Gwalior. Then we go home and meet my mother. I can't wait to show you where I grew up.' The enthusiasm in my voice is genuine; I've dreamed of bringing Shruti home, of seeing my childhood world through her eyes.

I notice her eyes brimming with tears. But she blinks them away. 'I feel horrible about lying to my parents, Aman,' she confesses. 'I've never done anything like this.'

The weight of her deception plays on both our minds. She has told her parents that she is attending a work conference this weekend.

'Shru, darling,' I say, squeezing her hand gently, 'I was ready to come and speak to your parents properly. You're the one who stopped me.'

The reminder, despite my gentle words, sounds sharp. Her fear of their disapproval, their potential rejection of me because I'm not from their community, their likely insistence that she marry someone from their community—these are her usual concerns.

'I know. It's just that I'm scared about what my parents will say to you,' she whispers, eyes downcast. I immediately feel I shouldn't have said it. We're both well aware of the unspoken reality.

'Okay, let's park that,' I suggest, sensing we're venturing into territory too fraught for this moment. 'This is our first flight together. Let's try to enjoy it, okay? Your parents aren't going to find out. And my mother is so excited, you have no idea! Just do this for my sake, please?'

Shruti falls silent, lost in thought. The engines roar to life, and she clutches my hand. When she finally speaks again, something has shifted in her demeanour. Her shoulders have relaxed slightly, and there's a new resolve in her voice.

'You know what? You're right,' she says, summoning a small but genuine smile. 'We must live in the moment. Let's just enjoy our flight.'

She turns to me and I see a glimmer of the carefree girl I fell in love with at the quiz competition all those years ago. 'You know, I'm very excited to see Gwalior and meet your mother.'

I lift her hand to my lips and press a tender kiss against her skin, overwhelmed by the quiet faith she's placing in me. 'Thank you,' I whisper.

As the plane ascends, the world below blurs into a patchwork of green and brown. The sky outside turns a brilliant, uninterrupted blue. For the rest of the journey, we remain seated in silence, our hands intertwined, a quiet tether between us. When we're closer to landing, the clouds thin and the contours of Gwalior begin to emerge. Shruti's eyes take in the shimmer of rivers, the neat geometry of fields and, finally, the imposing silhouette of the ancient fort, rising up like a sentinel from the rocky ridge. It commands the landscape, timeless and majestic. She is delighted. She looks at me and smiles as my city, steeped in history, welcomes us.

When we arrive at my childhood home an hour later, my mother is waiting at the door. Before Shruti can even set her bag down, Ma steps forward with an aarti thali, its copper surface gleaming, a small oil lamp flickering in the breeze, flanked by vermilion powder and sandalwood paste. With a graceful move, she circles the lamp in front of Shruti, then presses a thumb smeared with sandalwood to her forehead in a gesture of blessing, one usually reserved for daughters-in-law.

Shruti stands still, caught off guard. When she looks at me across the threshold, there's so much in her gaze—love, awe, a flicker of disbelief—that my heart clenches. I ache to pull her into my arms and whisper that this welcome is not merely a gesture. That she belongs.

But before I can move, my mother sets the aarti thali aside and envelops Shruti in a warm embrace, as if she's known her for years. 'Welcome, Shruti,' she says, her voice thick with emotion. 'I've heard so much about you. It feels like you're already a part of our family.'

'Aunty, same here,' Shruti responds. I can tell she is moved. 'I have heard so much about you too,' she says.

Our small living room opens onto a massive balcony that serves as a terrace. As we enter, Shruti's eyes are immediately drawn to the vibrant explosion of my mother's prized hibiscus collection. The flowers seem alive in the afternoon light. Scarlet, peach, yellow and white blossoms nod in the gentle breeze, as if acknowledging Shruti's presence.

Birds flit about freely; bright green parakeets, grey doves and speckled mynahs visit the ornate birdbath my father had installed before he passed away. The entire space is a visual symphony, a lovingly cultivated sanctuary in the middle of the bustling city. My mother has decorated the area with hand-painted garden ornaments, a copper wind chime that catches the afternoon breeze and tinkles, and strategically placed lanterns that will illuminate the space after dusk. Ma is proud of this space that has won prizes from the Gwalior Horticulture Society for the 'Best Home Garden' several years in a row.

Shruti steps towards the garden, drawn in by its quiet magic, her eyes widening with childlike wonder. This is one of the many reasons why I love her—this ability to find joy, to notice beauty and express herself, uninhibited by what others might think.

'This is incredible!' she exclaims.

The garden, my favourite space in my home, truly feels like something out of a storybook, what with jasmine-covered trellises, a tiny path that leads to a hidden nook and a weathered wooden bench that is perfectly placed beneath the shade of a sprawling parijat tree growing in a large metal drum that Ma has painted with ethnic motifs.

Ma follows her in, beaming with quiet pride. For years after my father passed, this garden was her refuge, her way of turning sorrow into something that bloomed. And now, watching her share it with Shruti, I feel a lump rising in my throat.

'Aunty, this is so, so beautiful,' Shruti says, her voice reverent as she gently touches the edge of a blooming hibiscus.

My mother's face glows. 'This is just the small garden,' she says, waving a hand dismissively. 'All the vegetables and fruits are growing on the terrace upstairs.'

'You've created something magnificent, aunty,' Shruti says. 'It feels … peaceful. Sacred, almost.'

My mother nods, adjusting her chunni. 'It saved me,' she says simply, her eyes scanning the blooms. 'After Aman's father passed, I didn't know what to do with the silence. So, I started planting. One pot, then two … and soon it grew into this.'

Shruti nods and for a moment, they both stand still, in quiet understanding. I watch them with my heart full. These are the two women who have shaped me in such different ways, and I cannot believe they are together. Finally.

'Will you show me the terrace, too?' Shruti asks.

Ma's eyes light up. 'Of course! Come! There are guavas nearly ready to pick and the mint has taken over one whole corner.'

They walk up the stairs together, chatting easily. As they begin to discuss the intricacies of urban gardening, their voices blend in animated conversation. I follow behind, unnoticed for once, and glad for it.

Ma guides Shruti through the terrace garden, the late afternoon sun slanting through the leaves and casting dappled shadows across Shruti's face. She turns back to look at me, her eyes finding mine with quiet certainty. Her smile is radiant.

In that moment, the noise of the world fades away. Her parents' disapproval, the weight of tradition, the uncertainty of what lies ahead. None of it matters. Not here. Not now.

Right now, there is only this: sunlight, birdsong and the girl I love, standing in the heart of a garden that has known both grief and growth. And deep in my soul, I know that we will find our way through it all.

Dinner that night is laid out on a low table in the flower garden, the cool Gwalior breeze washing over us. Ma had set up the table while I took Shruti to the Gwalior Fort. She loved every moment of the sound and light show that narrated the history of the fort. 'How lucky you are, Aman, to grow up in this place that is steeped in history!' she had said as we returned on Ma's scooter.

Ma had warned us not to eat outside, and I can now see why she said that. Fragrant matar-paneer rests in a gleaming brass bowl along with crisp aloo-gobi in a copper kadai, rotis puffed to perfection and a tangy mango chutney that Ma has made. She has gone all out for this dinner, and she has even made kheer, flecked with slivers of almond and cardamom.

Shruti sits across from me, freshly showered, dressed in a pale green kurti. She looks so beautiful I cannot take my eyes off her, and I can see that she is having the same magical effect on Ma.

'This is all so delicious, aunty,' she says, breaking off a piece of roti and reaching for the aloo-gobi. 'Honestly, I don't remember the last time I felt so at home.'

Ma smiles, pleased. 'I'm glad you like it.'

Shruti hesitates for a moment. Then she says, 'I just wish my parents could be like you.'

Ma looks at her for an explanation.

'They're very … conservative,' she continues, her eyes fixed on the edge of her plate. 'Rigid, sometimes. I don't even know how I'll bring this up with them. They expect me to marry someone from our community. Someone they approve of. Not someone I choose for myself.'

I reach over and place my hand over hers.

Ma just nods. There's no judgement in her eyes, only a quiet understanding.

'People are different, beta,' she says. 'Parents, especially. They carry the weight of generations. Sometimes they don't realize when their love becomes a cage ... But when the time is right, I'll meet your parents and I'll speak to them. I will tell them what I see when I look at you two.'

'What do you see, Ma?' I ask, curious.

Ma looks at me the way she always does when she understands more than she says.

'I see two people who care deeply for each other. Who are willing to try, to listen, to grow. That's rare. And it's worth standing up for.'

Shruti swallows hard and nods.

The conversation shifts gently after that and goes back to childhood stories, to the time I fell into a ditch trying to climb a guava tree, to the neighbour's dog that used to wait by the door and tear up any mail the postman brought.

Later, as we linger over bowls of kheer, there's a lightness in Shruti that I haven't seen in days. And for the first time in a long time, I let myself believe that maybe this won't be a battle. Maybe it will be a bridge.

SHRUTI

The Crack

'AMAN, IT'S TOO soon,' I protest, my voice barely audible over the gentle clinking of fine china and the muted conversations surrounding us. The afternoon sunlight, filtering in through the glass panels on the roof, casts a warm glow across our table, highlighting the tension in Aman's face. He has chosen this luxurious place, The Olive, with its beach-like ambience and Mediterranean cuisine, to celebrate my promotion to senior branding strategist. But what should have been a celebration with champagne toasts has turned into yet another argument about our future.

Aman sets down his fork, his baked brie almost untouched. 'It's been almost a year, Shruti,' he says, his jaw tightening. His eyes now hold a determination that makes me nervous. 'Almost a year since we visited Ma. What exactly are we waiting for? I see it as a godsend that she's travelling to Bangalore.'

'But she is not coming to meet my parents, Aman,' I respond. Then I take a sip of water.

'Yes, Shruti, she is not.' Aman's patience is worn threadbare; I can hear it fraying with each word as he explains things for what must be the fifth time that week. 'She's coming to attend that conference at the Indian Institute of Horticultural Research because she has been nominated by the state government. But what I have been trying to tell you is …' he pauses, running a hand through his hair, '… that this is a golden opportunity. You haven't once raised the subject with your parents. Now I want to come and meet them with my mother, and you have a problem with that too?'

The frustration in his voice makes me wince. Aman rarely shows his anger, which only amplifies the weight of his words now.

'I know, I know,' I admit, tracing patterns on the film of condensation on my glass. 'I know I haven't once introduced you to my parents, and that's not fair to you at all. But Aman, I know how my folks are. Especially my mother.' I look up at him, willing him to understand. 'She's been going on and on about my marriage lately. Traditional marriage. South Indian groom, preferably from our community, the whole works.'

'Yes, Shruti. I've been hearing this for a few years now. All the more reason to tell her about me as soon as possible.' His words are clipped. 'You chickened out and said there was nobody in your life when she asked you. How could you?'

The accusation stings because it's true. Amma had kept going on about meeting potential grooms and I had refused. In frustration and anger, she had asked if there was 'any special someone' in my life. I had lied smoothly, the denial slipping from my lips before I could stop myself.

'Yes, Aman, I did … and I'm sorry. I admit it. I did chicken out.' My fingers reach for his across the table, but he subtly shifts his hand away. 'It's only because I want to avoid confrontation. I don't want to do anything to rock the boat. You know how my work has been going really well. This promotion to senior branding strategist is everything I've worked for. Our relationship has been so wonderful …' I trail off, aware of how hollow my excuses sound. 'I feel like I need more time to make my parents understand how much you mean to me.'

Even as I speak, I realize that Aman is right. If I haven't found the courage to mention him in the four years we've been together, how will I suddenly find it later?

'Shruti,' Aman says, the hurt remaining etched in his eyes, 'there's never a perfect time for marriage. Once you've decided who the person is, I don't see any point in waiting.' He looks directly into my eyes, a cold piercing stare replacing the earlier vulnerability. 'Unless, of course, you're having second thoughts about me.'

'No! You know it's not that.'

'What else am I to think, Shruti? Every single time I bring it up, you make excuses.' He counts off on his fingers. 'First it was "let me find a job", then it was "let my probation period get over". Now every single thing you've been waiting for has happened.' He exhales deeply, a man at the end of his patience. 'Anyway, leave it. I will not keep bringing this up. Think about it, and if the answer is yes, I'll tell my mother. She's eager to meet your folks and has been constantly asking me about this. I need to give her an answer.'

He signals for the bill. There's a finality to the gesture that makes my chest tighten. The server brings the dark brown folder, and Aman slides his credit card in without looking at the total. He's very upset now, and I hate that I've made him feel this way. This man has stood by me through every career setback and has celebrated my smallest victories as if they were his own. He doesn't deserve this.

We ride home in a silence that stretches between us like a physical barrier. My hands are on his shoulders, but he is a million miles away. Cubbon Park blurs past, couples stroll hand in hand, groups of friends laugh. Reminders of what our evening should have been like. Aman's profile is rigid as he navigates the evening traffic, his jaw clenched tight.

He stops at our usual spot, a block away from my apartment complex, another concession to my fear of discovery. When I tiptoe to kiss him goodnight, a gesture so routine it's become reflex, he moves away. The rejection feels like a physical blow.

'I can't keep doing this, Shruti. Parking away from your house and hiding like I'm a fucking thief,' he says, his voice low and strained. 'All I want to do is marry you. It can't be that terrifying a prospect to even speak to your parents about us.' He pulls the visor of his helmet up so I can see the mixture of hurt and resolve in his eyes. 'Call me once you've decided.'

He drives away, revving his bike a little louder than necessary. In all our years together, I have never seen Aman this upset. As I walk the familiar path home, past the flowering gulmohar trees and the security guard who nods in recognition, I replay everything he said in my head. Each word rings true. This is definitely on me. He has been patient and understanding to a fault. I feel miserable as I realize that I have taken advantage of his love, hiding behind excuses that grow thinner with each passing month. I am a coward, and I need to change this.

'Hi, kanna! How was dinner?' my father greets me as I walk into our home, the familiar scent of jasmine incense and my mother's cooking enveloping me. He's in his favourite armchair, reading glasses perched on his nose, the television muted while a cricket match plays on.

'It was okay, Appa,' I manage, trying to keep my voice steady. I have lied to my parents, telling them that it was a celebratory dinner with my colleagues for my promotion.

'Only okay? You should be overjoyed! You worked hard for this!' His pride in me is evident, making my deception feel even worse.

'Yes, I am. I guess I'm just tired,' I reply, setting my purse down and slipping off my heels. 'Where's Amma? And have you eaten?' I ask, trying to divert his attention from my obvious distress.

'Yes, we both had an early dinner. Amma went to bed early. She's visiting the Ashtalakshmi Kovil with the ladies' group and has to wake up at 4.30 a.m. tomorrow.'

'Okay, Appa. I'll see you tomorrow. Good night,' I say, retreating to my room before he can see that I'm on the verge of tears.

Once inside, I sink into my bed, still in my celebration outfit, a midnight blue silk dress that Aman had once said brought out the depth in my eyes. I feel terrible about Aman being angry, more so because I know he's completely justified. If I were in his place, I wouldn't have been this patient with someone who had kept me a secret for four years now.

I text him, but there's no reply, and the message sits unread. I know I have to speak to my parents about him. I have to tell Aman that his mother can meet my parents. It's time I bite the bullet and do what must be done.

I decide that I will speak to my father tomorrow itself, even if my mother is not around. In fact, it might be better if I can convince him first. Perhaps he can advocate on my behalf, soften the ground before the inevitable storm with Amma.

I keep checking my phone, but there's radio silence from Aman. A dull ache settles behind my ribs. Each time my phone buzzes, I pick it up eagerly, but there are no messages from him. Finally, unable to bear it any longer, I text him. 'I'm sorry, Aman. I'll speak to my parents tomorrow itself. I promise. I love you.'

Then I drift into an uneasy sleep, my dreams filled with disappointed faces and ultimatums.

The next morning, sunlight filters through my curtains in golden streams, a direct contrast to the sinking feeling I experience. I bide my time until after breakfast. My father makes casual conversation as our cook prepares fresh dosas in the kitchen, the familiar ritual of spreading batter on the hot tawa bringing a momentary calm.

'Did you see the bitter gourds growing in the garden?' Appa asks as he awaits another dosa at the breakfast counter. 'And

Pillai has become the new president of the residents' welfare association. Oh, and the maintenance charges are being revised next quarter.'

I nod and respond appropriately as I eat my dosas in silence while rehearsing the various ways in which I can begin the conversation.

Once my father has had his breakfast, he settles down in his usual spot by the open balcony, newspaper in hand. The morning sun spills in, painting shifting patterns on the cool marble floor. I approach him with two tumblers of filter coffee—I've taken extra care to make it just the way he likes it.

He takes a sip of the coffee, closing his eyes briefly in appreciation. 'Aha, this is wonderful, Shruti! Did you make it? Or was it the cook?'

'I made it, Appa.'

'You've mastered the art from Amma. It's even better than what she makes, but don't tell her I said that!' He smiles.

My heart hammers against my ribs as I sit down opposite him.

'Appa, there's something I want to tell you.'

He puts his paper down, instantly alerted by my tone. His reading glasses slide down his nose as he looks at me over them. 'What is it, Shruti?' he asks, giving me his full attention.

'It's ... it's about my marriage.' The words feel thick in my mouth.

His face lights up immediately as he slaps his thigh. 'Finally! I've been telling your amma that we should not keep pestering you. I had predicted that you would bring it up yourself.' He sets his coffee down, looking animated. 'You're well settled in your job now. There's a fantastic proposal which has come. The boy is an IIT graduate and works in a multinational. The family is excellent. Your amma wanted to tell you a week ago, but I told her to hold on.'

The excitement in his voice is unmistakable, and I realize with sinking certainty that he has assumed I'm going to agree to the arranged marriage route, the path of least resistance that would make everyone happy. Everyone except Aman and myself.

'No, Appa … I mean …' I struggle to find the right words.

'What? Nothing to feel shy about.' He waves away my hesitation. 'If you have any conditions or preferences, we can accommodate that. We've been told that the boy's family is very progressive.'

I take a deep breath, gathering every ounce of courage. 'No, Appa. There's someone I like … I mean, I love. I … I would really like to get married to him.'

My father stares at me like I've sprouted wings. The silence does not merely sit between us. It swells. A living thing. Damp and breathing.

'Oh,' he says finally. Then he removes his glasses, wipes them methodically with a corner of his kurta and puts them back on, as if the action might change what he just heard. Then he looks at me expectantly, waiting for details, his newspaper lying forgotten by his side.

'His name is Aman,' I say, my voice a bit shaky. 'And he is … I mean, he was from my college. We've been together for around four years now. It started in my second year. He has a job at a multinational … and … I … I really love him, Appa.'

'Is he from our community?' my father asks, cutting me short, his voice carefully neutral.

I swallow hard. This is the moment of truth, the cliff I've been avoiding all these years.

'No, he isn't. He's north Indian.'

My father shakes his head slowly, and I watch as the warmth in his eyes dims, replaced by something I've never wanted to see directed at me. Disappointment. Judgement. I've been condemned without a trial. It cuts deeper than any words could.

Appa says nothing, absolutely nothing, and the silence destroys me. We both know what I've done. The one thing I was never meant to do. The one line I wasn't supposed to cross.

I have stepped outside the community. Wanting to marry for love.

In my parents' eyes, this is not a decision; it is a betrayal, the ultimate one. I might as well have driven a knife through their hearts.

Appa doesn't ask anything more about Aman, and I don't offer anything. There's nothing left to say. The words stay lodged somewhere between my throat and my heart, refusing to come out.

What surprises me most is the shame. This unbearable, suffocating shame. It presses down on me, relentless and sharp, even though I know, rationally, unequivocally, that I've done nothing wrong. I'm a financially independent woman. I've built a life for myself, made choices with intention. I have every right to love and marry whomever I choose. But logic doesn't stand a chance against emotion.

And right now, the emotional part of me is crumbling. That part is replaying every sacrifice my parents made, every hope they pinned on me. I drown in the guilt of having let them down.

My father is the gentler one, more forgiving. If his silence feels like this, I can't even begin to imagine what Amma's reaction would be like. Her words will cut deeper. Her disappointment will burn longer. And it's coming. I know it is.

'I'm sorry, Appa,' I mutter, my voice barely audible. 'I … this was not something I had planned.'

At first, he doesn't look at me. When he finally speaks, his voice trembles with tightly reined fury. 'This wasn't something you planned?' he scoffs, eyes narrowing. 'You hid it from us for four years. Since college, Shruti! What in the world were you thinking?'

He begins pacing the length of the living room, his hands clasped behind his back, fingers clenched so tightly the knuckles have gone white. I've never seen him like this before, so distraught, so visibly shaken. I cannot bear to watch the pain on his face.

'Appa, please. I … I just couldn't—'

'What couldn't you do?' he snaps, cutting me off. His voice rises, raw now. 'Don't tell me you "couldn't help falling in love". Spare me that nonsense. Love isn't some accident that just happens. Every step you took, you chose it. You chose him. And by doing that, you chose to betray us.'

His words land like slaps. I flinch but say nothing. Shame engulfs my chest, creeping up to my throat, pinning my words down before they can rise.

Just then, Amma walks in, chatting on the phone. But the moment she sees our faces, her expression changes. She pauses mid-sentence and quickly tells the person on the line, 'I'll call you back.' She hangs up, her eyes darting between Appa and me. I am already bracing for impact.

'What happened?' she asks, her voice tight, uneasy.

'What hasn't happened?' my father thunders. 'Ask your daughter.'

I turn towards her, already defeated. 'I'm sorry, Amma,' I say. The words feel inadequate. Pointless.

'What is it?' she asks.

'She's in love with some north Indian boy,' Appa explodes, the veins in his neck protruding. 'And now she wants to marry him.'

Amma stares at me as if I've just confessed to a crime. Her eyes widen in horror, and then, her voice shaking, she asks, 'Are you ... are you pregnant, Shruti?'

'No!' I cry out, mortified that this should be her first concern. 'Of course not.'

I think I hear Amma exhale a sigh of relief; her shoulders drop ever so slightly.

'Ah! Then that's fine. She can break up,' she says, just like that. Dismissed. Final. As if she's deciding what to cook for dinner.

I stare at her in disbelief. The casual ease with which she brushes aside everything I feel stings so sharp that I find it hard to breathe. Not one question about Aman. Not his education, not his family, not his values. Nothing. Just his origin. And that alone is enough to condemn him.

Anger rises in me, sharp and sudden, like fire licking at the edges of my restraint.

'Do my choices not matter at all?' I finally ask, trembling.

Amma storms closer until she's inches from my face, her breath hot against my skin. 'Look at you. Shameless!' she spits. 'You do this behind our backs and now you have the audacity to talk back? We should have gotten you married long ago. Like Aishu.'

'And this has been going on for four years,' my father says to her. 'She's been fooling us all this while.'

They speak about me as if I'm no longer in the room.

A ghostly hush sweeps in. Something has died. An illusion they once held of me, their perfect, obedient daughter. We sit in that stillness for what feels like an eternity. Then I gather every ounce of courage I possess and speak.

'Amma, Appa … I know you're both hurt. I know you wanted me to marry the man you chose. But I can't. I simply can't think of marrying anyone but Aman. He's a good man. A kind, loving, principled man. And I don't believe language, or geography, should decide love.'

'It's not just the language,' my father says quietly. There is something eerie about the calm expression on his face, and it terrifies me more than his rage. 'It's the caste. The pedigree. We come from a long lineage of Iyengars. Our ancestors were temple priests and scholars. Don't you understand what you're doing? One selfish decision and you dilute generations of purity. You shatter everything we've preserved.'

I blink, stunned. I can't believe that these words are coming from him, the father I thought was the more reasonable of my parents. The one I always believed would understand.

But now I see it clearly. Their love is conditional. As long as I do what they expect, I am cherished. The moment I deviate, I become unworthy.

'Amma, Appa ... Aman's mother is in town,' I say, desperately changing tactics. 'Please. Just meet her once. She's a lovely woman. She's kind and grounded. Also strong. Amma, she reminds me of you in so many ways.'

Amma gasps, recoiling like I've struck her. She clutches her chest dramatically.

'You've met his mother?' she whispers, horrified. 'How could you, Shruti? Do you really have no shame? Is this how we raised you? Lying? Sneaking around?'

'I'm sorry,' I say, the tears finally breaking free, hot and relentless, and streaming down my face. 'I know I've hurt you. I know I've made mistakes. But please, for my sake, just meet her. Once. If you still feel the same afterwards, I'll reconsider.'

It's a lie. But I'm desperate.

The next five days are filled with pleading, arguing, tears and long silences. My voice grows hoarse. My heart feels bruised. My parents remain unmoved, resolute. They refuse to meet her, insisting it's pointless.

And yet I persist. Because I'm afraid. I'm afraid that if they don't meet her, Aman will walk away. He has had enough of being the unnamed villain in a story he never asked to be a part of.

Finally, they give in.

My father's voice is cold, clipped. 'We'll meet her. Once. That's all.'

I breathe out, relief flooding through me. But before I can say anything more, Appa adds, 'Don't mistake this for approval. This changes nothing.'

'I understand,' I say quietly. 'Thank you.'

But inside me, a tiny flame of hope flickers to life. Just a sliver of light breaking through the heavy walls. A hairline crack in their resistance.

For now, that tiny fragment of possibility is all I have to cling to.

And it is everything.

AMAN

The Meeting

MA IS OVERJOYED that we're finally meeting Shruti's parents. She takes her time choosing a saree from among the three options laid out on my bed. She finally settles on an elegant sea-green silk with delicate silver motifs, a departure from her usual comfortable salwar kameez. The way she stands before the mirror, adjusting the pleats for the third time, tells me just how important this meeting is to her.

'Is this saree appropriate? Perhaps I should have chosen something simpler,' she murmurs, examining her reflection in the full-length mirror attached to my wardrobe. The glass catches the worry lines etched around her eyes, lines that have deepened over the years.

'Ma, you look splendid! Baba would've approved,' I say gently as I sit on the floor, helping her adjust the pleats so that they fall perfectly.

She smiles, but there is a trace of sorrow in her eyes. 'You think so? He always did like this colour on me.'

She had arrived in Bangalore a week ago, and after attending her conference, which wrapped up in three days, she had then moved into my place. But this meeting with Shruti's parents is the highlight of her trip. She is doing this for me. And Shruti.

Shruti had messaged me a few days back:

> Finally got them to agree to meeting you and aunty. But they're furious with me. So, it's best if I don't see you for a few days. Please apologize to aunty for not greeting her at the airport.

When I had relayed the message to Ma, she had just shaken her head. 'Who cares for such formalities? I'm just grateful that this meeting is finally happening. Anything for my son.'

Ma and I hire a cab to go to Shruti's house. She is carrying gifts that include sarees and sweets. She has brought a box of gajak and kaju katli from Sharma Halwai, which is the finest sweet shop in Gwalior. As soon as she had arrived at my place, she had also pulled out two Chanderi sarees from her bag. The one in pastel peach with golden butis is for Shruti, and the other in a greyish-blue is for her mother.

'Ma, that is so generous of you!' I had exclaimed.

'We cannot go empty-handed, can we? It's just a small token from our side. These are hand-woven, too,' she had explained, smoothing the tissue paper. I had then helped her gift wrap them individually in silver paper that she had brought along.

The drive to Shruti's place takes over forty-five minutes, much longer than I'd anticipated. The traffic today is unusually sluggish, and I can't help but compare it to our usual rides on the bike. On two wheels, I've done this route countless times, and rarely has it taken more than thirty minutes. Every time I dropped Shruti off, it was at the same spot, our designated point, a shaded curve near a row of Eucalyptus trees, just far enough from the entrance to her residential complex so that she doesn't run into anyone she knows. I've never asked to go further, and she never invited me to. It is an unspoken boundary, one I never even thought of crossing.

But today, the cab doesn't slow down at the familiar corner. It rolls past our drop-off point like it's irrelevant. I shift slightly in my seat, a vague unease settling in my stomach. As we approach the tall iron gates of her complex, fortified and gleaming, I feel a flicker of disorientation. It feels like I'm stepping into forbidden territory.

Guards stop us, and I tell them we're heading to H Block. I show them the access code Shruti had texted. They nod and wave us through. Then my breath catches as my eyes fall upon what lies ahead.

The road opens into a wide, tree-lined avenue which stretches for at least a kilometre. It is flanked by ornamental streetlamps and perfectly manicured gardens on both sides. Sculpted fountains send arcs of water glittering into the air. With rows of flowerbeds meticulously planted in geometric patterns, the front lawns look like they belong to a royal palace. The sheer scale of everything is overwhelming. This seems less like a residential complex and more like a fortress of opulence. It is practically a private kingdom.

Beyond a certain point, visitors' vehicles are not allowed. An electric buggy awaits to drive us towards H Block. The buggy driver introduces himself.

'Hello, sir, I am Nilesh. I will be driving you to your destination today.'

'Thank you, Nilesh,' I mutter, a little stunned. I wasn't expecting a five-star-hotel-like ambience.

Most buildings our buggy glides past are identical. They all have grand stucco archways with framed tile courtyards. Rows of white lilies stand in full bloom, creating a fragrant carpet along the borders. Everything exudes sophistication and wealth.

'Good lord, look at those lilies! And that Hawaiian hibiscus! And oh, that's a shade of frangipani I've never seen before!' Ma exclaims, her face lit up with the delight of a botanist in paradise as she gazes at the gardens we pass.

'First time here, sir?' Nilesh asks, politely smiling at Ma's enthusiasm.

'Yes,' I say curtly.

Nilesh puffs up with pride. 'The gardens here are one of the best in the city, sir. We also have the largest clubhouse in Bangalore. It is 70,000 square feet. An exclusive movie theatre for residents, our own grocery store, spa, salon, everything is here.'

'How many flats are there in this complex? And how big is this entire property?' I ask Nilesh, trying to gauge the scale.

'It's a twenty-two-acre estate, sir, with just 280 exclusive flats spread across fourteen buildings,' he replies. 'All are four- and five-bedroom homes, starting at 3,000 square feet. Everything here is bespoke; luxury at its absolute finest. The first time I visited, even I was stunned, sir. But you soon get used to it.'

I cannot help comparing this to our modest two-bedroom flat in Gwalior, nestled in a crowded, noisy, dusty lane, where buildings lean into each other and everyone knows your name.

I feel blindsided.

I had always suspected that Shruti came from money, but this? This is a different world altogether. Shruti had never so much as hinted at it. And now, standing here, I feel stupid for not seeing it sooner.

A spark of anger flickers inside me. Why has she never once spoken about this life, the sprawling estates, the gleaming opulence? Is she embarrassed of it? Or is it the brutal contrast to my own cramped, humble home that kept her silent? It makes me question everything. How well do we ever truly know someone? I've been with Shruti for over four years. Four years! Her wealth shouldn't matter. I know that. I believe that.

And yet, it does.

The realization hits me harder than anything else; the fact that it matters to me more than I want to admit. And what scares me the most is not the fact that Shruti has kept this a secret, but this ugly, burning feeling inside me. This gnawing sense of betrayal, of not being enough.

When we arrive at H Block, a uniformed receptionist greets us in the lobby. A receptionist. For an apartment building. She smiles warmly from behind a gleaming marble counter and offers us a chilled, perfumed towel. I can hardly believe this kind of luxury.

'Good afternoon, sir. The Srinivasans are expecting you. Please proceed to the fourteenth floor,' she says with a polished smile.

As we step into the mirrored elevator, even the air inside smells rich. Teakwood, fresh polish, and something else I can't name, something that whispers quiet, effortless wealth.

Our reflections multiply endlessly in the mirrors. I shift uncomfortably, nerves buzzing under my skin. Ma, however, radiates grace, though she does fiddle a little with the folds of her saree again.

The elevator doors glide open soundlessly into what looks like a private foyer. No corridor, no neighbours, just a direct entrance to Shruti's home. I glance around and spot a sleek security console on the side wall that sports an array of CCTV screens quietly displaying footage of the entire complex. One of them shows the grand main gate we entered through barely ten minutes ago. I feel a strange chill crawl up my spine.

And suddenly, so many things begin to make sense.

Shruti's carefully maintained distance. The insistence that I drop her off a few hundred metres away. The way she would change the subject every time I asked about her home. The absolute silence about her family's wealth. All this time, I thought she was just painfully private. Shy, perhaps. But now it feels like something else entirely. As I stand here, surrounded by all this wealth, it's like I'm seeing a version of her I'd never imagined. Maybe she was never hiding this from me out of embarrassment, but because she *knew* I wouldn't fit in. That no matter how much I loved her, her world and mine were never meant to overlap.

This place now feels like an impenetrable citadel designed to keep people like me out. The realization lands like a blow I never saw coming.

We've been together for four years. I've shared everything with her. My life, my truths, my dreams. And yet, here I am, stepping into her world for the very first time, and it's like discovering a whole other story she had been living. I feel foolish. Cheated. Like I've been part of a relationship built on selective revelation. Where the love was real, but the terrain had never been level. What else don't I know?

A dull ache begins to form at the base of my throat. My mother stands beside me, oblivious to my thoughts, clutching the gifts she has wrapped with love and hope, her face glowing with warmth and joy. And me? I'm feeling smaller with every passing second.

The door swings open before I can ring the doorbell. Shruti stands there, her eyes wide with anticipation, nerves thinly veiled by a smile.

'Aunty! Please, come in,' she says warmly, bending down to touch my mother's feet. But Ma immediately pulls her into an embrace. 'No need for formalities, beta. It's so nice to see you again.'

Behind Shruti, her parents sit rigidly on a plush sofa, their faces impassive and unwelcoming. They are stoic, silent, statuesque. They don't rise. They don't greet us. They don't smile. The contrast between Shruti's warmth and their coldness feels jarring. My heart sinks.

'Please, come in. Please sit,' Shruti says, trying hard to bridge the awkwardness.

Ma and I follow Shruti.

'Amma, Appa, this is Sunanda aunty, Aman's mother,' she introduces, her voice slightly higher than normal. 'And this is Aman.'

'Namaste,' Ma greets Shruti's mother with folded hands and a genuine smile.

Mrs Srinivasan merely nods and deliberately averts her gaze. The dismissal is so blatant that I feel heat rise to my face. What kind of people treat a guest with such disrespect? Ma, gracious as ever, chooses to ignore the frosty reception. I have to hand it to her; she remains calm, whereas I am already bristling at their behaviour. Like we are unwelcome guests.

'Please sit,' Shruti says unnecessarily, gesturing towards the seating area.

We sink into the luxurious Italian leather sofas. The living room is massive, dominated by an eighty-two-inch television mounted on a wall, at least twenty-five feet away. Crystal chandeliers hang from the ceiling. Every surface gleams with polished perfection. Mr Srinivasan continues to glare at me, his contempt barely concealed.

Ma reaches into the bag she has brought along and takes out the gifts. She leans forward with the packages in her hand. 'This is for you,' she says warmly, extending the gifts towards Shruti's mother. 'A small token from Gwalior.'

'What is this?' Mrs Srinivasan asks, not moving to accept the offerings.

'Chanderi sarees and some traditional sweets from Gwalior,' Ma explains, still smiling. 'The peach one is for Shruti, and the greyish-blue one I thought would be perfect for you.'

'I'm sorry to be blunt, but we cannot accept this,' Mrs Srinivasan replies, her mouth tightening into a thin line.

'Excuse me?' Ma falters, her hands still holding out the gifts. I hate to see her this way. I want to leave right this instant, but I control myself, trusting Ma to handle the situation.

'According to our traditions, such gifts are given only after a marriage is finalized, not before. It would be inappropriate,' Mrs Srinivasan says with finality.

Ma's smile dims, but she recovers quickly. 'That's what we're here to discuss, isn't it? The children's plans?' She places the packages on the coffee table, her dignity intact despite the rebuff.

Mr Srinivasan clears his throat. 'I don't know what Shruti has told you,' he says, 'but both Meenakshi and I are not in favour of this match. The only reason we're meeting you is because Shruti insisted on it, to the point of threatening to take drastic measures if we didn't.'

The bluntness of his statement leaves me speechless. If this was their position, why had they agreed to meet us at all? Why put Ma through this humiliation?

I glance at Shruti, who looks pale and stricken. Ma, however, still remains composed. She smiles even as I sense her hurt. My blood boils at their callousness.

'I understand that you were hoping for a groom from the same community,' Ma says quietly. 'That's natural for parents. But compatibility and love? Isn't that what marriage is truly about? Our children have made their choices freely and with love. As far as I'm concerned, my son has chosen Shruti and that's good enough for me. Ultimately, what matters in a relationship is that the two people in it love and respect each other. It's not about the parents' egos at all. It's about honouring our children's right to build their own happiness. With whomever they choose.'

'Ego? Is that what you think this is about?' Mrs Srinivasan scoffs, her bangles jingling as she sits up straighter. 'Who said anything about ego? See, we are Brahmins, and for us, caste is paramount. Also, we are Iyengars, one of the most respected castes. In our family, nobody marries even Iyers, although they are Brahmins too. We have very strict customs and traditions, like our thread ceremony and the dietary restrictions we follow. That's how we have raised Shruti. From what I understand, you Mathurs are Kayasthas and that's not even a Brahmin community.'

'Amma!' Shruti interjects, her voice sharp with dismay. 'How can caste possibly matter? This is the twenty-first century! These distinctions are meaningless now.'

'Meaningless?' Mr Srinivasan's voice booms. 'You know very well how much it matters, Shruti! How dare you speak to us this way! We've given you everything, and this is how you repay us? By bringing shame to our family name?'

The tension in the room is suffocating. I want to leave immediately and spare Ma further insult, but she remains seated, her face not revealing the slightest emotion. When she speaks, her voice is gentle yet firm.

'All these caste distinctions might have had their place once,' she says slowly, 'but times change, as they should. And, regarding food preferences, there are many Brahmins today who eat non-vegetarian food. As long as Shruti and Aman decide together what they want to eat and how they want to live their lives, would external opinions really matter?'

Mrs Srinivasan's nostrils flare. 'Yes, they absolutely will matter! We have a certain status in society. People know us.

What will they say? And Shruti is accustomed to a certain level of comfort and luxury.' Her gaze flicks dismissively around the room, as if to highlight the contrast between their wealth and our presumed lack of it. 'Will your son be able to provide all that? What does he even do?'

My mother's face falls, the insults finally breaking through her composed exterior. Before she can respond, Shruti jumps in, 'I don't care about luxury, Amma! I've never cared about any of this.' She gestures wildly at their opulent surroundings. 'I don't want Aman to "provide" me with anything except love and respect, which he gives me in abundance.'

Mrs Srinivasan turns to her husband and speaks in Tamil, probably assuming we wouldn't understand. 'How do these people even have the audacity to come here and talk about marriage? Do they think our daughter is so desperate? How dare they!'

But I understand every word. Growing up in Gwalior, I would spend hours at our neighbour's place every day as I waited for my mother to return from work. The Ramanathans were the kindest Tamil family you could meet. Over the years, I picked up the language to the point where I can speak it effortlessly. I know everything from drawing kolams to celebrating Pongal and all the Tamil traditions.

And what I've just heard is the final straw.

My anger explodes. I shoot to my feet, my rage burning through me like wildfire. My voice trembles with fury. 'You think we came here begging for your approval? I lost my father when I was seven. My mother worked herself to the bone with no help from anyone, to raise me. She built our home in

Gwalior brick by brick with my father, saving every rupee with pride, not pity. And your daughter? She's been to our house. She loved it. Every damn corner of it. So, no. You don't get to look down on us. Not today. Not ever.'

They stare at me, stunned. But I can't stop. My fists are clenched as I continue: 'Every single thing in life cannot be measured by money. You might have luxurious gardens here, but they're all maintained by the labourers you hire. In our home, every plant, every flower has been tended to by my mother herself. I don't think you would even begin to understand the value of such things.'

My voice drops, heavy with contempt. 'You might have money and your so-called superior caste, but I'm sorry to say, you have no class whatsoever. This is not how we would treat a guest in our home. You have failed to show us even the most basic courtesy of offering water. In our "modest" home, no visitor leaves without a meal, regardless of their background.'

'Aman!' Ma gasps, mortified. 'Apologize this instant! That's not the way you speak to your elders!'

'Ma, these people don't deserve our respect,' I retort, beyond caring about propriety now. 'What are we even doing here? Let's go.'

I stand up and march towards the door. I feel my entire body tremble with rage. Shruti's parents look thunderstruck, clearly unaccustomed to being spoken to in such a manner. Ma hesitates for a moment, torn between social etiquette and pride. Then she rises and follows me.

Shruti rushes after us into the foyer. 'Aunty, I'm so sorry! I never thought it would pan out this way. Please forgive my parents. I'm so sorry. I apologize on their behalf,' she pleads, tears streaming down her face.

Ma gently pats Shruti's shoulder. 'It's all right, beta. Different families have different values. This isn't your fault.'

Shruti turns to me, 'Aman, please …'

But I'm beyond consolation, consumed by a white-hot fury. As the elevator doors begin to shut, I see Shruti's devastated expression and her father appearing in the doorway behind her, his face rigid with anger.

'You foolish, selfish girl. Do you have any idea what your mother …'

The rest is swallowed by the gentle thud of the doors closing.

In the descending elevator, Ma stands silently beside me. A deep, raw ache rises in my chest. The buggy ride back through the beautiful gardens feels surreal now, tainted by the ugliness we have just experienced.

Once we're back in a cab heading towards my apartment, I explode again.

'Fucking pretentious people!' I slam my fist against the seat. 'How dare they treat you that way? Who do they think they are?'

Ma sighs deeply. 'Beta, I've learnt that wealth and education don't automatically confer wisdom or compassion.'

I'm still seething, my jaw clenched. 'They humiliated you, Ma. Right in front of me. Like we were dirt beneath their feet. All because we don't have the same amount of money or their fucking Brahmin lineage. I should've walked out the moment she opened her mouth.'

Ma is silent for a long time, then says quietly, 'To be honest, I'm shaken too.'

I look at her, startled.

'I've faced judgement before. So many times, after your father died. People have gossiped all sorts of things about me. I've learnt to not bother with any of it,' she continues, her voice calm but tinged with weariness. 'But something about today, their tone, their eyes … I don't know what it was, but it cut deep. I felt like we didn't belong in their world. Like we had no right to even sit on their fancy sofa.'

I reach for her hand. 'They are bloody arrogant, entitled fools. They don't deserve to even breathe the same air as you, Ma. You have more dignity in you than they have in their entire bloodline.'

She smiles faintly, but the smile doesn't quite reach her eyes. 'Shruti is a good girl. I can see that. She has a kind heart and she loves you deeply. But if this is the family she comes from, then this is the world you'll have to be a part of …' she trails off, shaking her head.

I feel something shift inside me as she continues, almost to herself, 'I feel a bit foolish now. Dressing up, going there with hope, thinking I'd speak to them and that everything would be sorted.' She gives a small, bitter laugh. 'Silly, isn't it?'

I press her hand tightly now, the words stuck in my throat.

We ride in silence after that, two hearts bruised in different ways, staring out at a city that suddenly feels colder than ever before.

The cab moves steadily through the dense Bangalore traffic, carrying us away from the manicured elegance of Shruti's world and back towards the quiet reality of our own. I stare out the window, and I can't help but wonder: Can love bridge a gap this wide? Or are some distances just too great to ever be crossed?

SHRUTI

The Parting

IT'S STRANGE HOW time quietly reshapes our perspective. What once felt unimaginable, slowly integrates into the fabric of our everyday lives. We adapt to circumstances beyond our control more quickly than we realize, as if acceptance were hardwired into our very being. When life hurls its fiercest storms our way, we discover a quiet, steadfast resilience we never knew existed. It is in these moments of chaos, when we are shaken, tested and tossed by forces far greater than ourselves, that something extraordinary rises from within. A hidden reservoir of strength. And then, suddenly, everything changes.

Even six months ago, if someone had told me that Aman and I would barely be speaking, I would've laughed. 'Impossible,' I would've said.

I couldn't imagine my life without him. And yet, here I am.

How does a love story of four years simply … end? In retrospect, perhaps it had been too perfect, too untested by the storms that eventually ravage every relationship. We had been cocooned in our bubble of mutual adoration, blind to the differences that would eventually tear us apart.

I close my eyes and memories cascade through me like a film reel playing at high speed. Aman's expression when he opened the scrapbook I had made for his second birthday since we started dating. I had collected mementos from our dates: movie tickets, restaurant napkins, polaroid photos, handwritten notes.

'What is this?' he had asked, voice hushed with reverence, as he turned the pages.

'Open it and see,' I had whispered, watching his face go from confusion to astonishment.

'You made this? All of this?' His fingers had traced the outline of the logo on a paper napkin from the Dhaba Café that I had glued to the page, a souvenir from our first date.

'Every night, for many months,' I had admitted. 'I had to hide it from my parents. They thought I was working late.'

He had looked at me then, his eyes shining with something so profound it had sent a delicate, undeniable shiver through me. 'No one has ever loved me like this,' he had said. And then he had kissed me. A kiss that felt like a promise.

A promise that was now about to be broken.

The gifts he had given me over the years now sit in a box under my bed. Exquisite crystal earrings for our first anniversary, a small diamond pendant when I got promoted, a tiny robot figurine because I had once mentioned my childhood fascination with them, a copper Buddha from McLeod Ganj when he had visited, clothes he had picked out saying, 'This colour brings out your eyes, Shruti.'

What does one do with such things when the relationship that birthed them dies? Even if I gave away every physical object, what will I do with the memories that burn through me like acid? How do you erase four years of your life?

I haven't slept properly in weeks. Food tastes like cardboard. I move through my days like a ghost, present but not there. I catch colleagues exchanging concerned glances when they think I'm not looking. My boss had pulled me aside last week.

'Take some time off, Shruti,' she had said gently. 'Whatever's going on, you need to address it. Your work is suffering.'

But how do you explain that your life has split into a before and after? Before, when I believed in fairy tales and perfect endings. After, when I realized that happiness is merely borrowed time.

It's been four months. To be precise, it's been one hundred and thirty-six days since Aman and his mother walked out of our home. My world had crumbled into unrecognizable fragments that day. And their walking out was not the cause at all. It was something much bigger.

It was the day I discovered what my parents had been hiding from me for several months. Every excruciating detail of when Aman had stormed out comes flooding back. I had chased after him and his mother, my voice trembling with apologies for how my parents had treated them. Just as I had reached the elevator, my father had yanked me back. The doors had slid shut, cutting me off from Aman, his face cold, unreadable, already hardening into something I didn't recognize.

'You foolish, selfish girl,' my father had hissed. 'Do you have any idea what your mother has been going through all these months?'

'Appa, whatever she's facing, it still doesn't justify the way you treated them. It was wrong. Plain and simple.'

'Wrong and right are subjective, Shruti,' he had said. 'From our point of view, the way you have been treating us is wrong. You've been so self-absorbed, doing exactly what pleased you. You even met his mother in Gwalior without telling us. That's what that boy said, didn't he? That you loved their house? And all this while, your mother is battling cancer.'

The word had hit me like a physical blow. Cancer?

'What are you talking about, Appa? I live in the same house. How could I not have known about this?'

'You would've known,' Appa had said quietly, shaking his head, 'if you had bothered to spend time here. You were always drowning in office work. And come weekends, you were always away. You always had things going on.'

Guilt had come crashing down on me. Crushing. Relentless. He hadn't been wrong. Every little slice of free time, every long weekend, every moment that had not been bound by deadlines, I had spent with Aman. Not with my parents. Not at my home.

'I'm sorry, Appa.' I had been so shocked I could barely speak. 'But … still, you should have told me earlier.'

'We're telling you now,' he had said flatly. 'The doctors have advised a lumpectomy.'

The shame had hit me so hard then that I froze, standing rooted to the spot. I had pushed them, relentlessly, into meeting Aman's mother. I had pleaded, begged, insisted, even when they were clearly not in the right frame of mind. And they had agreed. Only because I had made them.

Now, I feel sick with guilt. If I could go back, I would never have forced that meeting. I wish I had seen what they were going through. I wish I hadn't been so blind.

The surgery had already been scheduled. I had had no time to digest the news, no pause for panic or prayer. But what was supposed to be a straightforward lumpectomy spiralled into something far worse. When they opened her up, they found a tumour that was nearly twice the size of the one visible in the scans. Instead of removing one lymph node, they had had to take out eight.

I sat for hours in the freezing hospital waiting room, head in my hands, phone buzzing with Aman's messages.

> Shruti, I'm still processing everything that happened that day. How are you holding up?

Then a week later:

> Are you really not going to talk to me now?

And finally:

> Beginning to get worried. At least let me know you're okay.

But how could I tell him that nothing was okay?

That while I was dreaming of forever, my mother had been quietly preparing for the possibility of no tomorrow.

After the surgery came the chemotherapy. I watched helplessly as the strongest woman I knew withered before my eyes. Her glorious hair, those thick black curls I used to braid as a child, fell out in handfuls. Her skin turned pale, almost grey. And the body that had once carried me, held me through sleepless nights and growing pains, now trembled under the weight of every toxic drop meant to heal her.

And just when we had thought that the worst was over, the doctors delivered the final blow.

'A mastectomy is necessary,' they said, 'to reduce all future risk. To be certain.'

The chemo had done its part. It had shrunk what it could, slowed what it couldn't. But the tumour's aggressiveness, and what they had uncovered during the first surgery, left the doctors with no choice. A mastectomy was the only way to be absolutely sure. They didn't want to gamble with margins or hidden cells. Neither did we.

Clinical words. A cold delivery. But irreversible consequences.

Through it all, Amma never complained. Never cried in front of me. Just once, late at night, after the mastectomy, her body fragile and stitched up, her spirit fraying, she took my hand in hers and whispered, 'Forget about that boy, Shruti. He's not suitable for you. Please listen to your amma. I have only your best interests at heart. Rishabh is from a good family … known to us for generations. You will be happy with him.'

I opened my mouth to protest but she squeezed my hand with surprising force.

'My only wish is to see you married. To someone who will take care of you when I'm gone.'

'Don't talk like that, Amma,' I had said, clutching her hand. 'You're going to be fine. You have to be.'

But her eyes told me she didn't believe it.

And in the deepest, darkest part of me, I wasn't sure I did either.

When she finally came home after the mastectomy, I broke down completely. I would have given anything to have my old Amma back, the one who yelled at me for not clearing my plate from the table, who dragged me to weddings just to 'bump into' eligible boys, who was sharp, sarcastic and fiercely herself. Not this frail shadow lying in bed, pleading with me to meet a boy she believed would save me.

That night, I cried into my pillow until it was soaked. I cried from the guilt I couldn't scrub clean, for the mother I had almost lost and for the fragile thread she now clung to.

I'm an only child.

Their only hope.

Their only legacy.

And somehow, in my desperation, I convinced myself that if I granted her this one wish, she would heal. As if love could be exchanged for life. As if sacrifice could buy back strength.

And then I cried harder; broken, heaving sobs for Aman. Because deep down, I knew I would have to end it.

The day I agreed to meet Rishabh, I saw something I hadn't in weeks. My mother smiling. Not the tired, forced kind. A genuine smile. One that reached her eyes.

'I'm so happy you have agreed to meet him. Just one meeting, kanna,' she said, her voice trembling with hope. 'That's all I want.'

One meeting had turned into two, then three. And, irrationally or illogically, I felt that every time I met Rishabh, Amma seemed to be getting better. He was kind, educated, stable. He understood my mother's illness. His own father had battled cancer years before. There was no spark, no butterflies, but perhaps that wasn't the point anymore. Perhaps love was a luxury I could no longer afford. Last week, I had finally nodded when my parents asked if they could proceed with the engagement talks.

And now, here I am at a café, about to tell Aman that I am walking away. That I have agreed to marry someone else. That our love story, which had once seemed destined for a forever, is over.

The memory of his last text message is burnt into my mind:

> Whatever has happened between our parents, we can work through it, Shruti. Four years can't just disappear. Please talk to me.

I had replied with a clinical detachment that disguised the trembling of my fingers:

> Let's meet. Tomorrow. 3 p.m.

His response had come instantly:

> Yes! I love you, and I have missed you so, so much. Name the place and I'll be there.

His eagerness had felt like a knife twisting in my gut. The hope in those words had killed me.

The café bustles with afternoon customers, their laughter and conversation a cruel counterpoint to the hollowness inside me. I check my watch again: 2.47 p.m. Thirteen minutes to go before I shatter what remains of Aman's heart. Thirteen minutes until I say the words that will finalize the death of something I once believed to be eternal.

I spot him the moment he enters the café. Even after four months, my heart lurches at the sight of him. He has lost weight. Dark circles shadow his eyes, and his usually meticulously styled hair is slightly longer. But his smile when he sees me is radiant. It lights up the whole world. God, that smile still has the power to undo me.

'Shruti,' he breathes, sliding into the seat across from me.

I open my mouth, but no words come out. What can I possibly say? How do you begin a conversation that will end everything?

He reaches for my hands across the table, but I pull them back, tucking them under the table where he cannot see them trembling. His smile falters, and the distance between us feels immeasurable even though we haven't moved an inch.

'You ... you look different,' he finally says, his eyes searching my face.

I nod slightly, eyes fixed on the untouched glass of water in front of me. I say nothing. I am unable to.

'I've missed you terribly,' he continues, his voice barely a whisper. 'These four months have been hell.'

I swallow hard, still not meeting his gaze. Our table sits like a still point in the middle of all that noise. The clinking of cups, laughter from a nearby table, the hiss of the espresso machine, all seem to be mocking me.

'Aman, I ...' I start, then stop. The words are stuck in my throat.

'What is it, Shruti?' he asks. 'I know what happened that day between our families was terrible. But I think, ultimately, it is you and me who have to live with each other. I will apologize to your parents, ask for your hand in marriage, explain how much you mean to me and tell them that we cannot live without each other.'

I finally look up at him, at the hope shining in his eyes. The hope I am about to extinguish.

Forever.

'It's not that simple,' I whisper.

'Of course it is,' he insists, suddenly sounding resolute. 'We love each other. That's all that matters. We can start afresh.'

I shake my head slowly, my gaze dropping again to the table.

Neither of us speaks. It feels heavier this time. I can feel him waiting, his body tense with anticipation.

When I do not respond, he sighs.

'Are you even going to talk to me, Shruti? Four months of saying nothing, and now ... you won't speak?'

I force myself to look at him. 'My mother is battling cancer,' I finally say.

His jaw goes slack with shock. 'What?'

'Breast cancer. I found out about it the day you came home with aunty.'

What follows is stunned, horrified stillness. I watch his expression shift as he processes the information.

'Oh God,' he finally says. 'But why didn't you tell me?'

'I don't know, Aman. It was all too much.'

'Shruti, I'm so sorry.'

I wrap both hands around my glass of water, needing something to hold onto. He waits as I gather courage to speak the words that will destroy us.

'My parents want me to marry someone else,' I manage to get the words out, staring into the water as if it might offer some escape from this moment. 'His name is Rishabh. His family has known ours for generations.'

Aman goes completely still. His breathing changes, becomes shallower, more rapid.

'And?' he asks. That single word is loaded with fear.

I cannot bring myself to continue. The truth sits between us. Unspoken. Unchangeable.

A tear slips down my cheek.

'You're going to do it,' he says. Not a question. A realization.

I nod almost imperceptibly, still not looking up.

'Just like that?' His voice is sepulchral, heavy with disbelief. 'Four years, just … gone? Because your parents found a more suitable match?'

'It's not that simple,' I say again. 'My mother's one wish is to see me settled before …' I cannot finish the sentence.

The air is charged with tension. I can feel the weight of the emotions radiating from him. But when he speaks, his words are controlled.

'Why agree to meet me if you'd already made this decision? You … you could have messaged me. We did not need to meet.'

I finally look up at him. His eyes are a storm of pain and confusion. I feel everything he is going though. Like a punch to my gut.

'I needed to tell you in person,' I say quietly. 'You deserve that much.'

'How considerate,' he says, bitterness oozing out of his words.

We don't speak. A waiter approaches our table, sees our faces and wisely retreats without a word.

'Is there nothing I can say?' Aman finally asks. 'Nothing I can do?'

The weight of his question kills me. I stare at a small section of the tabletop that has chipped away, tracing it with my fingertip.

'She might be dying, Aman,' I whisper. He has to strain to hear me. 'The doctors say her prognosis is good now, but what if it comes back? What if these are her last months?'

'And what about your life?' he asks. 'The rest of your life?'

His words pierce me, but I have no answer for his question. Somewhere behind me, a woman laughs at something. A cup is set down. The world carries on, entirely unaware that mine has fallen apart.

'Do you love him? Will he be able to make you happy?' Aman finally asks.

I don't answer immediately. The truth feels too cruel.

'That's not the point,' I say eventually.

'It's exactly the point!' he says, his voice rising slightly before he controls it again. 'You're throwing away real love for a convenient arrangement.'

'I'm choosing my family,' I correct him, trying to look steadier than I actually feel. 'I'm choosing to be the daughter my mother needs right now.'

I drop my gaze to his hands that are resting on the table—hands that have held mine countless times, hands that I know as well as my own—and watch them clench into fists, then slowly relax.

'And what about being the woman you need to be?' he asks. 'The woman I fell in love with? Strong, independent, unwilling to compromise on what matters?'

His words hit me like a blade, cutting into my soul. He's right, and I can't deny it. I have compromised. I have surrendered to fear, to obligation, to the desperate need to hold onto something that feels safe. I have no defence, so I offer none. Everything I am not saying, says it all.

'So that's it?' he asks. 'We're over?'

I nod, unable to trust my voice, unable to say anything more.

He sinks back in his chair, defeat etched into every line on his face. For several minutes, neither of us speaks. What is left to say?

After what feels like an eternity, he stands up. The scrape of his chair against the floor makes me flinch.

'I hope ...' he starts, then stops and swallows hard. 'I hope your mother recovers fully.'

'Thank you,' I whisper, looking up at him one last time, trying to memorize his face.

He hesitates, as if there is something more he wants to say. Then he looks at me and I see it. The rawness, the love and the hurt. It is unbearable.

'Look, Shruti,' he says, almost pleading, 'you know what we mean to each other. You know you are my life, and I cannot imagine a future without you. You know where to reach me; you have my numbers, email, everything. If you change your mind—and I'm hoping that you will—please come back to me. I'll be waiting to welcome you with open arms. But I, on my part, will never ever contact you or stand in your way. That is a promise.'

I break down then, overwhelmed by the weight of everything. I stand up and go to his side, put my arms around him in a desperate embrace. But Aman is too angry, too hurt to hold me back. His hands hang limply by his sides as I sob into his shirt, my tears soaking through the fabric.

He gently disentangles himself from me. Then he nods once, a quiet acceptance, before walking away. No dramatic exit, no final declarations of love or anger. Just absence.

I watch him leave, his shoulders slightly hunched, his steps measured. He doesn't look back.

Outside, it begins to rain; soft at first, then a downpour that matches the storm inside me. I sit there long after he's gone, staring at the empty chair across from me. I think of my mother at home, frail but fighting. I think of Rishabh, kind and stable, waiting for my call. I think of the life that stretches before me: safe, approved, dutiful.

I think of Aman, walking away in the rain, carrying pieces of my heart with him.

Eventually, I pay the bill and step into the rain. Not to the future I had once dreamed of, but to the one I have chosen out of duty and the desperate hope that, sometimes, sacrifice brings its own kind of peace.

AMAN

The Geography of Heartbreak

THERE MUST BE at least thirty people crammed into our small home right now. The living room buzzes with conversation. It feels as though every house on our street has sent at least one member from their home to bid me farewell. Aunties in their fine salwar kameezes, uncles in their kurtas, children darting around Ma's garden with their tetra packs of Frooti. I stand at the centre of it all, smiling mechanically, nodding at congratulations that wash over me like tepid water.

I catch Ma's eyes across the room. Her face is radiant with pride, chin lifted slightly as she answers a question Gupta Uncle from three doors down has asked about my 'prestigious foreign posting'.

For these few precious moments, watching the joy illuminate her tired features, I can almost forget the hollowness that has carved itself into my chest these past six months. Almost.

'London mein toh bahut thand hoti hai, na?' Mrinalini aunty is now asking me as she presses a samosa into my hands. 'Have you packed enough warm clothes, beta?'

I nod. I don't correct her. Norwich or London, it doesn't matter. To everyone here, the UK is a distant, glittering dream, and all of it is 'London'. Their pride in me, the boy from their lane, the one they've watched grow up with scraped knees, is effusive and sincere. And it moves me. I take the samosa and chew it dutifully, though everything I eat has tasted like sawdust since February. Since Shruti.

Her name still triggers a physical reaction, a sudden tightening in my chest, as if invisible hands are squeezing the breath out of my lungs. Four years. Four years of loving her, of building dreams, brick by fragile brick, of shared weekends, quiet mornings, late-night conversations and the countless promises that we would always be there for each other. And then everything unravelled in the space of a thirty-minute conversation in a crowded café.

I can still feel her tears soaking through my shirt, and the way her body trembled as she struggled to say the words. She couldn't look me in the eye when she said she was choosing to marry someone else. I couldn't hold her, couldn't speak. I was hollowed out, gutted. I had nothing left to give her, not comfort, not anger, not forgiveness. And yet, I told her that I would wait. That if she ever came back, I would be standing right there, with my arms open. It was desperate and undignified, but I had meant every word.

Every single day since then, I've hoped for a message. Something. Anything. A sign that she regretted it. That I still mattered. Every day, I've checked my phone with a kind of quiet, private madness. And every day, there's been … nothing.

The memories strike without warning, sudden, sharp and cruel. I excuse myself from a conversation I was barely a part of, step out into the terrace garden and draw in deep breaths of the evening air. Below me, Gwalior stretches out, sprawling and indifferent. Cars honk, lights flicker on, laughter drifts out of a nearby window. Life goes on, relentless. As though my world hasn't shattered.

In a few hours, I'll board a plane; first to Delhi, then to London and, finally, a train to Norwich. An expat posting that nobody my age has ever secured from the company. A lifeline thrown by Vikram, my boss and mentor, who saw me drowning and refused to let me sink.

After that day in the café, I had become a ghost in my own life. I went through the motions, showing up at work with bloodshot eyes and crumpled clothes. Vikram had noticed immediately. He took me to a bar after work one evening, poured three fingers of Glenfiddich into a glass and said simply, 'Talk.'

And I had. Words had poured out like blood from a wound. I held nothing back. I told him how Shruti's parents had found me lacking, how they had insulted my mother when we had formally visited them, questioned my family's status. And how Shruti had gone silent after that. Yet, I had not given up hope. I had genuinely thought that everything would be all right once we met. That all she needed was time. That we could still convince her parents.

'But her mother's illness, it's a ticking clock,' I had told Vikram, staring into the glass of amber liquid. 'Still, I never thought that Shruti would ...' I couldn't finish.

Vikram had patted me on my back and waited till I regained my composure.

'She didn't just leave me,' I had continued after a long silence. 'She's marrying someone else. Within months of ending things with me. Four years, Vikram! Four years of promises, broken in less than forty minutes.'

Vikram had insisted that I take time off. He told me to book my leave for two weeks. I went back to Gwalior, to Ma. I spent most of my time in bed, curtains drawn against the sunlight that felt like a personal affront. How dare the world remain beautiful when everything inside me had turned to ash? Ma had tried to console me, sitting at the edge of my bed, stroking my hair like she had done when I was a child with a fever.

'Aman, what is not meant to be will fall away,' she had said wisely. 'All the connections we form in our lives are karmic. They remain only till the karmic debt is paid. When that business finishes, no matter how strong your connection is, it breaks.'

I had turned away from her, trying not to let her see the tears streaming down my face. 'I don't know about all of that, Ma. All I know is that I feel betrayed, cheated. Look at how her parents insulted us. Still, I was ready to fight for her. I was a fool to be so madly in love with her.'

'Beta, she is not responsible for her parents' behaviour. She did run after us, apologizing.'

'I know, Ma ... It's just that this is so hard to bear.' My voice had cracked, a grown man reduced to a wounded child.

'I know, beta, I know,' she had said, her eyes full of tenderness. 'What do you think I went through when your baba died? I was angry for years. Angry that he died. Angry that he left me. I was angry with someone who was dead. Imagine that. But gradually, I learnt to accept it.'

'How did you manage, Ma?' I had asked, desperate for some formula, some solution to this unbearable pain.

She had said sadly, 'I learnt that in life, every relationship carries a purpose. Some people are meant to stay forever, while others come only for a little while. It's a soul contract. Like I said, when the purpose with which a person came into our lives is fulfilled, the invisible bond you had with them breaks. It's not betrayal. It's simply the natural course of spiritual growth. Only when you accept this and let it go will you start to heal. Instead of holding onto the pain, be thankful for what you have experienced. Understand that you have grown.'

I had nodded even though the wisdom had felt hollow against the sharp edges of my grief. How could something that still felt so right be over? How could Shruti go from being my future to being nothing at all?

After returning from Ma's, I had reached out to my old friend Chandan after nearly a year of sporadic contact. He was in Bhutan, happily married to the woman he had loved since college. She had just given birth to twins. His voice over the phone had been buoyant with joy, his world blooming with new beginnings, while mine quietly shrank inwards.

'Come to Bhutan,' he had urged. 'Stay with us for a while. The mountains heal everything.'

But I couldn't bear to. His happiness contrasted too sharply with my devastation. Also, I was tired of running. I had to face this pain, walk through it somehow.

When I got back to Bangalore, I joined a local gym and worked out like a man possessed, pushing weights until my muscles screamed louder than my heart. I became every cliché of the heartbroken guy at the gym with my protein shakes and obsessive workout routines. My biceps grew while my emotional wounds remained untreated and festered. My body transformed, but the bone-deep ache persisted.

Work became my sanctuary. I turned into a machine. Efficient, focused, devoid of feeling. I arrived before anyone else and stayed until the security guards began eyeing me with quiet concern. I volunteered for extra projects, said yes to every business trip, all to avoid the silence of my apartment where memories of Shruti haunted every corner. The blue ceramic mug she had gifted me still sat untouched in the cupboard. I couldn't bear to use it. Nor could I bear to throw it away.

I didn't let my mind idle for even a second. If I did, the pain attacked with fresh vigour. Unbearable thoughts would flood in: Was she going out with him? Was she happy with him? Did she think of me? Had our years together meant nothing to her? Was her mother responding to treatment? Questions with no answers; questions that gnawed at me in unguarded moments.

Then Vikram had called me into his office one rainy afternoon. 'There's an opening in Norwich,' he had said without preamble. 'International team, prestigious position. Nobody your age has ever been considered for it, but I've put your name forward.'

It felt like the first ray of light after an endless night, a chance to escape, to start over in a place untouched by Shruti, where streets didn't echo with memories. What followed were multiple rounds of interviews amidst fierce competition with candidates from across the globe. I approached each one with the desperate determination of a drowning man clutching at a lifeline.

And somehow, improbably, I had made it. Four relentless months of paperwork, visa formalities and endless checklists had brought me to this moment—my living room buzzing with well-wishers, Ma's face lit up with pride and my suitcases lined up by the door, packed for a journey across the ocean.

Now, on the balcony, I feel someone join me. It's Ma, holding two cups of chai.

'They're asking for you inside,' she says, handing me a cup. 'Gupta Uncle wants to take photos of you to show to his grandson in Mathura.'

I nod, sipping the warm tea. I've somehow become the poster boy for what a small-town boy can achieve, and their pride in me is fierce and unquestioning, their stories of my success already woven into local legend. And yet, none of them know the truth. That behind the applause and the packed suitcases stands a man gutted by loss, carrying a grief too private for photographs and praise.

'Are you having second thoughts?' Ma asks quietly.

'No,' I say firmly. 'I need this, Ma. I need to go someplace where everything doesn't remind me of her.'

She studies my face, reading the grief that I know is still written there despite my efforts. 'Just remember, beta, that even though it is a new beginning, the pain will still come. Sooner or later, you will still have to face it.'

'I know,' I whisper, looking out at the sky, which is beginning to turn a brilliant orange. 'But maybe, from a distance, it won't feel like it's killing me.'

She takes my free hand, her palm warm against mine. 'When your father died, I thought I would die too. The pain was physical, like someone had carved out half of me. But here I am, still standing. And one day, you'll look back and realize that you, too, have survived. You will be fine. Now go make all of us proud. We're all counting on you.'

I squeeze her hand, unable to speak past the lump in my throat.

We stand in silence for a moment, the sounds of celebration floating out from inside. Then Ma straightens, adjusts her chunni. 'Come. They're waiting for you. Your send-off party.'

I follow her inside, the smile back on my face, effortlessly slipping on the mask I've worn so long. As I move through the crowd, accepting blessings and good wishes, I'm filled with a strange blend of tenderness and desolation. These people love me. They're genuinely proud. And somewhere within the echoing hollowness of my chest, a trickle of gratitude begins to flow; hesitant, but real.

Later, as the car pulls away from our narrow lane, I wave back to the hands raised in farewell. I rest my forehead against the cool glass of the window. Norwich awaits with its quiet streets, its ancient cathedrals, its blank slate of anonymity. A place where no one knows of Shruti, of the man I was beside her or the shell I've become in her absence.

As my flight takes off from Delhi's Indira Gandhi International Airport to London, I keep telling myself that this is a fresh start.

I have to heal. I have to get better.

The words loop in my mind like a prayer as the airplane lifts into the sky. Land slips past the window; fields, rooftops, a country that once held all my dreams, everything shrinks beneath me as I rise above the geography of my heartbreak.

Whether healing is truly possible is a question I leave suspended in the clouds behind me.

To know what happens to Aman and Shruti, meet them again in *The One You Cannot Have*.

THE ONE I ALMOST MISSED

LIVING MY DREAM

'ANJALI, WHAT HAVE you got?' Nimmi's voice slices through the office buzz like a surgical blade. It's the kind of voice that commands attention the moment it's heard, piercing through distractions, silencing side conversations.

It's 9.32 a.m. on a Friday, and we're assembled for the tri-weekly morning meeting she insists on having even though none of us quite understand why it needs to happen three times a week. It's not like we are writing news that changes fast or launching space missions.

I straighten up in my chair, pushing my mug of chai out of sight like it's contraband. 'I'm working on the promo piece for Amara Jewellery,' I say, trying to sound both efficient and enthusiastic. 'And I've started compiling the content for the sex-ed feature, "One Thing I Wish I Knew about Sex".'

Nimmi drums her immaculately manicured fingernails against her brushed steel water bottle. Tap. Tap. Tap. It's the kind of rhythmic disapproval that tightens your spine even when she hasn't said a word.

'Is that it?' she asks, arching a perfect brow. 'That's hardly a day's worth of work. I want pitches for both Luminous Skincare and Elysian Resorts. Make them relatable but aspirational. For Luminous, think modern goddess meets girl-next-door who uses the right serum.'

Her eyes have already moved on to Ishani before I can respond.

'Yes, Nimmi. I'll send them over by EOD,' I mumble, scribbling notes like a student who knows the teacher won't wait.

Ishani is working on 'How to Get Your Glow Back in Your Thirties' and a promo article for a luxury spa chain in Coorg. Mahima is handling a destination wedding story set in a boutique hotel overlooking the Powai Lake, plus a lifestyle piece on 'Cool Dudes Who DJ: Bangalore's Hottest Nightlife Tastemakers'. We're all juggling at least two stories, three deadlines and one rapidly fraying sense of identity.

Neither Ishani, nor Mahima, nor I have been given our own columns. We're elves in Santa's workshop. Except there is no snow and no joy. Just three twenty-something women churning out content for *Tiara*, one cleverly disguised clickbait at a time. Our byline reads 'By Our Columnist', as if we're some hive-minded organism sharing a single keyboard and a single extra-caffeinated brain cell.

We write it all. From '10 Ways to Tell If He's Into You' (spoiler alert: if you have to ask, he's probably not) to 'Superfood Spotlight: Is Your Smoothie Missing This Ancient Grain?' (spoiler alert: yes, it is, and it will cost you more than your monthly internet bill).

Nimmi is terrifying in the way only women who have nothing left to prove can be. She wears her ambition like other people wear perfume. Intense, unapologetic and impossible to ignore. You could follow her by the trail of deadlines and fear she leaves in her wake.

'More ideas, girls,' Nimmi says, scanning the room like a general inspecting her troops. 'We're not clocking in hours. We're creating culture. We're shaping young women.'

If she could crack a whip without violating HR policy, she would.

Still, there's a part of me, hopeful, foolish, determined, which believes that if I keep saying yes, if I keep smiling on cue and keep delivering flawless copy, someday I'll be rewarded. A column with my name on it. My voice. My space. My words. Someday.

But don't mistake my frustration for ingratitude. I do absolutely love my job. I'm writing for *Tiara*, for God's sake. The magazine that helped me navigate the emotional landscape of my teenage years like it was a secret map for the lost and heartbroken. It was *Tiara* that saw me through my first real heartbreak when I was in Class IX, when Karun Khanna picked M. Jyotirmayi, the leggy volleyball captain with a perpetual annoying giggle, over me. It was *Tiara* that taught me how to talk to boys without sounding like a total nerd. And it was *Tiara* that guided me through my awful flannel shirts-and-tights fashion era with kind encouragement and a voice that told me that no matter what I wore, confidence was my best accessory.

When I was still in boarding school, my friends Latika and Sriram and I would smuggle in copies of the magazine.

Latika and I would read it under our blankets at night, with our torchlights on, after which we would pass it to Sriram. Latika and I absorbed every word, like the magazine was our gospel; Sriram, I suspect, only wanted to look at the pictures. The nuns who ran the school hated it. Too many articles about sex, orgasms and female pleasure, they said. Things we weren't supposed to know, let alone enjoy. But for us, *Tiara* was freedom on glossy pages.

And now? Now I'm the one writing those pages! Sometimes I still can't believe I managed to get this job after slogging it out for a mere six months at a local newspaper, right after my media and journalism course. This is indeed my 'dream job'.

When I leave office that evening after submitting everything Nimmi had asked for, I find that the Bangalore traffic gods are being unusually kind. I make it home a lot earlier than I normally would. As I approach the house, I spot Mr Joshi, my landlord, watering the plants on his front porch with the same stern dedication with which he approaches gossip and dishing out unsolicited advice.

'Back early?' he asks.

No, I'm the evil twin, I want to say. *The real me is still being slowly crushed by capitalism.*

But I don't. Joshi Uncle is my father's distant cousin and, in his mind, that makes him the family-appointed guardian of my virtue. One wrong word, and he will have my mother on the phone faster than you can say this-is-what-happens-when-girls-write-for-*Tiara*.

I smile, nod and climb the stairs two at a time, grateful for my rented solitude.

My parents only agreed to let me live alone because Joshi Uncle's house was available for rent, and because he and his wife live downstairs, offering the kind of 'proper supervision' that makes my parents believe will prevent drunken nights and bad decisions. What they don't realize is that after years of shared dorms and hostel food, even with a nosy landlord, having my own one-bedroom apartment feels like owning a luxury penthouse. This space is mine.

Yes, I know that the bedroom is roughly the size of a spacious closet. And yes, the kitchen barely fits my gas stove and fridge. But the terrace? Ah! The terrace is my sanctuary. It's not massive, maybe thirty by twenty feet. But it's mine. A private patch of sky in a city of chaos. My kingdom. A respectable size for a queen who rules over precisely no one except the occasional pigeon and the crow that stops by to judge my life choices.

I pour myself a cup of masala chai and collapse onto one of the two plastic deck chairs I dragged here from a closing sale. My faded yoga mat lies next to me, having seen far more chai spills than sun salutations. The sunset turns Bangalore into a hazy watercolour, with rooftops tinged with terracotta and neon signs blinking like they are tired of their own hustle.

Up here, above the madness of the city, above the constant clamour of deadlines and decisions, I can breathe. I stretch my legs, warm my face in the last of the slanting sunlight and cradle my journal in my lap. Its faux leather cover is peeling at the edges, worn soft from use. Writing here has become my ritual, the hour I protect like a secret. The one thing in my day that is entirely, unquestionably mine.

The evening sky turns a shade darker as I flip through pages filled with my tiny handwriting. But my phone buzzes, shattering the moment.

6 p.m. tomorrow, at Wicked Wench?

I stare at Vinay's message, feeling that familiar knot of dread tighten in my gut. Potential match number five in nine months. At this rate, I would have rejected half of Bangalore's eligible bachelors before the year ends. I toss my phone aside and close my eyes, mentally cataloguing my dating fiascos so far. Two were full-blown disasters that had me sprinting for an autorickshaw before we reached dessert. The other two were … well, mediocre at best and soul-crushingly boring at worst.

'Maybe I'm the problem,' I had confessed to Latika and Sriram over filter coffees and masala dosas during our last catch-up at India Coffee House. The three of us meet regularly, even if it's only for an hour, at one of the numerous cafés dotting Church Street or MG Road. The commute from our respective corporate dungeons is equidistant and mercifully short.

'Yes, absolutely, you're the problem, Ms Picky-Choosy-Queen-Can't-Get-Anyone-Good-Enough,' Sriram had teased in a singsong voice, dramatically flipping an imaginary scarf over his shoulder, imitating Poo from *Kabhi Khushi Kabhie Gham*.

Sriram was always performing, which is not a surprise considering he spends most weekends with a local theatre group. Secretly, he dreams of television stardom, but until that dream materializes, he remains a corporate slave like the rest of us. I must have looked genuinely dismayed because Latika had rushed to my defence.

'Of course not! What are you even saying, Sri? You know it wasn't because of that. The guys she has seen till now were all walking red flags.' She had squeezed my hand across the table. 'Trust me, you're not the problem. *They* are.'

But how would I know? I've never had a 'real' relationship, never had my heart properly broken. Maybe it was because I had witnessed too many girls in my hostel go through painful break-ups, sobbing into their pillows at 3 a.m., that I never ventured into the capricious waters of commitment. I knew how to console, knew how many tubs of ice cream it took to patch a cracked heart. Now, however, I cannot help wondering that maybe, deep down, I'm not meant for all of this. Maybe I'm not relationship material.

I flip open my journal and skim through the postmortems of each date, hoping to find a pattern. If there's something I can fix, perhaps I'll stand a better chance next time. Something that might lead me to a man whose company doesn't immediately trigger my SOS protocol: a single stop sign emoji, our agreed-upon distress signal, sent to Sriram; it prompts him to call or turn up with an elaborately fabricated emergency. Our little system has saved me from further torture with these men I have gone on dates with.

9 January, Rohan

Coffee at Third Wave. Sir arrived 20 minutes late with no apology. Zero points for dressing up well too. He had hardly made an effort with a faded T-shirt that had seen better days and a pair of crumpled, oversized three-quarter pants. (What the hell! Who even wears those to a date these days?) I felt stupid to have worn a nice dress.

Then he spent the next hour talking about his startup. Every question I asked somehow circled back to his 'revolutionary app that will disrupt the organic food delivery space'. When the bill came, he calculated my share down to the last rupee, including the exact percentage of the service charge I should pay. Kept calling the waiter 'boss' in that fake-casual way that people trying too hard have. Finally, when I couldn't take it anymore, I had sent Sriram the stop emoji.

Sriram had called, pretending to be my cousin from Chennai, and screamed something about our grandmother's hip replacement surgery. I rushed off, clutching my bag like I was running to catch a flight.

And as if his behaviour wasn't obnoxious enough, Rohan later sent me a 500-word WhatsApp essay titled 'Why You're Sabotaging Your Own Happiness'.

I've blocked him.

Not worth my time.

4 February, Arjun

Dinner at Ebony. Perfectly nice on paper. Doctor, well read, decent taste in music, well dressed. But something felt off. It seemed like he had rehearsed what to say and how to behave, like he was performing 'good date' rather than having one.

He made the right comments about the wine and asked the perfectly correct questions about my job. When I mentioned how I get bored within a few days every time I visit my parents in Muscat, he nodded with such practised sympathy, I could practically see him mentally checking off 'showed empathy' on some internal spreadsheet.

When I asked questions about his job and what it felt like to barely get any sleep (he was doing his residency at St. John's), he said that 'it's challenging but rewarding' in a tone that suggested he'd given this answer a hundred times before. Nothing he said felt 'genuine'.

Later, when the waiter accidentally spilled some water on the table, I caught a flash of annoyance cross his face before he quickly rearranged his features into understanding patience. That split second had revealed more about him than the previous hour of conversation.

By this time, the alarm bells had started going off in my head, my imagination getting the better of me. Maybe he was a serial killer. Maybe he would kill me and dismember my body. Maybe I will end up in the hospital morgue. I had shuddered.

Halfway through dinner, I texted Sriram from the bathroom. 'He's a serial killer. Help me.'

Sriram stormed in fifteen minutes later, dishevelled and dramatic, yelling, 'Anjali! How could you? After everything we shared at the art therapy retreat in Auroville?'

Arjun looked like he wanted to melt into the tablecloth. I made my escape. We never spoke again.

18 March, Dev

Disaster from start to finish. Met at Toit, where he proceeded to order for me without asking what I wanted. Spent forty-five minutes explaining cryptocurrency while checking out every woman who walked past our table. Then had the audacity to ask if I wanted to 'skip drinks and head back to his place' because he had 'an early morning meeting tomorrow'. When I declined, he looked genuinely shocked, as if his crypto monologue was some sort of foolproof seduction technique. I didn't have to call Sriram. I simply said 'no thanks' and walked out. It's something I've never done, but I was disgusted by his behaviour.

I blocked him even before I made it out of the restaurant.

27 April, Karan

Lunch at Fatty Bao. Sweet guy, painfully shy. Very well dressed. Smart casuals, right shirt, right shoes.

But he was so shy that I found myself filling every silence, eventually just monologuing about work while he nodded. I ended up rambling about everything from my childhood to the Joshi surveillance system at home just to create some sound, some noise. I could feel my throat going dry by the time the food arrived.

I didn't even need to call Sriram. He turned up on his own, claiming he 'just happened to be in the area'. He sat down at our table, stared Karan dead in the eye, and said, 'So, you're the guy trying to steal my woman?'

Karan blinked three times, said 'I'm sorry,' and left.

Poor, poor Karan. I feel bad for him. But not bad enough to endure him.

Later, Sriram and I called Latika. We all laughed till our stomachs hurt. I asked Sriram how he had walked in at the right time. Turns out, he had indeed been telling the truth. He had come to meet a friend close by, and when he was done, he had decided to swing by Fatty Bao as he had a hunch that I would need him.

I close the journal with a sigh and look out at the Bangalore skyline, now dotted with twinkling lights as darkness falls. I cannot find any pattern in any of my dates. Maybe Latika is right and I was just plain unlucky.

And now there's Vinay's text that's begging to be answered. Honestly, I am tired of these dates, tired of men who don't measure up. But Latika will not take no for an answer. She insists that I give this a shot. She has vouched for Vinay since he is her husband's colleague at a tech company in Whitefield. She assures me that 'Vinay is different', 'not like the others'. I, however, remain sceptical.

My phone buzzes again, but I don't check it. Instead, I watch a flock of birds wheel across the darkening sky, moving in perfect synchrony. How do they know which way to turn, when to swoop, when to soar? What invisible thread connects them?

I think about cancelling tomorrow's date, then remember Latika's half-pleading, half-threatening face. Besides, a tiny, traitorous part of me whispers, what if this one is different?

If he isn't, it will be just another diary entry.

One more date. One more potential disappointment. One more story to tell.

THE OKAY-OKAY GUY

BOTH LATIKA AND Sriram cannot believe that Vinay isn't out on strike one. He has surprisingly lasted for two whole dates, which is something of a record given my dating history. The three of us are sitting at our usual corner table at Cobalt on Church Street, the evening bustle of Bangalore unfolding outside the floor-to-ceiling windows. The café smells of fresh coffee and buttery croissants while soft jazz plays in the background, barely audible over the chatter of other customers.

'So, do you like him? I told you he was different,' Latika says triumphantly, stirring her cappuccino with the air of someone who has just won a bet. Her dark hair is pulled back in a sleek ponytail; her eyes sparkle with curiosity.

'Well, I do not dislike him, but I'm not sure I really like him either,' I say as I sip my masala chai, letting the spicy warmth of it slide down my throat. The ceramic mug feels smooth and comforting in my hands.

Sriram, Latika and I are meeting after nearly twenty days, and, needless to say, we're all excited about the meet up. It's a

Friday evening and the whole of Bangalore is vibrating with weekend energy: office workers flooding out of glass buildings, traffic snarls in every direction, restaurants filling up with people ready to decompress after a long work week.

'I must say, this guy knows how to keep you on your feet. No pun intended,' laughs Sriram as he fiddles with the case of his sunglasses. He looks happy. He's wearing a new shirt, which looks flamboyant but totally suits him.

'I must say, he knows how to fly a kite and how to play games,' I imitate Sriram in mock anger, waving my hands in the air dramatically. 'Ha ha ha!'

For our first date, Vinay had suggested we go to Ulsoor Lake. He had brought two kites along, bright blue and yellow paper diamonds with long tails that danced in the wind. It was surprisingly fun, and he ended up teaching me how to fly a kite, standing next to me, giving me instructions as he guided his own kite on the string, demonstrating how to catch the wind just right.

'Pull back when you feel the tug,' he had said, never taking his eyes off his kite. 'Don't fight it, work with it.'

'Like life,' I had quipped. But I don't think he had heard. He had been so focused on his kite. Still, it had been fun. A low-pressure, relaxing activity, something I had never done before and which I enjoyed. Full marks to him for creativity. Afterwards, we had some chaat from a cart outside. Tangy pani puris and spicy aloo tikkis that made my eyes water, and then we left, with promises to meet again soon.

For our second date, he asked if I would be interested in a treasure hunt organized by Bootleggers, a liquor company.

The game involved decoding clues that would lead us to various locations across Bangalore. At each stop, we would have to complete a small task before moving on to the next destination. Missing a task meant losing points, so it was a fun mix of adventure, challenge and teamwork.

The clues sent us from Indiranagar to Church Street to Cubbon Park, making us weave through the city like excited children. One of the tasks was to get a picture of any food item. It had to be a real picture, not a photo on a phone. We had both desperately rushed to a local Udupi restaurant and asked for flyers of their takeaway menu, earning confused looks from the waiter in a crisp green uniform. Then we had torn out the picture of sambar idlis.

Another task was to record a ten-second video of ourselves dancing to a popular song. We managed to complete that as well by performing an impromptu jig to 'Chaiyya Chaiyya' in front of the Vidhana Soudha, earning amused glances from passersby and security guards alike.

We were the third to finish, and we had won gift hampers filled with branded merchandise: T-shirts, caps, bottle openers and a small bottle of champagne. That had been a lot of fun. We had also dressed up in matching clothes: black T-shirts, blue jeans and white shoes. Everyone had thought it was cute and said we made a good couple.

'See, the thing is, I've only flown a kite and gone on a treasure hunt with him,' I say, helping myself to the French fries that we've ordered. 'I haven't got to know him at all. I don't feel any sparks or butterflies in my stomach, that's for sure.'

'All of that only happens in the movies. Real love grows slooooowly … slowwwwly. Tu original piece hai, maloom hai na tujhe?' says Sriram, using a dialogue from the film *Jab We Met*, complete with Shahid Kapoor's exact intonation and hand gestures.

Both my best friends are so excited that I haven't rejected Vinay yet, which, in their eyes, practically counts as a 'committed relationship', that they have elevated this one to 'meet the parents' territory.

'Enough of my dating life. What's new with the two of you?' I ask, eager to shift the spotlight away from my romantic uncertainties.

'I was waiting for you to ask,' Sriram says, leaning forward with a twinkle in his eyes. 'Guess who just shot for the next commercial for Ajanta Paints?'

'What? Wow!' Latika says, her eyes widening.

'Wonderful, Sri!' I exclaim, both of us speaking at the same time, our voices overlapping in excitement.

'Well, it's not like it's a role in a TV series, but still nice to do on the weekend,' Sriram says with feigned modesty, though I can tell he's thrilled.

'What was the shoot like?' I ask, genuinely curious. I've always wondered about the behind-the-scenes of commercials.

'It was all very professional. We shot at Innovative Film City,' he explains, gesturing animatedly. 'The female lead kept messing up her lines. I mean, it was such a simple shoot. We were playing a couple who had just bought their first home, and instead of saying, "This colour brings life to our living room," she kept saying, "This colour brings our living room to life," which led to so many retakes. The director was getting visibly frustrated with every retake, but all in all, it was a nice experience.'

Latika also has news to share. 'Manish's niece is coming over and will stay with us for a month or maybe more until she finds her own apartment. She has landed a job in Bangalore,' she sighs and rolls her eyes, her gold earrings catching the light. 'My husband is so excited about it,' she continues. 'How does he think three people will manage in a six-hundred-square-foot apartment? As it is, I've been telling Manish that we should move to a bigger place. It's a tight squeeze even for two people.'

'Can't she find a paying guest accommodation or something?' I ask, knowing how particular Latika is about her space. Her apartment may be small, but it's meticulously organized, with everything kept in its designated place.

'She's coming from Shimoga, and she's a "paavam" thing from what I've been told,' Latika says, using the Tamil term for a naive, innocent person. 'So, I feel bad for being mean, but I'm mostly worried about being late for work as we have only one bathroom, and all of us will have to leave at the same time.'

'Wake up at 5 a.m. and have a bath,' Sriram offers unhelpfully, and both Latika and I glare at him, our eyes narrowing in perfect synchronization.

'Better yet, what if I move into your apartment, Sri?' Latika says, batting her eyelashes in mock flirtation.

'Of course, you're welcome anytime. I don't have to leave for work until ten, so you can hog the bathroom all you want,' he says with a generous wave of his hand.

But we all know that Latika would never go for it. As much as she likes to grumble, she would never want to spend time away from her husband Manish, even for a day. She's madly in love with him. And has been since they were introduced to each other by their parents five years ago. It was one of those arranged marriages that worked out perfectly, like a key finding its lock.

Our conversation continues about both mundane and important things, like Sriram's ageing parents in Chennai, Latika's upcoming promotion, my rant about Nimmi and work. The evening light softens, turning golden as it streams in through the café windows. Coffee cups get emptied and then refilled. We dig into chocolate pastries that taste divine.

When it's time to leave, we linger outside the café, the evening air cooler now. My friends hug me goodbye and, as they pull away, they say in unison, 'Keep us posted about Vinay.'

I smile and nod, but I already have a feeling about this one. I only have to say yes to the third date with Vinay to see if I am right.

2 June, Vinay

Yet another entry in my graveyard of dates. This one was out at strike three.

The first two dates with him were good, no doubt. Flying a kite and then the treasure hunt was fun too.

Great as those experiences were, there's more to life than fun and games. I want conversation. I want to get to know the real person behind the fun facade. I want to hear about his childhood, his dreams, what keeps him up at night, what books have changed him, what he believes in.

But Vinay insisted that we go to an arcade for our third date. When he suggested it over text, I responded saying I would prefer if we could sit down somewhere and talk. A quiet dinner, perhaps, or even a walk in Cubbon Park. He promised we would talk after the arcade.

The arcade—Bang 'Em Cars, roulette, billiard pool, shooting games, dance machines with their flashing lights and tinny music—all of it was fun in a nostalgic way. I found myself laughing as we competed for tickets, his competitive side emerging as he insisted on winning me a stuffed dinosaur from the prize counter. But throughout the evening, I felt a certain hollowness to our interaction. The noise and the lights were too much, making real connection impossible.

After two hours, I gently suggested that we grab dinner and talk. We were at the food court, surrounded by families and teenagers, the smell of fast food hanging in the air. I looked at him expectantly, ready to finally have a real conversation.

And the guy bolted. Really bolted.

Maybe he had a female version of my Sriram feeding him lines in his ear, because he suddenly got a call and the next thing I know, he's telling me his 'roommate was locked out of their apartment' and he had to leave immediately.

What the hell? This was not what I expected at all. Still, I texted him the next day, asked about his roommate's situation, if everything was okay, giving him the benefit of the doubt. And he ghosted me. Complete radio silence. It made me mad. Made me question if I had imagined the connection during our first two dates.

Then, a whole five days later, he replies saying 'he got caught up', wants to set another date, this time at Wonderla Amusement Park.

I begin to think he wants an activity partner, not a date. Someone to do things with, not be with. It's like he's afraid of stillness, of the quiet moment when two people look at each other and see what's there between them.

I end it right here. Life is too short, and Bangalore traffic is too long to waste time on someone who can't even sit across a table from you and have a conversation.

I deleted his number. Blocked him on WhatsApp.

Next, please!

Or maybe I shouldn't date for a while.

I am disappointed.

THE ELEPHANT MAN

THE SOUND OF childish giggles echoes through the spacious bedroom as I sit perfectly still, surrendering myself to the whims of my cousin Dipika's children. The twins have decided that I'm in desperate need of a makeover with stickers, sparkles and a questionable number of hair clips that they have pinned onto my hair. With matching ponytails bobbing on either side of their heads—like tiny fountains of chaos—and expressions of fierce concentration on their faces, they look so utterly adorable that stopping them would be a crime against cuteness.

'Ria, Rima! That's quite enough of decorating Anjali didi with glitter. Go to the bathroom right now, both of you. Shikha didi is ready to wash your hair,' Dipika announces as she storms in, trying to sound stern but barely masking the amusement in her eyes.

In response, her four-year-old twins giggle and proceed to ignore her completely. Ria carefully piles on more glitter pins into my already bedazzled hair while Rima applies a generous dusting of silver glitter, with surprising precision, directly onto my nose. I catch my reflection in the ornate mirror hanging on the opposite wall and burst out laughing at the spectacle they have created.

My hair is covered with multi-coloured butterfly clips and star-shaped pins that sparkle, my face is painted with swirls of iridescent powder that makes me look like a bizarre fairy princess who has taken a tumble through a craft store.

Dipika sighs dramatically before picking Rima up, who immediately protests with a high-pitched wail.

'Mummy, five more minutes! Anjali didi doesn't mind,' she pleads, her bottom lip quivering in that performative way children perfect so early on.

Dipika hands her over to Shikha, their live-in house help who is also a nanny to the girls. Then she swoops in for Ria, hoisting her up as the child squirms in her arms.

'But we're not finished! Anjali didi needs a crown too!' Ria protests, reaching out towards me with a handful of glitter as her mother carries her away.

Dipika looks back at me and shakes her head, unable to contain her smile.

'You're worse than these two. If you weren't my favourite cousin, I would've banned you from playing with them forever. Now good luck washing all that gunk off your face and hair!' She laughs as she disappears down the hallway.

I had arrived at their place last evening to stay over after several weeks of Dipika's persistent follow-ups. 'It's been ages since we had a proper conversation and caught up,' she had insisted. 'The girls will go to bed by eight, and Vikram is coming back only tomorrow. Come,' she had pleaded, and I had finally relented.

We had spent the previous evening watching a soppy romantic comedy, laughing and talking away like we were children again. Among all my cousins, Dipika and I share a special bond even though she's a good nine years older than me. Whenever I couldn't go to Muscat for my summer holidays, I would spend those long, lazy days at Dipika's home in Chennai. It was usually because both my parents would be travelling for their respective jobs, which was one of the main reasons why they had put me in a boarding school in the first place.

Dipika was the older sister I never had. When she was in college, I was privy to all her secrets, her boyfriends, her heartbreaks and her dreams of becoming a fashion designer. I was her little messenger when she was grounded for sneaking out to attend a concert with her then-boyfriend. As I grew up, the age gap between us began to matter less and less, and I became her confidant, friend and, as implausible as it might sound, even her relationship adviser.

When she met Vikram at a mutual friend's wedding, it was my opinion she sought first. And it was because I said that he seemed to be genuinely in love with her, unlike her previous boyfriends who seemed more interested in how she looked on their arms, that she agreed to marry him.

Vikram rose remarkably in his career and is the chief operations officer of his company now, which means they lead a luxurious lifestyle. They live in a penthouse on the fifteenth floor in one of the premium residential properties on Sarjapur Road in Bangalore. She has a home theatre, a private pool and all the trappings of wealth, a far cry from the modest apartment her parents own in Chennai. Despite Dipika asking me over many times in the past, it was only this weekend that I had been able to get away after meeting all my deadlines and finishing my stories for the magazine.

I glance at the glittery chaos Ria and Rima have left on my face and hair and grimace. Since looking ridiculous is more fun when shared with friends, I click a selfie and send it to Sriram and Latika on our group chat. We call ourselves 'The Triumvirate'.

Sriram texts back with a few laughing emojis and writes:

> You can audition for a glitter commercial with your bird's nest hair. 😄😄😄

Latika asks:

> Jeez! Will it wash off?

And I reply:

> If it doesn't, Nimmi is going to have heart failure when I walk into office on Monday. 😄

I spend the next hour in the guest bathroom detangling my hair, prising out the clips carefully, and discovering that the glitter the twins have used is worse than superglue.

Scrub. Rinse. Scrub. Rinse. Scrub. Rinse. Yet it clings to me like a toxic relationship, sparkly, persistent and unwilling to let go. Even after my thorough cleansing, worthy of a crime scene cleanup, parts of my face still shimmer under the bathroom light.

When I finally emerge and walk into the guest bedroom, Dipika is lounging on the sofa by the window, scrolling through her phone.

'Ha! I warned you,' she says triumphantly as she looks up at my face.

'Is it too bad?' I ask, rubbing at my cheeks.

'No. Only that you look like a disco ball,' she says, and I playfully throw a decorative cushion at her, which she dodges with ease.

'It's not *that* bad,' I mutter as I examine myself in the mirror, tilting my head to catch the subtle shimmer that still clings to my skin.

'Vikram says that he's inviting a few colleagues over for dinner.' Dipika makes a face as she delivers this news. 'Three people, small gathering, he says. Please stay for it?'

'What? Today?' I turn to her in surprise.

'Yeah, he told me just now. He's on his way back from the airport. I already told him you're staying.'

'Why did you do that? I don't want to socialize with Vikram's colleagues,' I protest, already feeling weary at the thought of making small talk with strangers.

'As if I want to!' Dipika makes a face. 'Stay, Anjali. Help a girl out. At least it won't be too boring with you around,' she says, clasping her hands together in mock supplication.

And that's how I find myself roped into a 'casual house party' with Vikram's colleagues and my cousin on a Saturday evening.

The doorbell rings.

'Daddy's home! Daddy's home!' the twins shriek, tumbling into the living room like a pink tornado. They're wearing matching frocks, hair still damp from their bath, soft curls framing their identical, heart-shaped faces. They are so adorable it makes me want to have my own children someday.

Vikram walks in beaming and drops his laptop bag just in time to swoop both girls into his arms like a proud superhero coming home from battle.

Then he notices me. 'Anjali! So nice to have you over. Glad you're staying for the get-together.'

'Oh, me too,' I lie with a straight face as I exchange a knowing look with Dipika.

Dipika, naturally, is in full command mode. She's the kind of hostess who can plan a wedding in her sleep and still make it look Instagram-worthy. Groceries are ordered with military precision. The cook receives step-by-step instructions on what to cook. Fresh flowers arrive from the florist and are magically arranged, one bouquet in every bathroom (yes, really!) and a grand one for the living room. The day-maid is briefed on table-setting like she's prepping for a state banquet. I watch in a mix of awe and mild panic, wondering if I'll ever manage to adult with this much finesse.

When it's finally time for the guests to arrive, Dipika emerges from her room in a beige chiffon saree and a halter-neck blouse, looking like she's just stepped out of a Sabyasachi ad. Vikram and I both whistle in unplanned but perfectly synchronized admiration.

'You look gorgeous. Now I feel underdressed,' I admit, glancing down at my deep blue dress, the only remotely decent outfit I had packed. Everything else in my suitcase screams 'pyjama life'.

'You look great, girl,' Dipika says and flashes me a reassuring smile.

Vikram chimes in, 'Yeah, don't worry, it's not formal or anything.'

Which, of course, only makes me wish all the more that I had at least packed a better dress.

The doorbell chimes at around seven, announcing the arrival of the first guest.

'Ria, Rima, we need you to be on your best behaviour. Do you know what that means?' Dipika asks, smoothing down her daughters' matching dresses.

'Yes, Mummy,' they chorus in unison. 'We have to greet the guests and be good.'

'Yes, good girls,' Dipika beams with maternal pride while I wonder how much wine I can have to make it through the evening without getting drunk in front of Vikram and Dipika's guests.

Vikram welcomes his colleague, a tall, slender man with carefully styled blond hair and a perpetually amused expression. He is wearing a suit that probably costs more than two months of my salary and is carrying a bottle of wine that I instantly recognize as the overpriced Bordeaux that Vikram had once lectured me about for forty-five minutes.

'Vikram! How lovely to see you,' he says in that perfect French accent that somehow makes everything sound like an innuendo.

'Likewise, Pierre,' Vikram says as he shakes his hand with the enthusiasm of someone who's just been told he's getting a promotion, which, knowing Vikram's talent for strategic socializing, might not be far from the truth.

When Vikram introduces Dipika, Pierre kisses her hand with flair, and I mentally prepare myself for the same treatment. Sure enough, when Vikram introduces me, Pierre promptly takes my hand in his and brushes his lips against it while maintaining uncomfortable eye contact. I smile politely, calculating how quickly I can excuse myself to wash my hand without seeming rude.

The next one to arrive is Relia Ionescu, who is from Romania. She is statuesque with platinum blonde hair and is dressed so immaculately that I think Nimmi would be pleased to feature her in *Tiara*. I make a mental note of suggesting a feature titled 'What to Wear to Work to Look like a Million Dollars'. It's funny how my mind never stops working and is always coming up with more ideas for pieces for *Tiara*.

Vikram introduces all of us again. Relia already knows Pierre from work and greets him with air kisses.

'You have a wonderful home, Dipika,' she says, glancing around with carefully calibrated enthusiasm. I wonder if she means it or if she is simply being polite.

The third person to come in has me sitting up in sudden, embarrassing interest. Vikram introduces him as 'Aman Mathur, our bright, young rising star, who is based in Norwich.'

Aman is tall, taller than Vikram by at least a few inches. He has warm, deep brown eyes and a smile that seems genuine rather than a polite social one. There's something so compelling about his face that I can't help staring for a moment too long. Then I become aware of my inappropriate attention and force myself to look away. Just in time, too, as Ria and Rima appear together, so well-behaved and 'proper' they might as well have stepped out of a Victorian-era children's etiquette manual.

'Hello, I am Ria,' says one.

'And I am Rima,' says the other with perfect timing.

It looks as though they have practised the words. Maybe being a good host is a genetic trait because the twins seem to have inherited their mother's people skills. I notice Vikram beaming with pride.

Relia makes a show of being charmed, her hands clasped beneath her chin, as though witnessing something unbearably precious. Pierre chuckles indulgently, the laugh of someone who interacts with children approximately twice a year.

But Aman? Aman kneels on one knee, bringing himself to their height, and says with utter seriousness, 'I'm very honoured to meet you both. Thank you for welcoming me to your home.'

I watch Ria and Rima blossom under his sincere attention and find myself liking him instantly. I can't help but think how sweet and genuine Aman seems, so different from the polished corporate types I've met so far.

The get-together unfolds into an unexpectedly memorable evening filled with laughter and moments that linger in my mind long after we say our goodbyes. When I leave the next morning, the warmth of those interactions, especially Aman's endearing playfulness with the girls, follows me home like a pleasant shadow.

As soon as I close my apartment door behind me, I drop my overnight bag in the hallway and head straight to the kitchen to make myself a cup of chai. Then I walk to my desk. My fingers find my journal, its pages a sanctuary for thoughts too perplexing to leave floating in my mind. I pick it up and make a beeline for the terrace. I need to capture these impressions while they're still vivid, to examine this curious lightness in my chest before returning to the drafts of half-finished articles that Nimmi has assigned.

19 June

Just got back from D&V's suburban paradise. It was such a lovely stay. And the twins, Ria and Rima? Absolute menaces that come in the most adoring, angelic packaging imaginable. Last night's party was equal parts chaotic and charming.

I'm writing this entry at 11.30 a.m., the moment I have walked in through the door. Not because I'm particularly sentimental, but because my brain won't shut up about this man I met last night. Aman.

The evening started predictably enough with Dipika playing the flawless hostess, brushing off my attempts to help with a firm, 'Don't worry. Shikha and I have it under control,' which is basically code for 'Stay out of my kitchen; you're more hindrance than help.' Vikram was at his usual station, pouring drinks with his signature heavy hand. Relia and Pierre launched into a string of office anecdotes that only became funny sometime after my second glass of wine.

When Dipika slipped inside to check on dinner, the conversation veered into quarterly projections. It was my cue to make a quiet exit. I figured I'd peek in on the twins, kill fifteen minutes and be back before the biryani hit the table. I expected them to be fast asleep.

Except, the twins weren't sleeping. The door to their room was ajar. I looked in and froze.

Ria and Rima were floating beside their bed, in mid-air, one behind the other, swaying and giggling uncontrollably. For a second, I genuinely wondered if the wine had been spiked with something hallucinogenic. I blinked, trying to make sense of the scene. And then I saw him.

Hidden behind the bed, crouched on all fours like some benevolent jungle beast, was Aman. A grown man in crisp chinos and a sky-blue shirt, giving what could only be described as the world's most patient elephant ride to two gleeful children.

When he saw me, his face flickered with embarrassment, eyes widening, cheeks colouring slightly, but he didn't stop. And I? I burst out laughing. Of course, I reached for my phone and snapped a few pictures. That kind of adorable absurdity needs to be preserved forever.

'Ria, Rima, why are you torturing poor Aman?' I asked, still chuckling and snapping away.

'We're Princess Ria and Princess Rima,' they announced with the imperial confidence that only four-year-olds can muster. 'And this is our Amanelephant. He is our royal elephant!'

'I think poor Amanelephant might need to be taken to the Royal Hospital if you don't get off this instant,' I said, noticing his knees pressing into the hardwood floor.

The girls looked momentarily troubled by this revelation. The concept of human-elephant discomfort had clearly not crossed their minds. They dismounted immediately. Aman straightened, brushed off his knees and took the deepest, most theatrical bow.

'Your Majesties, it has been my humble honour to serve you both. I hope your journey was satisfactory.'

The girls squealed with laughter. And then Ria, who normally treats new adults with the kind of wary suspicion reserved for broccoli, climbed onto her bed, threw her arms around his neck and kissed him on the cheek. 'You're very sweet. Thank you, Aman uncle,' she declared.

Not to be outdone, Rima did the same. And I swear, Aman's face lit up like he'd just won the national lottery.

'These two here insisted on showing me their sticker collection and refused to go to bed till I agreed. Dipika was so hassled, but I told her I didn't mind,' Aman said, grinning sheepishly.

That's when I knew. This wasn't just another one of Vikram's boring work colleagues. This man was *different*.

'You're amazing with kids,' I said. 'You'll make a great father someday.'

The words tumbled out before I could catch them, making me immediately want to rewind and swallow them. I must have sounded like some desperate twenty-something trying to flirt without finesse. Totally in contradiction with *Tiara* principles.

But Aman just shrugged, unfazed. 'I've had lots of practice. Back home, our street's like one big, boundaryless family. There were always kids around at my home.'

By then, the girls had abandoned us for their dollhouse, so we leaned against the doorframe and talked. I discovered that this man reads. Really reads. He had thoughtful, original takes on Murakami that didn't sound like they'd been lifted from a podcast. He was funny, reflective and at ease with himself. Effortlessly engaging. And the kicker? He's *not* on social media!

'What's your Insta ID?' I asked.

'I'm not on social media,' he said simply.

'At all? What are you, a Soviet spy? A time-traveller from 1955?'

He laughed. (God, that laughter! How I loved it.)

'Never really got into it. It's mostly noise. Kills real connection.'

No pretentious speech about digital detoxing, no holier-than-thou attitude. Just a simple statement of fact. So there I was, desperately wanting to send him that absurdly cute elephant picture, with no modern way to do it.

'How will you see this blackmail-worthy photo then?' I asked.

'Email still exists, you know,' he said with a teasing smile. 'Some of us dinosaurs still use it.'

And that's how I ended up with Aman's email address, scribbled with a crayon on a pink Hello Kitty notepad which Rima insisted was 'fancy paper'.

It's been three hours since I got home. I've typed and deleted seventeen versions of what should be a simple 'Here's the photo' email.

Why am I acting like a teenager? I have a career at *Tiara*, for God's sake. Why is my heart fluttering like I'm in high school?

Is it because he got down on all fours to be an elephant for two kids he barely knew? Or because he spoke intelligently without trying to impress? Or because he smells like cedar wood and something else I can't quite name and haven't stopped thinking about?

I'm sending that email before I lose my nerve. And maybe, I'll casually ask how long he's in India.

God, I'm transparent.

Well, I hit send. Now to obsessively check my inbox every thirty seconds like a rational adult woman.

From: Aman Mathur <aman.mathur@zmail.com>
To: Anjali Prabhu <anjali.prabhu@tiara.com>
Sub: re: Photos of Amanelephant

Hey Anjali,

Thank you so much for the photos. They're wonderful. I don't quite know how you managed it but you've made even an elephant-on-all-fours moment look somewhat dignified. Quite a feat.

You asked about my travel plans. I'm in India for just a short while, unfortunately.

I'm currently in Gwalior, spending time with my mother, and I head back to Norwich in about eight days. I was only in Bangalore for a day, though I wish it had been longer.

It was truly lovely meeting you.

Warm regards,

Aman

From: Anjali Prabhu <anjali.prabhu@tiara.com>
To: Aman Mathur <aman.mathur@zmail.com>
Sub: re: Photos of Amanelephant

Hey Aman,

You're welcome. I take great pride in capturing rare wildlife, especially talking elephants who willingly offer piggyback rides to shrieking twins.

Dipika tells me that Ria and Rima haven't stopped talking about it. You're now a bedtime story legend and possibly will soon be elevated to god status. Good luck with that responsibility.

I must admit, the photos came out even better than I had expected. Something about the combination of your defeated posture and the twins' maniacal glee made for excellent composition. *National Geographic* would approve.

I've attached one more photograph. You're smiling in it, possibly because the twins dismounted without breaking your back. Or maybe because you're absurdly nice and don't mind becoming a part of other people's legends.

Gwalior sounds intriguing. So lovely that you're spending time with your mother. What's she like?

I've never been to Gwalior, but I hear the fort is great for brooding walks and existential thoughts. Do send a report. Bonus points for dramatic weather or philosophical squirrels.

Anjali

From: Aman Mathur <aman.mathur@zmail.com>
To: Anjali Prabhu <anjali.prabhu@tiara.com>
Sub: re: National Geographic-worthy content

Hi Anjali,

I've been called many things, but bedtime story legend is a first. Possibly a career highlight. Please inform Ria and Rima that their personal elephant sends a dignified trumpet in return.

Also, thank you for capturing my moment of heroic defeat (I just couldn't say no to the twins) with such flair. That smile? Pure spinal relief. There was a very real chance I would've ended up permanently horizontal after that ride.

Gwalior's great! I love being here. I've mostly been at home with my mother who, by the way, is a true force of nature here. Her garden looks like it could host state functions. It's home to hundreds of discerning butterflies and birds, bougainvillea, roses, jasmine, hibiscus and an aggressively ambitious lineup of brinjal, chilli, bitter gourd and pretty much any vegetable that you can think of. She's won prizes, though she shrugs them off like they are no big deal. She talks to her plants, and I'm 90 per cent sure they talk back.

We're very close. She's sharp, endlessly kind and has a sixth sense for what's going on in my head, usually before I've figured it out myself. Being here with her feels like the world has paused for a bit. Which, in this speed-run of a life, feels rare. I'm already sad about leaving India and heading back.

The fort, by the way, is as dramatic as you imagine. I get a great view of it from my home. Haven't spotted any philosophical squirrels yet, but I live in hope. Possibly wearing tiny glasses.

Tell me, do you always click photos of people just as they're losing the last shred of their dignity and then pretend you're just documenting wildlife?

Aman

From: Anjali Prabhu <anjali.prabhu@tiara.com>
To: Aman Mathur <aman.mathur@zmail.com>
Sub: Garden adventures of a non-nurturer

Aman, Aman,

An elephant man who trumpets in return? I'm not sure if the twins can handle this upgrade. The next thing you know, they'll be demanding pet elephants for their birthday. I'll be sure to tell Vikram and Dipika that I'm pre-emptively blaming you for their developmental trauma.

Your mother sounds absolutely magnificent. A woman who communes with plants and dominates local gardening competitions while maintaining perfect nonchalance? I'm taking notes. My houseplants stage collective suicide whenever I walk into the room. Last week, my supposedly 'unkillable' succulent somehow developed what I can only describe as plant depression. If your mother has tips that don't involve actually developing nurturing qualities, I'm all ears. The only thing that has thrived under my care (or rather neglect) are the palms that dot my terrace. I sit between them like a benevolent dictator, ruling my leafy queendom, writing in my journal while watching Bangalore sunsets and pretending I have things under control.

As for your question about my photography habits, I prefer to think of it as 'capturing authentic human experiences'. There's something poetic about the exact moment a grown man realizes he's made a terrible decision but is committed to seeing it through. Your face has great storytelling abilities.

How many more days until you leave? And what awaits you back in your non-elephant life? I realize I know very little about the man behind the trumpeting.

Anjali

PS: If you do spot a philosophical squirrel, please document immediately. I suggest luring it with existentialist nuts.

From: Aman Mathur <aman.mathur@zmail.com>
To: Anjali Prabhu <anjali.prabhu@tiara.com>
Sub: re: Garden adventures of a non-nurturer

Hi Anjali,

Your plant depression diagnosis made me laugh. My mother would be equal parts horrified and intrigued.

I suspect, however, that she would prescribe compost, classical music and daily pep talks.

As for me, I head to Norwich day after tomorrow. Back to work, real life and a to-do list that seems to have grown a mile long in my absence.

No philosophical squirrels yet, but I did spot a monkey looking pensive. Might have been the heat.

Bye!

Aman

I read Aman's email for the third time, scrutinizing every word as if it were an ancient text hiding coded meaning. Three pithy paragraphs. No questions, no follow-up. Just that terse 'Bye!' at the end with an exclamation mark. It feels like a door slamming shut.

But why the exclamation mark? Was it a friendly banging of the door? Is this a cheery send-off, a dismissal? Is this the end of our correspondence?

Argh, this is maddening.

For the next entire week, my inbox sits still and sullen. I scroll through our email thread, analysing our exchanges with the intensity of a literary critic. Our conversations had evolved from casual observations to something I looked forward to each day. He wrote about his mother with such tenderness that I could almost see her garden blooming across my screen.

This had become my evening ritual: come home from work, make myself a cup of masala chai, settle into my deck chair among my palms and craft replies that I hoped were witty and engaging. I would spend my commute mentally composing lines, testing phrases in my head.

And now, this abrupt shift. A handful of sentences, one pensive monkey, zero emotional breadcrumbs. No invitation to continue.

Now, every evening, I still make the chai. I still sit in my deck chair, nestled between my palms, and pretend I'm not waiting for another email from him. But I am. I hate how much I am.

What was once a casual correspondence has become something I carry around like a folded note in my pocket. His words echo, his silences stretch. Even at work, I catch myself glancing at my phone, half expecting an apology, an afterthought or simply a 'PS' that changes everything.

By Monday, I cave and call Latika during my lunch break.

'Am I overthinking this?' I ask after explaining the situation.

'You're asking me if you, Anjali Prabhu, the writer, is overthinking something?' Latika laughs. 'Girl, that's like asking a fish if it's wet. Of course you are.'

'But look at how short his reply is,' I insist, reading it to her verbatim. I even leave dramatic pauses between sentences.

'Mmmmm ... He's a man about to travel. They get weird and distracted before trips,' she says. 'Suddenly, socks are more important than feelings.'

'So, you think I should write back?'

'If you want to. But keep it light. Don't compose a thesis in response to his paragraph.'

That evening, I meet Sriram for coffee. Latika cannot come as not only are they moving houses, but she has also been roped into helping her husband's niece shop for a lehenga for a 'traditional wear' day at work.

Sriram listens to me vent with the patience of someone who has weathered many of my minor crises over the years. Then I finally stop talking.

'Maybe he sensed your interest and got scared,' Sriram suggests, stirring his coffee thoughtfully.

'Ugh. Great. So I was too much,' I mutter. 'Of course I was. One man I truly like, and I come on like a hurricane.' My face falls.

'Or, maybe, he's just busy packing and didn't realize how his email came across,' Sriram adds hastily, noticing how sad I am.

'So, what do I do? Pretend I didn't notice the shift?'

'Write back if you want to keep the conversation going,' he shrugs. 'But don't invest too much in it yet. These are just emails, Anjali. Not vows.'

'But they were good emails,' I mumble.

'Then they deserve a proper conclusion, at least,' Sriram says. 'Write something short. Ball in his court. If he doesn't respond …'

'I know, I know. Move on,' I finish his sentence, feeling both annoyed and grateful for his pragmatism.

Back home, I stare at my screen. The cursor blinks accusingly. Should I match his brevity? Be deliberately casual? Pretend I didn't notice the change in tone?

I type. Delete. Type again.

What began as something spontaneous now feels like a game where I don't know the rules. And the worst part is how much I care about the outcome.

After three more days of receiving nothing more from him, I decide to write.

From: Anjali Prabhu <anjali.prabhu@tiara.com>
To: Aman Mathur <aman.mathur@zmail.com>
Sub: Re: Garden adventures of a non-nurturer

Hi Aman,

Hope you've reached back safely and that the journey was kind.

I now have a vivid mental image of your mother playing Beethoven to her bitter gourds. If she ever starts a podcast for emotionally complex plants, I'll be the first subscriber.

I've never been to Norwich, but I've read about its cobbled streets, antique bookshops and an unreasonable number of ducks. It sounds like a place where thoughts walk beside you and time slows down just enough. I hope the re-entry into real life isn't too hard. May your to-do list be merciful and your inbox less brutal than mine.

Bangalore, meanwhile, has entered that indecisive phase where the rain gods flirt but refuse to commit. It's excellent weather for nostalgia, book-reading and, of course, overthinking, which I've been doing with great dedication.

Anjali

PS: I bought a new succulent. Wish me luck.

I wait for three whole weeks, but I don't hear from him. Three entire weeks of complete silence. Twenty-one days of checking my phone like it's hooked to an IV drip, providing essential life support. Each notification on my email causes a small cardiac event until I see that it's just another irrelevant email from a clothing brand I bought one sweater from three years ago, or an email from Nimmi. I feel stupid doing this, but I'm unable to stop. It's like picking away at a scab even though you know you have to leave it alone if you want the wound to heal.

It takes every molecule of my willpower not to cave and write again. I've typed out fourteen different follow-up messages in a Word document, ranging from casual ('Hey, just checking in!') to passive-aggressive ('Guess your fingers broke?') to pathetically honest ('I keep thinking about our emails and wondering what happened').

But I know I will not send a single one. No way. I will wait, even if it kills me.

'Stop brooding over him. He's gone,' Latika says, waving her fork at me dismissively. 'Shall I set up the next date for you?'

Sriram, Latika and I are at our usual spot inside Café Hideout, at the dimly lit corner table that's witnessed countless collective dissections of the happenings in our individual lives. The wooden table between us is cluttered with half-empty coffee cups and the remnants of a lemon chiffon cake I've been picking at for the past hour.

'No!' I protest a bit too loudly. The couple at the next table glances over. I lower my voice. 'After that stupid Vinay, I am never trusting you again.'

'Come on, babes!' Latika rolls her eyes, leaning back in her chair. 'You lasted three whole dates with that one. Maybe on the next date, he would have had a real conversation with you. But instead, you decided to block him.'

'Shut up, Latika.' I stab my fork into what's left of the cake. 'That man had the emotional maturity of a six-year-old. You know very well that he only wanted a gaming partner, not a date. Do you know what he said when I asked about his family? "They exist." That was it. The full answer.'

Both Sriram and Latika laugh. I am too glum.

'You're too obsessed with Aman and his emails,' Sriram says. He suddenly straightens up, puffs out his chest and drops his voice an octave. 'Life is like a box of email drafts. You never know which ones will actually get sent,' he proclaims, doing his best Forrest Gump impression.

'But I still want the emails to continue,' I wail like a heartbroken teen, dropping my head dramatically onto my folded arms. 'They were the best conversations I've had in months. Do you know how rare it is to find someone who is kind, who reads and who writes well?'

My friends exchange that look. The one that says they're reaching the limit of their patience with my romantic melodrama. They've heard me analyse every word, comma and potential subtext in Aman's emails for weeks now.

'Then write him a novella,' Latika suggests, shaking her head. 'Get it out of your system. Write the great Indian email romance.'

'No way,' I sit up straight, suddenly resolute. 'I'm following the tennis ball rule.'

Sriram furrows his brow. 'Tennis ball?'

'Well,' I explain, warming up to my metaphor, 'we serve once. The ball is in their court. If they don't return the serve, you don't play. You never, ever serve a second ball. You don't ask why they aren't playing. You wait. Maybe they've walked off. Maybe they don't want to play. Maybe they're not even in the court anymore. If you serve another ball, you're only setting yourself up for more disappointment and looking horribly desperate. It's like breaking the fundamental laws of dating physics.'

My friends look at me like I've sprouted a second head. One that speaks exclusively in sports analogies despite my well-known athletic ineptitude.

Looking at their faces, I know that I have gone on and on. A bit too much. I decide to shut up. I'm not going to talk about Aman again. I deftly change the topic. We speak about Sriram's theatre group and Latika's upcoming travel opportunity. Her company is sending her to Belgium, and she is very excited about it. I look at my friends talking animatedly, feeling a surge of great affection for them, genuinely grateful that I have them in my life.

For the next two weeks, I pitch article ideas to Nimmi that have her nodding in approval with increasing enthusiasm:

- 'Why Twenty-Somethings Should Chase a Career and Not Men: A Survivor's Guide'
- 'Six Ways for a Girl to Reclaim Her Digital Dignity After Being Ghosted'
- 'How to Keep a Man Guessing (By Completely Ignoring His Existence)'

All the ideas I pitch get approved. I write. I bury myself in work. I become a productivity machine fuelled by mild rejection and the desire to prove that I'm absolutely, positively, 100 per cent fine. I'm so fine that I've started saying it out loud to my succulent, which is still alive despite my over-watering, a sign of my emotional state.

Even though I'm writing all this empowering content, it's hard to get over that little rejection, that no reply. It sits in my chest like a small pebble in my shoe that I can't quite shake out. Not painful enough to make me stop walking, but uncomfortable enough that I'm always aware of it.

Finally, after a month and a half, when I least expect it, his reply arrives. I'm in the middle of brushing my teeth when my phone pings and I lunge for it with toothpaste dribbling down my chin.

From: Aman Mathur <aman.mathur@zmail.com>

To: Anjali Prabhu <anjali.prabhu@tiara.com>

Sub: Re: The Non-Nurturer's Succulent

Hi Anjali,

Apologies for the long silence. Things have been non-stop since I got back. I've been meaning to write, but the days somehow kept vanishing.

Saw a tiny plant at the station yesterday that looked like it was questioning its entire existence. Naturally, I thought of you and your new succulent. Hope it's still alive and not plotting revenge.

How are things on your end? Still ruling over the leafy queendom?

Aman

I read it once. Twice. Thrice. Then I fume, pacing my tiny apartment like a caged tiger, still holding my toothbrush like a sceptre of indignation.

I expected a longer email. What games is this guy playing? Now he's inviting me to play when he's free, at his pace. After six weeks of silence? As if he can just waltz back into my inbox with a casual plant reference and pretend that everything's fine?

I glance at my succulent, which seems to be judging me from its perch on the windowsill. 'Don't look at me like that,' I tell it. 'He should've made a bit more effort and written a long email.'

Hmmph! No. I am better than this. I am NOT going to reply. Let him stew like he has made me stew. The tennis ball has rolled under a bench somewhere, covered in dust and forgotten. If he wants to play now, he'll need to come up with something better than a half-hearted apology and a plant joke.

I toss my phone onto my bed with dramatic flair, then immediately dive after it to make sure that the screen didn't crack. I've got dignity, but I also can't afford to spend a small fortune over a cracked screen.

The phone is fine. But I am not.

A YEAR LATER

From: Aman Mathur <aman.mathur@zmail.com>
To: Anjali Prabhu <anjali.prabhu@tiara.com>
Sub: Found our elephant pics! (+ some news)

Hey Anjali,

How have you been? I hope things are great on your end.

I was cleaning up my laptop today and guess what I found? That email thread with the me-as-an-elephant photos you sent! Made me laugh all over again. It instantly brought back all those fabulous emails we used to exchange. Isn't it crazy how time just zooms by without us noticing?

I've been wanting to reach out to you for ages, but you know how it goes. Work gets intense, life gets busy and somehow months fly by before you realize it. Reading those emails made me miss our conversations. Those mails were fun.

Wanted to share some news with you. I'm moving back to India soon! Will be moving to Bangalore. That's partly why I'm clearing out my digital life (getting a new laptop before the move). And thought I should drop an email and let you know!

Aman

20 May

Well, well, well. Just when I'd lulled myself into the comforting certainty that life had settled into predictable routines: almond milk cappuccinos, yoga stretches that I pretend are harder than they are and meeting my deadlines at work. And BAM! Life, with its trademark flair for drama, decides to stage a comeback. Got an email from Aman. After what, a mere 347 days of silence?

And no, it wasn't just any email. Subject line: 'Found our elephant pics! (+ some news)'.

Our elephant pics. Our. Plural. Possessive. Nostalgic. Dangerous.

So offensively casual that I almost snorted coffee out of my nose.

And the 'some news'? Oh, just this tiny, inconsequential detail that he's moving back to India. Bangalore. Information my body is still processing, heart pounding, eyes wide and every nerve on high alert.

My coffee mug was so excited it performed a graceful commando parachute jump in slow motion when I read that part. It shattered into five pieces. I haven't decided if that's a sign or just physics being a jerk. My succulent is watching me with suspicion.

I feel victorious. He served the second ball. I didn't. I had promised myself I wouldn't reach out again. Not after he took so many months to reply to my email. I stopped writing and felt absurdly proud for being stubborn.

And hurrah! Now here he is with an email!

I mentally congratulate myself for winning. So what if Aman had no idea we were playing?

The rational hemisphere of my brain understands that it is merely an email. Words on a screen. The irrational hemisphere is already scripting elaborate scenarios where we bump into each other at Dipika and Vikram's, having conversations like we did the last time, while leaning against doorframes with practised nonchalance.

I'll wait at least twenty-four hours before responding. Maybe forty-eight. Or I could reply immediately with something devastatingly casual.

Who am I kidding? I know I'll craft twenty different responses tonight with surgical precision, analyse each for subtext and send absolutely none of them. Then I will reply with 'Oh that's nice' or something equally lame. I don't know. I need to calm down!

The elephant in those photos isn't the only one in the room. I've missed him too. But he doesn't need to know that particular truth just yet. Thank God Dipika is coming over in three hours.

It's the perfect distraction from this emotional hand grenade he's casually tossed into my peaceful life.

I've already decided that if she brings up Aman, I'm playing it cool. Ice queen-cool. 'Oh, Aman? Yeah, he mentioned he's moving back,' I'll say, while internally screaming into a pillow. The thing about Dipika is that she is delightfully meddlesome, the kind who'll stir the pot just to see what floats to the top. And if she even suspects that I have feelings for Aman, she's likely to bring it up to him in passing, probably while pouring wine, and make it sound casual. And that, I cannot afford. Not now. Not when she's his boss's wife. The last thing I need is to become the subplot in his career prospects because I couldn't keep my feelings under wraps. Nope. I'm staying Switzerland. Neutral. Polished. Unbothered.

At least on the surface.

Dipika stretches her feet and arms, squinting as the morning sunlight plays hide and seek on her face. She smiles and asks for another cup of coffee.

'If it isn't too much trouble, that is,' she adds as an afterthought.

'Of course not. No trouble at all. I knew you would want more, so I made some extra. Let me pop it in the microwave,' I say as I walk towards my kitchen, which is just a few steps away.

'I so love your terrace, Anjali. It's incredibly peaceful. I think it's the best thing about the house. And these deck chairs are lovely too. I can never get this kind of peace at home. Ria and

Rima are really a handful,' she says, leaning back comfortably and closing her eyes.

'I know, but they're such moppets. Truly little dolls,' I reply.

'Yes, when they're asleep.' She laughs. 'God, Anjali, I so needed this break,' she says, eyes still closed.

'Anytime. You're most welcome here. Offer open only for my favourite cousin though,' I reply.

I return with the coffees and plonk down on the deck chair next to hers.

'You know, Anjali, I really wait for these getaways. I'm so fed up with my life. Sometimes I feel I've had enough of the husband and kids, the whole marriage thing.'

'Why? Why in the world are you fed up?' I ask, genuinely curious.

Dipika really has the best of everything—a wonderful husband, two lovely girls, a beautifully done-up posh penthouse, unlike my tiny one-bedroom where the only good part is the terrace.

'What you see on the surface really isn't the whole picture. You only see the shine, the sheen and the gloss. Beneath it, there's masonry, peeling plaster, shaky foundations. It's all dressed up and you never notice because of the sheen.' Her voice is laced with bitterness, and I'm surprised.

'Are we talking about building constructions here? Masonry, bricks and all that?' I attempt a feeble joke to lighten the mood, but Dipika doesn't smile.

'Do you know it's been about two months since Vikram and I even had a proper conversation?' she asks.

I don't know what to say. Secretly, I have wanted to have a marriage like hers. Dipika always teases me about how I haven't found Mr Right yet. And now here she is, telling me that her Mr Right is not so right after all.

'It's the monotony that gets to me. All I do is look after Ria and Rima, send them to school, go to the gym, work out, then come back home. Vikram is never around. My life is always the same old, same old. I really think men have a button that gets activated the moment they become husbands. They change so much. He was never like this before marriage,' she continues.

'Come on, Dipika. Vikram is babysitting today, isn't he? He is giving you a break,' I defend him. 'I know so many whose husbands don't lift a teacup. Vikram is sweet in comparison.'

'He would be sweeter if he were around. Most of the time he's travelling. Even when he comes back home, he hardly has time for me.'

I want to point out that it's because he works so hard that they lead such a fancy lifestyle. They vacation abroad every year and live in one of Bangalore's most enviable residential luxury apartments. But I don't think Dipika wants to hear that, so I stay quiet.

'Leave all that. Tell me, how are things with you? How are Sriram and Latika? And how's work? All good?' Dipika has taken the tone of a concerned older sister now. I don't mind, really. I like that she 'watches out' for me.

'Yes, all good. I met both of them yesterday. Sriram has broken up with yet another woman. And Latika's husband was out of town. So, it was just the three of us, instead of their respective partners tagging along. It was just like the old times.'

'You three have really been together a long time, haven't you?' asks Dipika.

'Yes,' I reply. 'Together since Class VI, when my parents decided to put me in that hostel in Bangalore. Sriram and Latika are truly my lifelines. I don't know how I would have survived school without them.'

Dipika smiles. 'I know about some of the crazy adventures you've had. You're lucky, really, to have such great friends. I'm barely in touch with anyone I went to school with. It all changes when you have kids.'

In that moment, I hope nothing changes between Sriram, Latika and me. I want nothing to come in between our friendship. And I don't know if things really change after people have kids. If they want to keep in touch, they'll always find a way. But I don't see any point in arguing with Dipika. She seems to be in a cynical mood today.

'By the way, it'll be great to have Aman back in India. The girls are so excited,' says Dipika.

'I know. I've been in touch with him on and off. He's so good with children, isn't he? So patient he was with Ria and Rima. Has it been almost a year now since that dinner at your place?'

'Yes, I think it's been just over a year. Do you remember how they were clinging to him and wouldn't let him go?'

'Of course. They both sat on his back, and it was really sweet of him to pretend to be an elephant and give them rides. His knees must have hurt,' I say and smile at the memory.

Dipika and I lie around on the deck chairs for some more time, chatting about everything. She calls it our 'hanging out' time. I rustle up some sandwiches for lunch. Finally, around four, Dipika says she has to leave; it's time to take both girls to their ballet lessons, and Vikram won't be able to manage their hair by himself since Shikha is visiting relatives.

After she leaves, I lie for a long time on the deck chair, reflecting on what she has said. I wonder if people really do change after marriage. She does sound down. She never used to be so cynical during her earlier visits, but lately, she seems more and more negative. I just hope it's a phase that will pass.

As the golden late evening light spills across the terrace, I absorb the silence, watching the gentle sway of my palms. The hibiscus plant Dipika gifted me a few months ago is in full bloom. Surprisingly, it has managed to thrive under my care. The flowers are bright red, unapologetically bold, almost as if they were reminding me that no matter how much life changes, beauty finds its way back. I close my eyes and let the breeze graze my face. There's something oddly comforting about this stillness.

Aman's email replays in my head again. A simple message on the surface, but underneath it, I can sense a ripple, a shift. I think about what Dipika said, how things lose their shine over time, how people change. But it is possible that some things don't fade. Maybe connections, true ones, hold their shape even when wrapped in silence for three hundred and forty-seven days.

I open my phone and scroll to Aman's email. My fingers hover above the keyboard for a few moments before I finally type.

From: Anjali Prabhu <anjali.prabhu@tiara.com>
To: Aman Mathur <aman.mathur@zmail.com>
Sub: re: Found our elephant pics! (+ some news)

Hi, Aman!

Good to hear from you. Welcome back! Let me know once you're settled in. We owe those elephant photos a proper sequel.

Anjali

I hit send before I can overthink it.

Sometimes, you don't need twenty perfectly crafted drafts. Sometimes, one honest line is enough.

I head back inside, humming to myself, feeling strangely lighter, as if something I didn't realize I was holding has quietly let go.

To know what happens to Aman and Anjali, meet them again in *The One You Cannot Have.*

ACKNOWLEDGEMENTS

TO MY FATHER K.V.J. Kamath, who believed in the writer in me long before I believed in myself. Everything begins there.

To Purvi. You read this first, fastest, and with the most generous heart. Your instincts are sharp and your enthusiasm is the kind a writer dreams of. Thank you for being my first reader, always.

To Atul and Satish, for being my home. I cherish the unique ways you show up for me.

To my mother, for her strength, her directness, her pride and her wonderful sense of humour.

To Prem, for being in my corner.

To Gayatri Goswami, Rashmi Menon and Wesley D'Souza. This book exists in its best form because of you. Your editorial eyes, your patience and your commitment to the work made all the difference.

To the team at HarperCollins, for championing this book with energy and care. A special thanks to Shabnam Srivastava and Nandini Tripathi for their passion and flair in taking it to the world.

To Saurav Das, for a cover that said everything I couldn't. The moment I saw it, I knew.

To Pranav Shah, for always being a calm, reliable presence when technology decides to be otherwise.

To my closest friends. You know who you are, and you know what you mean to me.

To Fareeda, for keeping everything running so I can keep writing.

To Kasper, Leo and Harvey, my three cats who kept me company through every page, every late night, every rewrite. And to Lossie, my dear dog, no longer here but never quite gone.

To my readers. You are why I do this. Every book I write is, at its heart, written for you.

ABOUT THE AUTHOR

Preeti Shenoy is one of India's highest-selling authors, with over a million books sold across eighteen bestselling titles. Known for her accessible yet profound storytelling, she explores complex themes including mental health, gender inequality, relationships and socio-economic divides with sensitivity and insight.

Featured on *Forbes*'s list of influential Indian celebrities, Preeti has represented India at prestigious international literature festivals in Birmingham, Sharjah and Abu Dhabi. Her accolades include the Popular Choice Fiction Award (2021) from *The Times of India*'s AutHer Awards, Amazon India's Most Popular Self-Help Book of 2021, and the Business Excellence Award from the New Delhi Institute of Management.

Preeti is a monthly columnist with *The Indian Express* and has contributed to the *Financial Chronicle*. An artist and long-distance runner, Preeti brings the same discipline, curiosity and resilience to her creative life that define her work. She lives in Bengaluru.

Connect with Preeti:

Website: www.preetishenoy.com
Email: ps@preetishenoy.com
Twitter/X: @Preetishenoy
Substack: preetishenoy.substack.com
Instagram: @Preeti.Shenoy and @Preetishenoyart
Facebook: preeti.io/fb
LinkedIn: linkedin.com/in/preetishenoyauthor

THE STORIES CONTINUE IN ...

It's All in the Planets

Meet Aniket. Twenty-seven, techie, Mr Average. His best friend is Subbu, a nerd who breathes, thinks and lives code. Aniket cannot believe his luck when he starts dating Trish—a stunning, sexy model, who is totally out of his league. But Trish has a list of things she wants him to work on, beginning with his pot belly and his geekiness.

Then there's Nidhi, thirty-two, who has quit her corporate job to follow her passion. She is engaged to Manoj, Mr Perfect—except for one aspect.

Aniket and Nidhi meet on a train, a chance encounter, and she agrees to become his 'relationship coach'. It's a decision that sets in motion a chain of events that will have a profound impact on the lives of all involved.

One man, two women and the trap called Destiny.

Some things, they say, are all in the planets.

The One You Cannot Have

How long does it take to heal a broken heart? Can you ever forget that one perfect relationship you had?

Anjali knows who she wants; she wants Aman. Aman too knows who he wants; he wants Shruti. Shruti and Aman were once inseparable. Theirs was a love that would last forever and more. Then, out of the blue, Shruti left Aman. A devastated Aman moved abroad in the hope of forgetting Shruti and to heal. Shruti married Rishabh. Now Aman is back in India and looking for a fresh start. But he is still haunted by memories of his love. Can he ever break free from it? His head tells him to move on, to find love with Anjali, but his heart won't listen. No matter what he does, Shruti's shadow looms large.

Can there be a happily-ever-after for any of them?

A straight-from-the-heart modern-day romance of unrequited love, of complicated relationships and about moving on when you realize that there will always be the one you cannot have.

HarperCollins *Publishers* India

At HarperCollins India, we believe in telling the best stories and finding the widest readership for our books in every format possible. We started publishing in 1992; a great deal has changed since then, but what has remained constant is the passion with which our authors write their books, the love with which readers receive them, and the sheer joy and excitement that we as publishers feel in being a part of the publishing process.

Over the years, we've had the pleasure of publishing some of the finest writing from the subcontinent and around the world, including several award-winning titles and some of the biggest bestsellers in India's publishing history. But nothing has meant more to us than the fact that millions of people have read the books we published, and that somewhere, a book of ours might have made a difference.

As we look to the future, we go back to that one word—a word which has been a driving force for us all these years.

Read.